HAND TALKER

THE LIFE AND TIMES
OF A MONSTER SLAYER

HAND TALKER
THE LIFE AND TIMES OF A MONSTER SLAYER

A NOVEL

JOHNNY DOESKIN

BLOODY TALES PUBLISHING

HAND TALKER: THE LIFE AND TIMES OF A MONSTER SLAYER

BLOODY TALES PUBLISHING (BloodyTalesPublishing.com)

Images and design:
Front cover foreground images by Vlue
Wraparound cover photograph by Pratchaya Ruenyen
Cover concept by the author
Cover design by Kostya (Getcovers of Ukraine) in collaboration with the author
Part 3 cover image collage from photographs by Maryam (Eastern Wind Studio of Canada) (*Silver Wolf Mask / Headdress Combo*) and creativemarc (*Fossil Skull of Homo erectus*)
Maps by the author using base layers created by Kaldari, Halava and Alehnia
Photograph of the author by Janey Doeskin
Horbse Textured font created by David Novrian and Ahmad Aswin

Cataloging-in-Publication data is available from the Library of Congress.
Subjects: | BISAC: FICTION / Literary. | FICTION / Coming of Age. | FICTION / Contemporary Native American.

First BTP edition / May 2024

eBook ISBN: 979-8-9899367-0-0
Paperback ISBN: 979-8-9899367-1-7
Hardcover ISBN: 979-8-9899367-2-4

Printed in the United States of America

THE HEALING PATH

i
am
here at
this place
yet again as
memories awaken
reopening old wounds
now flowing fast and free
painting these pages salty red
ripping ahead on the healing path

Contents

Part 3 - Monster Killin' Time

MAP OF NORTH AMERICA

PART I
RUNNIN' TIME

Final Entry
in Hand Talker's Journal

When I was growing up at the rez [Navajo Reservation], *I heard the old legends lots of times just like all the other rez kids did. And I always asked to hear my favorite one again. It was the story about the battle between the hero kid called Naayéé' Neizghání* [Monster Slayer] *and a horrible monster called Yé'iitsoh* [Big Giant].

I used to have a twin brother just like Naayéé' Neizghání did. That is probably why the story meant so much to me. My brother Shash Yáázh [Little Bear] *and I played all the time around the hogan. We pretended we were code talkers like our grandfather was in World War II. We went on play war missions together. We were the twin fighter kids just like in the legend. But instead of voice talking, my brother Shash Yáázh would hand talk his war code with me. Everybody in the family hand talked with me because I was born with no voice.*

But back when I was thirteen, Shash Yáázh and my dad Jess and my mom Nitzee got killed in a wreck when they were coming home from a sing near Gallup. Their pickup got hit head-on by a drunk guy. Because I was sick in the belly, I stayed in bed at the hogan with Shimásání [my grandmother] *that day. That sickness in my belly is the only reason I am still alive writing down these memories for anyone who cares to read them.*

Anyway, that story was always my favorite one. Sometimes I still see my brother Shash Yáázh in my dreams and we hand talk with each other like when we were little kids. But after he and my mom and dad died in the wreck, there was no one there to help me out when things got tough in life. I had to learn to take care of myself. I learned that monsters really do exist. I know because I killed one.

I

BLOOD TRAIL

DENVER, COLORADO
DECEMBER 15TH, 1999

ICY SNOW CRUNCHED beneath the reporter's feet like the sound of small bones breaking. She trudged ahead in near darkness, her eyes locked on the colorful flashing lights of the two squad cars. A pair of policemen stretched crime scene tape around the covered front entrance of a yellow-brick Romanesque-style building.

The young woman set down her bag and stood tiptoe. She leaned against the tape, notepad in-hand, camera at-the-ready. She checked her watch and jotted down the time: three minutes to midnight.

Blood was pooled around the base of the double-arched stairway, concentrated around a broken newel post. The white marble façade was splashed and splattered crimson. The more she looked, the more blood she saw. Even the snow-packed driveway was blood-sprayed. The reporter became aware of her gooseflesh. The scene sickened her. But, like she'd been taught in her journalism classes, she forced herself to contain her emotions and simply analyze what she witnessed. No sensationalism or embellishment. Just gather the facts and report the news. Don't *make* the news.

She adjusted her zoom lens and snapped a few images of the broken post and nearby bloody footprints. Then she spotted several tiny ivory-colored objects on the bottom step by the largest blood pool. She snapped another photo.

"What happened here Officer?"

"You with the press Miss?"

"Yes. Rocky Mountain News. What happened?"

"Not sure. We haven't found a body yet or any injured parties."

"Could I get your name and credentials please? For the story?"

"Officer M. Patricio Valdez. I go by 'Pat.' Denver PD. Badge number 1050. South Birch Precinct. I was first on-scene. Got here fifteen, maybe twenty minutes ahead of him." He gestured toward the other officer. "It's not much of a story though Miss. For a story you reporters need a body, right?

Anyway, try to keep the photos and questions to a minimum. We've got a lot of processing of the scene to do. You'll need to stay back and out of the way."

A cold breeze rustled the ribbon barrier.

The reporter was insistent. "Have you followed those tracks over there? They'll lead you to the person who's hurt, right? What if they need help?"

He ignored her questions. "Stay back behind the tape. Don't be pushing on it. The entire area is considered an active crime scene until we've collected all the evidence and cleared it."

Valdez placed yellow plastic evidence markers next to the impressions and blood pools in the snow. She noticed he'd gotten blood on the sleeves of his navy-blue coat. There was even some on his uniform pants. The woman watched as he stood back and snapped a couple photos while the other officer penciled a sketch of the scene on a little yellow notepad.

Doesn't seem very professional, she thought.

With her zoom lens she focused again on the tiny ivory-colored objects, then zoomed in further. One of the objects was different. It looked like a little gold nugget. The image blurred. When she leaned around the camera. Valdez stood there by the blood pool. He quickly shoved a hand into his coat pocket, then stared at her.

"Officer Valdez, don't the crime scene technicians normally do that sort of thing?"

"What sort of thing Miss?"

"Evidence collection and crime scene diagrams."

"Oh, right. They're tied up on another call. Couldn't make it to this one."

"Would you like some coffee?" she said.

"That sounds mighty good." He propped himself against a lamp post as she opened a thermos and poured him a cup. "Thanks. It really hits the spot."

"There's a big storm coming tonight—this morning I mean," she said. "That might affect the evidence. It seems like following those tracks in the snow and finding the person would be a top priority before it arrives, right?"

"Like I said Miss, don't worry. We'll get to it. Takes time, right? I've done it—we've done it before. We know what we're doing here."

"No offense. I was just thinking out loud."

"You'll get your story. Just be patient."

"How long will it take to process the scene?"

"Two—three hours max. Depends. If we find a body it'll take longer of course. Right now there's the possibility of a crime, but no direct evidence without the body."

"But that's a hell of a lot of blood, right?"

"The snow makes it seem like more. Soaks it up like a sponge."

"What do the tracks tell you? How many people were involved?"

"You know the routine Miss. Once we identify the suspect we'll release whatever information we're able to. Until then we can't say much."

"What makes you think there's a suspect? Did a crime occur?"

Valdez paused, annoyed with himself as much as with the reporter. "First, if it was a suicide, the body would still be here, right? Second, the tracks tell me at least two people were in an altercation of some kind—and I've already told you way more than you need to know. No more questions now Miss. Here's your thermos lid. Thanks again for the coffee."

"Some of those tracks—the smaller ones—look like bare feet," she stated. "What do you think it means?"

2

PIETÀ

THE HITCHHIKER GLANCED FROM SIDE-TO-SIDE, then grabbed a fistful of snow to clean the dried blood from the crevices of his nails. As it melted, the pink runoff dripped onto the brown slush stuck to the toes of his cowboy boots. He pulled his wide-brimmed felt hat low, tugged his collar high and balanced his duffel atop the guardrail and waited.

His hand rested atop a cross-shaped object inside the bag—the last thing he grabbed during his hasty departure.

A new storm arrived. It hit him full force. The Front Range winds sprayed him with freezing rain. Refusing to turn aside, he faced the rhythmic gusts and raised his numb thumb for each approaching motorist. An hour went by. Then two. He stomped his feet from time to time to drive away the creeping cold. Finally, a dark-haired lady in a red Camaro took pity on him and pulled over.

"C'mon Hon'. Get in. Where you headed?"

He stowed his drenched coat and duffel behind the seat next to a lump of fur and pointed north at the gray horizon.

She pulled onto the interstate. The windows began to fog, so she switched the defroster over to *'Max.'*

"What's your name?"

He withdrew a dog-eared notepad and scribbled an answer.

Davy

She smiled. "Hi Davy. I'm Donna. How long were you waiting there?"

He scribbled again: *3 hours maybe*

"Well, at least for now you'll be out of that nasty weather. I'm going as far as Billings. You're going that way, right? You're sure one lucky young fella. I don't usually pick up hitchhikers, but you looked so miserable out there. My ex-husband used to always say I could never pass a stray without stopping. I guess he's right."

Davy shrugged. He avoided her eyes and focused his gaze instead on the pale skin showing below the hem of her sapphire-blue outfit. She caught him staring there, so he shifted his attention to his hands and nails. He re-checked them for traces of blood. Then he noticed spots of blood-crust on his dark T-shirt.

Can she see it?

His vision blurred and his arm and neck muscles tensed. Without warning, a Pekinese shook its collar and shot forward from the backseat onto his lap. The fat little dog jumped up and licked his cheek. Davy jerked back.

"Get down Sophie. Don't mind her. So, Davy, what do you think about all this Y2K stuff, huh?"

He lifted his brows.

"Where have you been hiding? Under a rock or something? Y2K stands for 'The Year 2000.' People are predicting the water and power are gonna get shut off in a couple weeks during New Year's Eve. Planes are gonna drop from the sky. The computer programmers supposedly forgot to put some digits in their programs and there's not enough time to rewrite all the code. At midnight on the 31st—when the date changes—everything that's computerized is gonna crash. That's what some of the experts are saying anyway."

Davy shrugged.

"Where you headed Davy? You never did answer."

Sask. Canada

"Saskatchewan? That's quite a long trip for someone your age—all alone. Does your family know where you're at?"

He nodded and pointed at the notepad.

"If you don't mind me asking Hon'—because of your long hair and features. I'm guessing you're Native American?"

Davy nodded. He wrote some more words, then showed her.

Dené—Navajo & Apache & Buffalo River

"That's so cool. So, you're headed to see your family, huh? I thought the Diné people live in Arizona and New Mexico. You know we're going the wrong way, don't you?"

We live all over the place

Donna smiled and was quiet for a time. Finally she spoke.

"My ex was on the road awhile, same as you. About your age too. He was fourteen when *he* ran away. Said it was hard at times—real hard. But those were some of his best memories I think—talked about it all the time—being all on his own. Free to come and go as he pleased. He said he learned the ways of the world then. Learned to appreciate his family more because of it. Of course *we girls* couldn't ever do that sort of thing—hitchhiking all over the place. We'd have been raped and murdered for sure."

She paused for a moment while he stared at her thighs.

"Don't you get scared?"

He rubbed Sophie's tummy and shook his head 'no.'

The miles ticked by. Davy was beginning to doze off when something outside jolted him awake. His breath caught in his throat like cotton on thorns. A huge wolf-like creature loped along in the snowy field beside the highway. Its gray fur robe flapped in the storm. The creature looked over at him. Its eyes were fierce—yellowish. *What the hell is that thing?* he thought. *Are those claws?* An image from the Diné stories he'd heard as a young boy came to mind: yee naaldlooshii—a skinwalker. Davy knew about these legendary witch-wolves, but had never actually seen one. He rubbed the thin veil of fog from the window and pressed his nose tight to the glass. The thing bounced a bit and he realized it wasn't a skinwalker at all—just a giant tumbleweed racing across the snow-crusted field, scattering its seeds in the winter wind.

They continued north on the interstate. He drifted to sleep with Sophie curled on his soggy lap.

HE AWOKE AS THEY PULLED into a gas station in Cheyenne. Outside an orange plow skimmed the blowing, drifting snow from the road. He clutched the warm ball-like dog to his belly while the woman filled the tank and paid.

"Hey Davy, that attendant in there just told me there's a ground blizzard hitting on-up-around Sheridan—right where we're headed, wouldn't you know it. They're requiring chains on that section of highway. He said we should maybe find a motel in Casper and wait till it passes. You're welcome to stay there with me if you'd like."

He shrugged.

"Hon', when you need a little help, you need to let people help you."

Donna pulled into a restaurant. She talked about her son JJ and her ex-husband Joe while they ate. Davy studied her immaculate ivory skin, brown eyes, and long ebony hair—eyes and hair that reminded him of his deceased mother. Donna wore a tiny gold cross on a thin chain around her neck. There was a reddish knob on the bridge of her nose. She said she'd been divorced for about a year and was on holiday from her job at Boulder Memorial Hospital. She had spent the night with her sister in Lone Tree and was now on her way to visit her brother in Billings. Davy pulled out some bills to help pay for the meal, but Donna made him put them away. Before leaving, he pocketed a handful of jelly and sugar packets from the condiment caddy at the back of the table.

They got back in the Camaro and crossed over to a Kmart where he followed behind while she loaded heavy winter clothes into the cart: long johns; thick wool socks and mitts; an insulated bomber cap; and a pair of shiny black snowmobile boots. "You need these Hon'. You're not dressed right for this kind of weather. You can't keep warm in a cowboy hat and boots in the winter. Even cowboys know that."

At the checkout counter he pilfered a half-dozen free matchbooks and stuffed a few thin white plastic shopping bags in his coat pocket.

It was dark by the time the Camaro rolled into Casper. The sign at the motel said *'Vacancy.'* She entered the office alone, then quickly returned with a key.

"Sorry Hon', but the room only has one bed. It's king-size. Is that okay? I hope so 'cause it's the only room left what with the blizzard and all. Don't worry—I don't bite," she laughed. "And don't let-on about Sophie, okay? The motel rules say *'No Pets,'* so we're gonna have to park way in the back and sneak her in, okay?"

Davy nodded.

Donna pulled into the last empty space behind the motel.

"Wow, quite a storm, huh?"

She hooked Sophie to a leash and walked her around to pee while Davy hauled in his duffel and the lady's luggage.

Once inside, Donna flipped through a booklet of complimentary coupons. She called in an order for a large Canadian bacon and pineapple pizza plus a couple pops while Davy went in the bathroom to strip off his damp clothes and don the new oversized long johns.

"They call it Hawaiian-style," she hollered to him through the door. "I think you're gonna like it. I've had the Hawaiian before and it's really good. We'll have a luau party tonight," she laughed, "okay Hon'?"

Donna phoned her brother and rambled on to him about the day's weather delay and the next day's forecast. Davy emerged from the bathroom and spread his clothes over the heater and chair backs to dry.

She ended the call, then asked him for his family's phone number. After a few tries, she was able to reach his Auntie Millie and explain the situation about the snowstorm. Donna didn't seem too surprised when his aunt said she was unaware the teen was thumbing his way to her home in Northern Saskatchewan. Donna held the phone to his ear.

"Stay right there Hand Talker! I'm coming to get you," said Auntie Millie.

He shook his head 'no.'

"He says 'no,'" said Donna.

"You better be extra careful then," said his aunt. "I love you Kiddo."

He grinned and waved 'goodbye.'

"Davy says 'bye' and he'll see you soon."

When the pizza arrived, Donna handed him a pop. They sat on the bed and ate and watched TV. She plucked pineapple pieces from her pizza and chewed and swallowed them one by one. "When my ex and I vacationed in Maui I got to eat *fresh* pineapple every day. It was absolutely incredible."

At her encouragement, he changed into his shorts and they headed to the pool. Donna lounged poolside beneath some artificial vines. She admired the bronze teen with chiseled cheeks and long jet-black hair as he plunged in and stroked snake-like through the blue-green water.

He glanced at her now and then. After a while she got up and Davy followed her back to the room. He dried himself and once more donned the baggy white long johns. They sat on the bed and watched more TV.

"Mind if I get closer Hon'? The heater's on high, but I'm still cold to the bone. Seems like I'm always cold."

Before he could respond, Donna scooted over. She stared into his eyes and leaned on him for warmth. Once more he picked at his fingernails and focused his eyes on her pale thighs. He felt her body slowly drain the heat from his own. Together they watched TV for the better part of an hour while she flipped through the channels. By and by, he drifted to sleep.

Later that evening Davy woke with a powerful jolt. His heart raced. He'd dreamt of a tall demon with long yellow hair and a flying chunk of stone and spraying blood. He glanced around the room in panic, then remembered where he was. Donna was in bed beside him watching TV, but she'd changed into a blue nightie. She stared at him with deep dark eyes, fingering her little cross.

"Are you okay Hon'? You were just having a bad dream I think." She flashed him a smile, then slowly unhooked her necklace and set it at the back of the nightstand. Silvery-blue reflections from the TV screen flickered across her bare shoulders. The shape of her breasts was faintly visible to him through the flimsy fabric. She smelled good. Perfume. But there was a different fragrance about her too—something that triggered memories from his early boyhood at the Reservation. Davy trailed his eyes to the lower half of her nightie. He wondered what was underneath. Did she carry a little beaver fur down there like some of the women he'd glimpsed as they prepared for the Blessing Way ceremony when he was little—right before he looked away in embarrassment? Or like that girl Gabby Sanchez whom he'd been with behind the school gym a few months ago?

Donna's eyes searched his sweat-beaded face. A look of pity crossed her own. "Davy, I've got something to confess. You remind me of someone." She placed her hand on his shoulder.

Once more his vision clouded and his muscles tensed.

"It's okay Hon'. Like I said. I don't bite."

After a while he relaxed and allowed himself to lean against her. Together, they watched TV well into the night. Donna held him. She caressed his scalp and smoothed his long hair with her fingertips. Her gentle massaging calmed him—hypnotized him. After a spell, Davy fell asleep.

Later that night he was awakened again, this time by the lady's movements while she squeezed him and breathed heavily. The head of the bed lightly tapped the wall. She made little noises and gripped his body tighter and tighter, almost hurting him. Donna released a moan. Suddenly he felt it. Wetness. *What is it?* he thought.

Wary, Davy stared at her in the dimness. *What the hell is going on?* He hesitated, then reached up and touched her moist cheek and the bump planted there on the bridge of her nose long ago by her ex-husband.

"I woke you didn't I Hon'?" Her voice quavered. "I'm sorry."

He wiped tears from her marble-white cheeks and held her smooth hands. Then Donna held him to her breast—rocking—rocking—rocking, his lanky body draped across hers. She quietly sobbed and let loose another low, wounded moan. Eventually her shudders and sobs stopped.

She remained quiet for a time. Finally she spoke. "There's something I didn't tell you yet Davy. You see Hon', my son—JJ. He's dead. He was your age. He died two and a half years ago. His buddies told me and Joe it was an accident— that he slipped and fell in Boulder Canyon when they were up climbing on some rocks. But I know different because I work at the hospital you see. The other nurses tried to hide the truth from me. When they were at lunch, I opened his file and read the tox report. It was drugs. JJ was high on drugs when he died. That's why he fell off the rocks. Later I told Joe about the test results. But he wouldn't believe it—not about our boy JJ. Joe called me a liar. A no-good mom. That's what happened Hon'. JJ was in a coma for a week. Then he died. Joe left me and later filed for divorce. I got the house and his sports car. And now...

"Davy, will you pretend with me a minute—for just a minute—that I'm your mom? And you'll promise to listen to me? Okay Hon'?"

He nodded.

"Swear?"

He nodded.

"P-please. Just promise me you won't *ever* get hooked on drugs, okay?"

Davy promised.

Once more the mourning mother clutched the teen to her breast. He returned her embrace. They hugged that way awhile as Davy thought of his mother and Donna thought of her boy JJ. Sophie jumped up on the bed and licked Donna's neck and earlobes. She giggled.

"Thanks for putting up with me Davy," she whispered hoarsely. "I'm such a crybaby, aren't I?"

He patted her shoulders and nodded.

3

THE HEALER

NAVAJO RESERVATION
LATE OCTOBER 1990

"SHASH YÁÁZH, where's your brother?" said Jess.

"Out in the sheep pen."

"It's getting dark. Tell him to hurry up. The medicine man is ready."

The wind slammed the hogan door shut as the young boy left.

"I'll have him lie here in front of the woodstove so he won't get cold," said Sam. "Nitzee, have you got an old diyogí to put under him?"

Nitzee retrieved a thick wool blanket from her wooden chest and handed it to the healer.

The family members sat huddled together atop their beds, bundled in blankets. Lamplight illuminated their brown faces.

A gust stirred dust as Davy and his brother entered the hogan.

"Hey there," said Sam, "so, you're the one they call 'Hand Talker,' huh?"

Davy nodded and, out of habit, signed 'yes' to the man.

Sam turned to Nitzee, raised his eyebrows and put his hand to his mouth. "Can he speak?"

"No," she said. "When Hand Talker was a baby, a stray dog came by and licked inside his mouth. So he's never spoken a single word."

"The dog must have paralyzed his voice," said Sam. "There's probably no cure for that."

Sam turned to the boy. "Hey Hand Talker, your dad tells me you wanna be a tribal leader like him someday. Is that right?"

Davy grinned and nodded.

"'Aoo'," said Auntie Millie, "Hand Talker is honest. He cares about his people. And he's got a good head on his shoulders. He'll make a great Dené leader someday, eh."

"You mean Diné leader," said Sam.

"No Sam. Not just Diné [Navajo]. I mean Dené [all Athapaskan speaking people]. A leader of all of our people."

"Oh," he said. "Is that another one of those Dinénáhódlóonii [Northern Dené] ideas of yours Millie? Good luck getting everybody together." Sam turned to Hand Talker's brother. "And how about you Shash Yáázh? What do you wanna be when you're bigger?"

"A football player. I'm gonna play for the Chicago Bears."

Sam's infectious grin permeated the hogan. "Then you'll need to get a *lot* bigger. You might bring me some business, huh? Football players are always getting hurt, you know. You'll have to come back to the rez to heal up. Hey, you two boys might be naakishchíín [twins], but you're sure easy to tell apart. Hand Talker's got silver eyes instead of brown like yours."

Sam indicated it was time to begin.

"I laid out some fresh sand for you," said Jess.

"No Jess, I don't do the Yeibichai ceremony. My way is different—no need for a 'iikááh [sandpainting].

"Ha 'diijááh," said Sam as he motioned for Davy to strip naked and lay on the wool blanket.

'But they'll see me,' signed Davy. He pointed at the family's guests from Canada—his Auntie Millie and her young stepdaughter Macha.

Jess spoke up: "The other medicine men always cover up the sick ones. Can't you do it the regular way?"

Sam was insistent: "I'm not a medicine man Jess. I'm a healer. My ways are newer—better. I got my training from a curandero over in Las Cruces. For it to work, I gotta touch him. Do you want me to heal him or not?"

"Don't worry Hand Talker," said Auntie Millie, "Macha and I won't look."

The boy stripped and laid on the blanket.

"Which part of your belly hurts? Right there, huh?" The healer massaged Davy's lower abdomen while his relatives looked away. "Well, it's definitely not your appendix. And I don't think your farts are stuck in there. You've got something ugly stuck inside you. I'll need to remove it."

The healer sang an off-key song. He opened a hat-size wooden box he'd brought along and withdrew a little glass bottle and a small white bundle. "I stopped at the store on the way here. For some reason all the corn oil was gone. All they had left was this fancy stuff from Italy. It sure was expensive, but it'll do the trick." Sam liberally anointed Davy with the yellowish liquid, then pocketed the bottle. Next, he carefully unwrapped the bundle. Inside was a white hen's egg. The healer rubbed it on Davy's stomach and made sucking sounds with his mouth. When he'd finished, he re-wrapped the egg and returned it to the box.

"Okay Shash Yáázh, I got the ugly thing out of your brother. Take it out to my truck for me, huh? Tomorrow I'll find a safe place to bury it."

Sam carelessly flipped off the lid as he handed the box to the boy. When Shash Yáázh spied the bullsnake inside, he yelled and lurched back.

"What the hell Sam?" said Jess. A serious expression crossed his face. "Wolf Man Keetsal told me you could help."

"Yeah. I visit Wolf Man quite a bit. Pretty much every week I guess."

"He lets you heal him?" said Jess incredulously.

"Not usually. He gets migraines, but Wolf Man likes to play the tough guy part and won't admit he's sick in the head. We're mostly just good buddies. There's a group of us that get together every Friday night at his house when he fires up the grill and we do different kinds of games. He's really good at acting out the part when we play charades. We can get pretty rowdy, huh."

Nitzee spoke: "Sam, do you know Hand Talker is a healer too—with his music? Get out your ts'isǫ́ǫ́s [flute] Hand Talker and play something for Shimá [my mother]. Her knees are hurting her."

Davy sat beside his mother on the bed while his grandmother rocked in her wooden chair in front of them. The old woman fixed her gaze on the boy's bright eyes as he played her favorite song. Her leathery hand gripped his thin knee. She whispered: "Bik'i hodidoonih [he is the one]," then leaned back and slowly closed her eyes.

He played three more healing songs on his cedar flute. The haunting notes dipped and rose and reverberated in the nighttime desert air. The cedar logs rhythmically moaned with the wind. Outside, a rogue gust approached the hogan. It roared like a beast. The door groaned under the strain, then burst open. The three kids screamed and the tiny home went dark except for the dim glow of the embers in the stove.

"Yee naaldlooshii [a skinwalker]," stated Sam loudly.

The women shooshed him.

Jess found a flashlight, added a chunk of piñon to the stove and relit the oil lamp.

Nitzee shut the door and bent to retrieve her broken crucifix from the floor. Brittle from its years of hanging over the doorway in the desert air, two long conchoidal flakes had detached when it struck the hardpacked floor. The fractured base of the heavy plastic cross was now sharp and double-fluted like the stone blades once used by ancient North American mammoth hunters. The fresh edge immediately drew blood when Nitzee inadvertently brushed her hand across it.

"Ouch. Oh shoot. Look—it's broken."

"See Nitzee?" said Sam. "I told you that silly thing wouldn't keep yee naaldlooshii away."

"Oh hush Sam," said Auntie Millie. "Macha and the boys are already scared. Don't go making it worse, eh."

4

Incident at Crooked Creek: A Dog-Eat-Dog World

Victoria Outback Region, Australia
December 17th, 1999

SEARING SUNRAYS BIT at the parched river valley. Cloud wisps drifted off toward the horizon. The desperate young girl balanced herself atop the rickety picnic table and let out another holler for her dog. The last time she'd seen Willie was at breakfast time. He liked to roam of course, but always raced right back when she called him. This time he'd wandered out of earshot. The surrounding area simply had too many tempting scent trails of brush 'possums and wallabies for Willie to resist.

Her tall father strode into back into camp. He wiped perspiration from his neck and forehead with his 'kerchief and opened the cooler.

"Father, where is he? Where's Willie?"

"I don't know Bethie. The laddie must have gone downriver. We'll go have a look that way. But first some tummy-tucker and a drink, right?"

She hung her head. "Yes Father."

They sat side-by-side while they drank lemonade and munched sandwiches.

"Don't worry about the little bugger Bethie. He'll come on back when he gets hungry."

"I hope so."

"I wish that mum of yours was here. She'd figure out where the laddie ran off to. She sure knew her way around the bush." He fell silent. *She knew her way around the pubs too,* he thought. *What will it be now? Three years in September since she got hammered and wrecked the car—went and got herself killed. Why did she have to go and do that?*

"I miss her too," whispered Bethie. She intertwined her small fingers with his for a time.

They finished lunch and continued their search for Willie. The girl and her father covered nearly two kilometers along the dirt road. A battered truck rattled up from behind and slowed. They stepped into the shade of a eucalyptus.

"G'day Mate. Need a lift? I'm going on to Dargo. I've got room. I can take you there."

"No thanks," said the father. "We don't need a lift."

"Your camp is back the other way."

"Right."

"You look familiar," said the old man. He scrutinized the fair-skinned pair more closely. "I've seen you on the telly, right? Yeah Mate, I remember now. You were on the news. Did you and the young miss come out here to escape all those big city reporters?"

The father ignored him.

"You're one of them, aren't you? Part of the Family—the Royal Family? I'm telling you I've seen you on the telly. I'm sure of it."

The prince turned away, silent.

The old man studied the dirt-smudged tear trails on the girl's blonde-framed cheeks. By her features, he surmised she was indeed one of those Aussie girls of Royal Germanic descent.

"Have you seen my Willie Dog?" she blurted.

"So that's it. Right. Is he a dingo mix? I saw a ding—"

"No," she said. "He's a poodle—a white poodle."

The old man's brow crinkled. He stroked his whiskers, tipped his worn hat and pondered for a moment. "Little Miss, why don't you and your father get in and we'll go find your poodle."

"His name is Willie."

"I think my girl and I will check downriver."

"You might have better luck coming with me Son."

The two men sized each other up. Each thought he knew more than the other, but only one was right.

"Why not get in—rest your legs? It'll do her good. We'll head back toward Crooked Creek and see if we can't find that poodle of yours."

The prince relented. The old man gathered up some papers from the dusty seat and stuffed them in the glove box.

"I don't get many passengers out here in the bush." He patted Bethie's head. "Move your legs a bit now Miss so I can shift the gears. You know my wife had hair like yours. Pure gold. And her face—painted by God just like yours."

The prince stared at the tangle of animal traps around his feet. His face reddened. He glared at the old man and asked, "Any luck today?"

"A little," said the old man.

"Right."

Bethie wrinkled her nose.

"What is that awful smell?"

"Shh," said the prince.

"It's okay. That's my cat bait you smell Miss."

"You catch kitty cats?"

"Feral cats Miss. That's right. That's what I do."

"Do you catch them with traps?"

"Yes Miss."

"Why?"

"Shh."

"It's alright mate, I don't mind explaining. The feral cats are killing all the songbirds. Some of them might go extinct. So the Wildlife Department hired me to trap—"

"Father says that trappers are bloody evil. Isn't that right Father?"

"Hush now Bethie. That's enough."

"Where's my Willie Dog?"

"I have an idea where he might be. But listen now Miss, you need to prepare yourself. Your Willie Dog shouldn't have been roaming around—"

"What are you implying Old Man?" said the prince.

"Don't make this more difficult Mate. Nature's in charge out here in the bush. You'll just have to accept it. Up ahead is where they hang out—the dingoes."

The truck rounded a bend, then halted. The old man pointed to the edge of a clearing. Some gray birds flushed and flew to a nearby bluff.

"What makes you think he went that way?" said the prince.

"The young miss should stay here."

"Come on Bethie. Let's—"

"Listen mate. She *needs* to stay put."

The prince rolled his eyes. "All right then. Stay here Bethie. Roll up the window, but not all the way, okay?"

The old man gestured at the packed bare red earth around their feet.

"What do you see?" asked the younger man.

"Tracks."

"Of what? That ground is rock-hard. There can't be any tracks on that."

"A small dog—and other dogs. They crossed right here, then went that way."

"Hah—he's found some mates then. Let's go get him. Hey Willie," he yelled.

The old man followed the tracks. Another bird croaked and joined the group of birds atop the bluff. The small prints in the soil became clearer and even the prince recognized them as belonging to Willie.

"You know he's gone Mate," said the old man.

"Of course he's gone. If he was close by he would have come running."

"Gone forever I mean."

"What the—"

"He's dead Mate. Dingoes got him. Just look at the spoor. You'll have to tell her."

The prince was stunned. The old man continued to examine the churned tracks where the wild dingoes killed Willie and ripped him apart. But to the city man the marks were meaningless.

"Bloody ridiculous. My wife—a pretty fair bush-lady herself—wouldn't have said those scratches mean he's dead. Hey Willie? Come on Boy."

"Not just the tracks. Everything—the specks of blood—the hair. And look at the birds. You need to *see* what's around you and *understand* what it is you're seeing. Someday your sheila will be able to read the bush like me. It just takes a bit of practice Son."

"She can't do it *someday* because she happens to be dead. And I am not your son."

The old man paused. "Sir, your poodle is dead." He walked around and showed the prince some tufts of fluffy white fur snagged in the brush. He pointed out a stained spot on the ground with claw marks from the scavenger birds. For nearly an hour they searched for Willie's collar, but only found more bloody fur clumps and his saliva-soaked paw.

They trudged back to the truck. The girl was asleep.

With a thick, calloused finger, the old man brushed a yellow strand from her sun-reddened cheek. "We should let the young miss sleep, okay?" he said. "She doesn't need to see this."

"There's nothing to see."

The old man sighed and pointed at a faded photograph taped to the dash. "That's *my* sheila. I lost her last year. Pickled liver—you know—too much tipping of the bottle."

They drove back to camp in silence.

Bethie awoke as her father lifted her from the seat. "Where's my Willie Dog?"

Neither man answered.

"G'bye Mate. And g'bye to you Young Miss. I'm truly sorry for your loss."

Father and daughter watched dust billow as the truck rattled away.

"It was that bloody trapper wasn't it Father? He trapped and killed poor Willie, didn't he?"

The prince looked down at the packed red clay and reflected on his own father who'd abandoned him and his mother and returned to England many years before to further his own political career. He chose his words carefully.

"Yes Bethie. That's what he did. Willie's gone."

"Trappers are bloody evil," she shrieked.

5

LITTLE BIGHORN

MONTANA
DECEMBER 17TH, 1999

THE SUN WAS HIGH OVERHEAD. Yellow grass shielded the wind-whipped hills, the long blades slashing. The leafless limbs of cottonwood trees along the frozen creek reached skyward like dead, bony arms. A gray cloud-bank—a second storm—advanced from the west.

Davy scanned the faraway historic battlefield through the windows of the Camaro as they drove past. The sign beside the highway indicated it was now a National Monument. Donna missed the off-ramp for the Custer cut-off, so she slowed and pulled over to the snow berm. She pressed three twenties into his palm and gave him a quick hug. "Be careful now. Remember your promise, okay?"

Donna waved 'goodbye' and drove away. Davy got out a large black bandana from his hip pocket and tied it around his forehead in the manner of the men back at the Reservation, then put on his bomber cap and wool mitts. The teen trudged down the snow-packed on-ramp. A big rig rolled down the junction off-ramp toward him. Its jake brakes thumped like a Gatling gun. He followed the tractor-trailer to the nearby truck stop.

Inside, the clerk showed Davy a Chinese knock-off military fighting knife from the display case. To test its sharpness, the runaway rubbed its edge cross-ways on the skin of his thumb like he'd watched his father do. He purchased the knife along with a vinyl poncho, a folded Montana road map and a small box of uncooked mac and cheese. Before leaving, he grabbed a few condiment packets from the deli section and scrounged an empty coffee tin from the waste bin.

Outside, he opened the map, found the old battlefield and truck stop, then traced his finger along his intended route to the U.S.-Canada border. Davy shouldered his bag.

He followed the course of the Little Bighorn River on Route 47, holding out his thumb for every northbound motorist. A couple pickups slowed, but when he turned they continued past. After a while he gave up hitchhiking and simply stepped onto the snow berm each time a vehicle approached from behind.

The storm front drew closer. He tramped onward along the now-empty steel-blue highway. The packed snow powder on the road shoulder squeaked like old dry leather beneath his black boots to the drum of his heart. Ahead in the roadway, a lone magpie pecked at something furry and half-flat. The black and white bird squawked, then shot skyward. He bent to examine the remains of its meal: a gałbáhi [cottontail rabbit] with its guts ejected and smeared on the road. One of its bulging gray-blue eyes peered at him. He cut away and discarded the half-frozen entrails, wrapped the roadkill in a Kmart bag and stuffed it in his duffel.

The scattered cloud patches from earlier in the day were gone. Solid lead-gray formations now hid the sun. He marched past snowed-in ranch entrances and drifted over hayfields. At the base of a lone mailbox were some spiny twigs with small squishy red fruits poking out of the drift. Each fruit had a nipple-like end. Davy recognized them—wild rose hips—like the ones his mother showed him long ago during a foraging foray in the mountains of northern New Mexico—one of the few fruits available in wintertime. He quickly gathered a handful.

Back on the highway, the primal force of the storm slammed into him. Ice needles shot sideways—flanking and stabbing him and setting afire any exposed flesh they happened to hit. He trekked onward through the afternoon. The wind whistled and whipped with fury. Smoky-gray gusts buffeted him. The ground blizzard intensified. The temperature dropped.

As darkness closed in, he spied a group of shadowy figures crouched ahead in the roadside ditch. They leaned eastward—foreboding in the fading light and swirling snow. There was no way to avoid them. He removed a mitt, gripped his new knife and cautiously approached the nearest one.

He released his breath in a rush. *It's just a damn cedar!* These were the same kind of trees that grew back at the Reservation—gad ni'eełi—the ones said by his mother to be 'the tree of life and death.' He removed his other mitt and rolled the scaly leaves between his palms and inhaled deeply. The rich, musky scent carried memories of his mother's hogan—her earth-covered lodge built of cedar logs near the hill his family called Bááhkin.

Davy crossed the ditch, slid under the barbed-wire fence and descended a cedar-filled draw down to the river's willow-lined bank. At the mouth of the draw, he found a rock outcrop that overhung several large cedars—a place to shelter him from the howling wind. He broke dead lower limbs from a tree close to the rock face, scuffed away the thin layer of snow and, with his heel, piled-up a thick mound of cedar duff. He pulled the vinyl poncho and his sleeping bag from the duffel and laid them out on the makeshift mattress.

At the base of the rock, Davy fashioned a small stone fire ring. He broke more dead limbs, gathered kindling and tinder, then lit a fire. After rinsing the coffee tin with snow, he filled it with icicle chunks and set it in the fire.

He skinned and cleaned the scavenged cottontail, skewered it on a willow shoot, then whittled a spatula. The water soon boiled. He cooked the macaroni while the road-rabbit slowly roasted above the coals. Time passed as he alternately tended to the food, gathered firewood and organized his camp for the night.

When it seemed ready, he pulled a leg from the rabbit. The bony end was charred. The meat was chewy and smelled faintly of burst guts. He drained the softened noodles and stirred in the cheese powder. Some noodles had stuck to the tin and there was no milk or butter to add, yet, after the long march, Davy didn't care. He leaned against a nearby boulder and ate. In the end, the bones were clean and not a noodle remained.

He rinsed the can as best he could and melted more ice. When the water bubbled. He finger-crushed the winter-ripened rose hips gathered earlier that day and dropped them in one by one. Soon, fruity vapors wafted from the boiling tin while the trees around him creaked and groaned in the wind. He sweetened his aromatic brew with pilfered sugar, plucked-out some floating bits of scorched macaroni and set the tin aside to cool. He leaned against the boulder.

Wisps of cedar woodsmoke swirled through camp. *It smells like home—like hogan-scent*, he thought. He was at peace. Relaxed. But then, gradually, a nagging sense of dread crept along the margin of his mind. It was then that he pinpointed the source of his uneasiness: *What happened back there—back at school?*

Davy tried to reconstruct what happened the night he'd run away. He remembered being utterly dazed and becoming aware he was in the shower stall with bloody water circling his feet. And, after drying and dressing, he recalled shoving his sleeping bag and other belongings into his duffel and retrieving his father's yoostsah [ring] and his mother's crucifix. But what happened prior to his shower was missing from his memory. When he tried to remember the earlier events of that night, he just hit a wall of fear and horror—a barrier too terrible to breach.

He pulled the broken crucifix from his duffel. Davy recalled his mother Nitzee recounting how, when she was young, the federal government forced her parents to send her away to the residential school for Indian kids at Wingate operated by the Bureau of Indian Affairs. During her first few years there, she said they punished her whenever she spoke her native tongue or disobeyed the other rules. But later, a group of disapproving parents convinced the government to allow their native language to be taught and to hire Navajo aides to assist the non-Native teachers. When the speaking of her native tongue was no longer punished, his mother's treatment improved.

Nitzee described how incredibly lonely it was for her at the school—being separated from her friends and family and neighbors back home. One day soon after she first arrived, a Franciscan friar invited Nitzee and some of her classmates to attend catechism and mass at the local mission. It was there she said she met an elderly French nun. The nun treated her with kindness and gave her the plastic crucifix. She even taught Nitzee a few French phrases and encouraged Nitzee to teach her some Navajo words. After Nitzee graduated and returned home, she hung the plastic relic above the hogan doorway.

Now, as he looked closely, Davy saw smudges of blood on the sharp broken end of the cross and the handle-like top of it. He took out his hunting knife and held the two objects side-by-side. *They're exactly the same length*, he thought. *And both have blood on them.*

A torrent of dread flooded him. He clasped the crucifix tightly to his chest. His heart raced. His skin grew clammy. His head pounded and his body shook. *Why isn't it working this time? It always helps me calm down.* Confused, he shoved it back in the duffel.

Davy shifted his weight and dug deep in his front pocket. He pulled out the silver yoostsah [ring] that his father Jess gave him. It was the kind of antique Navajo jewelry referred to by traders as 'old pawn.' He turned it over in his hands and examined the turquoise inlay—a sky-blue stone—with six curved edges and six straight sides merged into a single shape. The ring was too large to fit any of his fingers. He polished it on his shirt till the silver gleamed brightly. Some of the stories surrounding the ring's history he'd been told by his father before his death. Later, at the boarding school, the principal, a priest named 'Father Phil,' confiscated the ancient heirloom and told him it needed safe-keeping and would be returned at the end of the school year. He remembered breaking into Father Phil's office the night he ran away. He'd found the ring in a locked drawer. Yet once more, he couldn't recall what happened earlier that night. A chunk of time was simply missing from his memory. It was as if whatever happened never happened at all.

His tea tin now empty, Davy pulled out his cedar flute and attempted a healing song. His spittle quickly froze in the mouthpiece, so he put it away.

He added wood to the fire and bedded down for the night. Tired, but alert, he listened to the groans of the cedars beside him and the roars of the wind gusts atop the outcrop. Snow pellets whizzed by, bombarding his small camp. And, occasionally, one made it through the tangle of overhanging branches and smashed into his sleeping bag like some gray kamikaze fly.

Davy slept fitfully.

Later that night he was roused by something peculiar—the distinct sound of adult male voices. He listened closely. Knife in hand, he rose from his bed. In the dim snow-glow he saw three men on horseback. They advanced across the draw toward him—a yellow-jacketed leader and two riders at his side with dark blue coats.

They must have seen my fire, thought Davy.

The ghostly trio reined-in their steeds and tethered them to some scrub cedars.

Davy eased his way along the rock face and backed into a dark cleft in the outcrop. He waited. And while he waited, the merciless cold bit at him. It seemed like every bit of gray and yellow and blue was moving about out there in the wind and snow and shadows.

The three men emerged from the trees and quietly encircled his small camp. They gestured among themselves and pointed at the runaway teen's makeshift bed. The leader's eyes were small and pallid and wafer-like. His long blond hair blew about under a dark, wide-brimmed felt hat. He wore a fringed coat and buckskin gauntlets and sported a thick mustache below his beak-like nose. But it was the saber in the man's hand that stopped Davy's breath—its blade gleamed blood-violet in the snowlight.

Yellow Jacket raised his saber high overhead, then let loose a guttural roar. He swiped at the teen's bulky bedroll in a frenzy. He slashed over and over. Then he halted mid-slash. Something was amiss. He kicked the empty bed. His companions milled about. Yellow Jacket barked orders. His men surveyed the camp for their missing quarry. They trotted around and jabbed at the snow and duff with their blades as they searched the surrounding tree wells and rock crevices for the runaway.

They found nothing. Yellow Jacket and the bluecoat with a short knife headed up the draw, back-trailing Davy's boot prints in the snow. The remaining bluecoat kicked at the fire ring. Then he bent and opened the duffel bag.

Davy sprang forward and buried his knife in the man's rib cage. He yanked out the wet blade. The bluecoat's shrill screech was cut short when the teen sliced open the man's throat. Hot blood spewed in the wintry night air. The man slumped to the ground. The young fighter retreated to the rock cleft and squeezed himself back into the crack.

When they heard their comrade's death cry, Yellow Jacket and Short Knife returned. They carefully skirted the camp. They waited—and watched—and listened. But the teen remained hidden in the rock cleft.

After a time, at his leader's urging, Short Knife re-kindled the fire. Yellow Jacket shoved the dead bluecoat's body aside. They rifled through the contents of Davy's duffel and scattered his belongings in the snow. The men broke branches, wrapped cloth around the ends and dipped them in the flames.

His torch raised high, Short Knife crept along the rock wall. He peered into the dark crack. The teen's knife flashed. It pierced the soldier's windpipe. Davy twisted the blade and peeled it to the side, severing the man's jugular. Blood geysered. Short Knife jerked back, dropped his weapon and clutched the gaping wound. He gulped for air and wheezed. Crimson froth oozed from his mouth. Wide-eyed with horror, the bluecoat turned to his leader, took a step and pitched forward—dead.

Yellow Jacket bellowed with rage. He rushed to the cleft and raked his saber left and right, showering sparks on his young enemy. Davy ducked and dodged from side to side then dove between Yellow Jacket's legs and sprang up behind. Yellow Jacket spun and swung wide as the runaway slashed deep across the man's belly. The leader released the saber and caught his escaping viscera in both gloved hands. Stunned, he stood in the firelight looking at Davy. As Yellow Jacket dropped to his knees, his arms fell away and his steaming guts gushed forth onto the churned snow and earth. He bowed his head. Then, ever so slowly, the man leaned forward and buried his face in the teen's groin.

Davy knocked the leader's hat aside, seized a fistful of blond hair and pulled back. Like a wartime surgeon, he cut quick and deep, circumcising his scalp. A loud *pop* sounded as he yanked it free, instantly converting Yellow Jacket into a bare-skulled monk of a man.

The young warrior toppled the kneeling corpse and raised the dripping scalp high to the sky. Davy snorted and silently roared his victory into the night air. His heart pounded. His lean muscles shook from rage and from the bite of the bitter cold. He felt the snow crunch beneath his feet. He felt the icy wind and flakes hitting his face. He grinned victoriously.

Then the night gradually changed. The firelight faded to just a glow from the bed of dying coals. And the bloody scalp in his hand was transformed to a jagged piece of bloody white fabric. The slain leader was gone. In his place lay the duffel bag. Yet Davy still stood there by the fire ring. And there in his hand was the knife. And there was blood. And there was pain. The base of his left middle finger was cut to the bone—the tendons cleanly severed. It hurt like hell. He felt a cold draft on his privates. His long johns were now crotchless. He was lucky to be intact, in fact, for during his dream, Davy cut his hand and nearly sliced his genitals when he scalped the ghostly leader.

Bewildered, he slipped the knife back in its sheath, then piled branches atop the glowing coals. Once the fire burned bright again, he wrapped his bleeding hand tightly in a sock, remade his bed and crawled into his sleeping bag.

The doctor who treated students at his school would have said he'd just experienced a hallucination due to 'REM Sleep Behavior Disorder,' a condition and diagnosis sometimes linked to severe emotional trauma. Yet Davy's dream was so vivid, he was still convinced it was real. The terrible gash on his hand was certainly real.

Deep in thought, he listened to the howling storm. His hand throbbed. A sharp pain bit hard when he moved it the wrong way. And yet, having just won the battle, he was exhilarated. His thoughts remained focused on the three dead men. *Why did they try to kill me? Are more of them coming?*

6

HOLE-IN-THE-WALL

MONTANA
DECEMBER 18ᵀᴴ, 1999

THE HARSH SCREAMS AND CROAKS of bickering magpies and ravens drew Davy's attention. He scrambled through the barbed wire and searched for the dead thing he knew must be there among the snow drifts where the birds were quarreling. He followed the blood trail to where she lay. The yearling doe mule deer had traveled about thirty yards and then piled-up in a sagebrush-lined barrow pit. One of her hind legs was broken, having been clipped by a truck while she licked the salted roadway during the night. The shattered femur and torn arteries sent the unlucky animal into shock. Her heart stopped within minutes of the impact.

As he'd watched his father do long ago, Davy dipped his fingers in her blood-slush, touched them to his tongue, then swallowed, allowing the doe's life-strength to flow into him. Favoring his injured finger, he trimmed off a big patch of hide from her back and exposed the sinew-sheathed backstraps. He scalped the doe and broke open her skull with a cobble. He wrapped the brain, sinew and backstraps in the piece of hide and stowed the soft bundle deep in his duffel.

THE DRIVER OF A THREE-QUARTER TON truck pulled over to the snow berm. Davy tossed his duffel into the truck bed amidst the scattered galvanized fence clips, hanks of orange plastic twine, and flakes of dried blood. He started to climbed into the cab, but hesitated when he spotted the blue heeler cowdog on the seat.

"Move over some Blue." said the cowboy. "Give 'em some room to sit. C'mon Boy. Git in."

Davy hopped in. He and the dog stared warily at one another.

"You spent the night out there, huh?"

Davy nodded at the hawk-faced man.

"Quite a storm last night," he drawled. "Reckon it was pretty cold. But that wasn't nothin' fer these parts. On *clear* nights it gits colder still. Yesterday I seen you south o' here walkin' this way. Thought you'd maybe stick out yer thumb or somethin' if you needed a ride. But I was headin' the other way," he said. The cowboy stroked his waxed mustache.

"I would've turned around too and picked you up Boy, but I had plans for drinkin' and whorin' last night—womanizin'. That's me. That's what I do." He paused. "Don't s'pose you ever been with a woman have you Boy?"

The runaway glanced over at the icy Little Bighorn River.

"Bet you're still at that chicken-chokin' stage o' life aren't you?" he chuckled. "I'd put twenty bucks on it."

Davy ignored him.

"You don't say much do you?"

He showed the cowboy his regular **'I'm mute'** note.

"Mute, huh? Well that explains it then. Why didn't you say so? How long you been that way?"

He scribbled: **Forever**

The cowboy paused and looked over at Davy. The man pinched the crease atop his brown wide-brimmed hat.

"You're Indian, am I right?"

He nodded.

"S'pose you know 'bout the battlefield down south then. Them Cheyenne and Sioux—they really kicked our 7th Cavalry asses, you know. During *that* battle anyway. Won the battle—lost the war."

Davy shrugged.

The cowboy spat tobacco juice into an empty Coors can. The long string of spittle snapped as he snugged the can back into the warmth of his crotch.

"What's yer tribe?"

Davy scribbled a note and showed him.

"Navajo, Apache and Buffalo River, huh? Ain't never heard o' no Buffalo River Indians. But them Apaches, sure. That Geronimo fella was one tough son-of-a-gun. And I know about them Navajo folks livin' down south. Looky here."

The cowboy held up a calloused hand with a silver ring on one thick finger. "Navajo," he declared. "Bought it at the Central Wyomin' Fair from a Indian gal when I was roughneckin' down there at the Oil Reserve."

Davy scrutinized his ring. *Those aren't Diné* [Navajo] *symbols*, he thought. *That's a Hopi ring.*

"Myself, I'm from East Texas. Grew up there. But ended up here followin' cattle jobs. Cowboyin'. I'm pretty traditional. I'm one o' them traditional buckaroos. Got a couple o' pack mules and a canvas officer's tent and all the old-style gear and tack. We git to do it just like back in the day with chuck wagons and tents when the corporate ranches do their roundups and trail rides. Shit like that. The name's Red McKinney. Call me Red. How 'bout you Boy? What's yer name?"

He scribbled and showed it to Red.

"Don't you got one o' them Indian names too?"

Davy scribbled again and showed him.

Red laughed.

"Hey, if you're a Indian, how come you got them gray eyes? Oh hell, ferggit I said that, okay Boy? It ain't none o' my beeswax."

Red motioned to the bloody sock.

"How'd you fuck up yer hand?"

Knife accident

"Hmm."

Red was quiet for a time before he spoke.

"Where you comin' from Boy?"

Davy scribbled.

"You go to school there?"

He nodded.

"What else you do—other than school?"

He scribbled.

"Hell Boy, you mean to tell me yer one o' them goddamn sheepherders? Lots o' damn sheepherders around these parts too if you haven't yet noticed. Myself, I'm a cattle man. Not a woolly maggot man like yerself. I work beef cattle. Don't have much use fer sheep—or sheepmen—or sheepherders fer that matter.

"You hungry Boy? Want somethin' to eat?"

He nodded.

"Okay, but we need to stop at my place first. Just 'membered—I gotta git somethin'."

On the edge of town, Red pulled into the unplowed driveway of an old white one-bedroom rental house with clapboard siding. Davy waited in the cab of the three-quarter ton while Red went inside. In the yard, the cowdog stared off into the distance. Davy looked too and realized there were sheep out there—hundreds of them—feeding far away on the snowy gray oil-shale benches and breaks of the winter range.

They do sort of look like woolly maggots out there on the land, he thought.

And then he saw something that gave him the willies. Beneath the bright blue sky was a sagging carcass-like figure—a scarecrow—strung-up on the fence, watching over Red's dead, weedy, unkempt garden. Davy reached under his coat for the knife handle to make sure it was still there.

Red stepped out the front doorway. He lingered there on the drifted-over porch and eyed the runaway. He gave Davy a twisted sort of expression. Then he spat in the snow and stepped forward. In his gloved hand he held a snake-like coil of rope.

"Ready," said Red. He tucked the rope behind the seat and flipped a rusty, palm-sized rod and hoop contraption onto the dash.

Davy looked at it.

"Know what that is Boy?"

He shrugged.

"Linchpin. It's fer lockin' the pintle hitch on—back o' the truck. Keeps whatever yer pullin' from gittin' away. Now that pintle hitch—it's gonna jerk you 'round some. Not like a gooseneck. That's what I really wanna git me one of these days. Next paycheck maybe. Ain't nothin' like a gooseneck hitch set-up. Smooth. Straddles the wheelbase. Pulls real nice. Myself, I much prefer a smooth ride to gittin' jerked. You with me Boy?"

Davy looked over at Red. A bit of light from the side mirror had settled on the man's forehead. The light-flick danced there for a moment like a tiny fiery cross, then slowly faded away. Red backed up the three-quarter ton and drove into town.

There were several pickups already parked in front of the café.

Red led the way to the entrance. "Git on in there Sheepherder," he said. He followed Davy inside. "Hey boys, looky who we got here," announced Red. He slammed the door. The bell jangled wildly. "A real live Indian—Apache and Navajo. And he's a damned sheepherder to boot."

The other cowboys laughed.

"Found 'em on the cut-off south o' here hitchhikin' our way. He's my special guest today. And I'll have you all know *I'm* the one that's buyin' 'em breakfast. Might be a while b'fore a hitchhikin' Indian gits another meal, am I right?"

Red and Davy sat down at a half-broken table across from a short man in a gray shirt. They ordered coffee and breakfast.

"Find any work yet Henderson?"

"Nope. There ain't shit for work around here this time of year."

"Well then, since you got time to kill, why don't you ride on up to Circle Town with me today—visit Cookie Monster? I got a delivery fer 'em. Sheepherder here is conveniently headin' that way too, so I figger we might as well drag 'em along," Red chuckled. "Might be somethin' in it fer you—might kill us a dog along the way, am I right?"

Red noticed Davy was watching the young waitress.

"Henderson, you had yerself a whore lately?" said Red. He slapped the table loudly.

"Nope. Not me. No money to."

"Well, like I was tellin' Sheepherder here, I had me one last night. Didn't I tell you that Boy? Twenty bucks. 'Course fer twenty bucks you don't actually know what yer gittin'. You see, they have this back room with a plywood wall with a hole in it. First they check yer pecker fer sores, then you pay 'em yer twenty bucks, and then they leave you alone. When they're gone you just stick yer pecker in the hole-in-the-wall. Coulda been yer gramma, Henderson. Coulda been that lard-ass sister o' yers. But most likely it was that plain jane waitress over there who was suckin' on me last night. Quit lookin' at her Boy—I'm talkin' to you."

"Might've been Sheepherder who was doin' it Red," said Henderson matter-of-factly. "You thought of that? You picked 'em up down south afterwards, right?"

Red glowered and lowered his voice. "Shut yer mouth Henderson—if you wanna live another day that is."

"Well, what d'you expect me to say when you talk that way about my gramma fer crissakes?"

1

KNOT A PROBLEM

DENVER, COLORADO
FEBRUARY 10ᵀᴴ, 2000

ARCHBISHOP JAMES MORENO WAS JOLTED AWAKE from his fitful sleep. Outside, the wind moaned. There'd been strange rustlings and things going jerkity-jerk, gaspity-gasp, bumpity-bump in the night. And now his phone was sounding off at 3 a.m.

"Really—she did? Memorial Hospital? Yes, of course. I'll meet you there."

He splashed cold water on his tired-looking face, squeezed an oil glob onto his palm and slicked back his thick black hair. This was one of those not-so-pleasant parts of his job—comforting the sick and performing the last rites sacrament at all hours, day or night. This particular request came from the well-to-do family of a woman who'd been quite generous to the archdiocese over the years. He didn't want to abandon her now in her hour of need. As he peered into the mirror, he pinched off a maggoty-looking little booger that clung there to a single nasal hair and flicked it in the general direction of the wastebasket. He clipped off the nasal hair, then adjusted his white slip-on collar.

The archbishop glanced at the clock again. He walked briskly down the rectory's long hallway, turned the doorknob, and stepped into the unlit oversized garage. Yellow streetlight streamed through the tiny windows. He felt his way to his black Lincoln, but tripped and fell over something. It clanked and scraped across the concrete floor. His eyes began to gradually adjust. In the dimness he could make out the shape of a steel folding chair. *Gilberto! Why can't that damned idiot put things away when he's done with them?*

When the archbishop got up he sensed hands grabbing him from behind. He spun in time to see a tall figure drawing back, ready to strike. But the shorter man struck first, his clenched fist catching the intruder under the chin. The figure absorbed the blow, then weaved and bobbed like an experienced fighter. The priest nailed the figure again with a hard right to the ribs, followed up by a bone-cracking left hook to the jaw. But the gangly intruder kept dodging and weaving and bobbing and holding his fists at-the-ready. The archbishop dove at him full force, headbutting his tenacious opponent, trying to tackle him. But he found himself clinging to the tall figure, spinning, as if on some wild carnival ride. In fear and anger, the archbishop reached up. He gouged and raked and clawed, going for the eyes. But the intruder seemed unphased. Then, in the dim light, he realized the two of them were swinging together—from the ceiling—from what appeared to be a rope.

He let go and made a quick break for the door. He flipped on the garage light as he re-entered the rectory hallway.

Looking back, he saw a slender corpse with long black hair swinging from an overhead beam. It created hideous shadows on the whitewashed walls, the grease-stained floor, and the shiny hood of the Lincoln. Then he recognized the corpse. It was that local Mexican-Indian mix kid—that transient—Johnny Deerskin or Doeskin or Elkskin—something like that. Johnny what's-his-face. That pesky lowlife alcoholic. The kid who kept penciling him those disturbing messages and showing up drunk at the main entrance every Friday night. *Why can't people simply forgive and forget and let sleeping dogs lie?* he thought.

The archbishop returned to the garage. He saw that Johnny's swollen bluish-gray face was now covered in scratch marks. His body was cold. Lifeless. He'd obviously been dead for hours. No use calling 911. Better to call the other number.

"GRAB HIS LEGS," said Officer Valdez. "Higher up. Now lift. Lift."

"Pat, can you do it?" said the archbishop as Valdez loosened the slipknot around the dead kid's neck.

"I'm off-duty in two hours. I just need to write a quick report, then clock-out. I'll be back soon. Just make sure to leave that side door there unlocked, okay?"

"I never lock it. Thank you Pat. I know it's a lot to ask. You've always come through for the Church."

"I'll put him in the regular place," said Valdez. "He's just a street bum, so he won't be missed. But if he *is* missed, he won't be found."

The archbishop got a pair of pliers from a toolbox and handed them to Valdez. "This kid's got one too. I'm the one who paid for it. I want it back. To square things up with the Church's dental office account."

Valdez spread Johnny's stiff lips. He pried the corpse's jaws open and twisted out the gold-capped incisor and plinked it into a plastic vial held by the archbishop.

"Wait a minute," said Valdez. "I've got another one for you. It's from that incident at the school in December. Forgot all about it." Valdez opened his rubber coin purse, withdrew a gold-capped canine tooth and plinked it into the archbishop's vial.

They laid out Johnny's body on a long sheet of polyethylene, then enshrouded it burrito-style. Valdez shoved Johnny's body into the shadows.

"Archbishop?"

"Yes Pat?"

"Don't go blaming yourself, okay? These stupid kids are making stupid decisions with their stupid brains these days. It's not your fault. He could've offed himself anywhere really. It's just a fluke he did it here."

"You're probably right."

"Archbishop?"

"Yes Pat?"

"About that other matter."

"Which one?"

The officer frowned.

"Oh, right. That one."

"Yes, that one. The parents are refusing to drop it. They want him brought up on charges for what he did to their kid."

"They do, huh?"

"Yeah. They say sending him off for treatment again and moving him to a different parish isn't right. So we'll need to have a meeting of the minds—work something out. Otherwise, they'll just take it on up the ladder. Go to the DA's Office. We'd lose containment. Wouldn't want that to happen, right?"

"I thought that might be the case. It's all about greed nowadays isn't it? Everybody's money-hungry." The archbishop retrieved a fat envelope from the Lincoln's glove box. "Here. I meant to give it to you yesterday. This should be enough to keep them quiet."

"What if it's not? What if we need more?"

"Not a problem," he said, rattling the plastic vial deep in his breast pocket. "My donors will gladly cover it."

8

KILL THAT DOG!

MONTANA
DECEMBER 18TH, 1999

THE NERVOUS MEN and high-strung cowdog scanned side-to-side as the runaway teen slept upright between them on the crowded seat. Red turned the three-quarter ton off the main highway north onto County Road 253. They entered a vast no-man's-land of windswept, snowed-over wheat fields and sagebrush country, an undulating ocean of yellow and gray and white waves. Red spat in his can, then snugged it back into his lap next to his upright rifle.

"I came through here 'bout the same time last year visitin' Cookie Monster," he whispered. "Killed me a goddamn dog right here. See them tall fence posts? I strung 'em up and peeled his skin off right there. Used a hollow-point bullet. Made a bloody mess of 'em. Pro'bly some bones still layin' out there. No traffic out this way. So it's a great place fer killin' one."

They drove a few miles farther. The cowdog's ears shot forward and the truck skidded to a stop.

"Git out—now!" said Red.

Davy dove over Henderson into the shallow drifts. Henderson was fast on his heels. Red leveled the rifle over the hood of the truck.

"Kill that dog!" yelped Henderson.

The long gun discharged. Davy felt the concussion. He slipped and nearly fell.

"Hurry Red, he's crossin' the damn coulee—he's gettin' away. Shoot again. Shoot 'em Red."

There was another *womp* from the varmint rifle and a telltale *thwop* as the bullet impacted the intended target. The gray blur out in the snow tumbled and lay still.

"Helluva shot," said Henderson.

"It was at that," Red grinned. "Make sure you tell the boys about it. Henderson, you need to earn yer keep. Git out there and fetch that songdog."

Henderson went and retrieved the dead coyote, slipping in the snow with each step in his slick-soled boots. When he finally returned, he was breathing hard.

"Dammit man, why'd you go and drag it? You pro'bly messed up the fur."

"What are the pelts bringin' this year?" said Henderson.

"Prices are still way down," said Red. "From what I hear, they're only payin' forty bucks a piece fer Montana pales like this. The off-colored ones are bringin' less."

"Good—that's twenty bucks a piece. You can use your half fer that plywood hole-in-the-wall you like so much."

Red laughed and hefted the big male coyote onto the truck bed. "Load up," he said.

They stopped at the next cattle guard. Red laid the bloody animal on the snow next to the H-brace. The heeler sniffed at it. Davy watched the part-time coyotero skillfully circumcise its anus. Red then hooked his blade up inside each hind leg and around its hocks and forelegs. He hung the dead canine from a post and, with his pliers and knife, commenced skinning it. After he freed the skin from the hind legs, Red stripped-out the tail, clipped off the penis and worked his way down to the shoulders. Using his knee for leverage, he pulled the skin down over the neck and cut deep at the ear butts and around the eyes. The naked, grey-hound-like carcass swung free and slapped the post as he swiped off the nose pad. He turned the pelt fur-side-out and scrubbed the bloody spots with snow. Finally, the cowboy whip-snapped it, rolled it into a fat cylinder and handed the bundle to Henderson.

"Sheepherder, go git me that coffee can—back o' the truck." Red latched onto the tufted anus with his pliers, pulled out several inches of butt gut, and sliced it off. He clipped some small bean-shaped glands from the back of the coyote's legs and tossed them in the can atop some other frozen shriveled anuses and glands. "O'Gorman makes a trappin' lure outta the assholes and glands," he explained. "Gives me a buck a piece. Cheapest piece o' ass in Montana," he laughed.

Red cleaned his hands in the snow. "Well, we're done here boys—now load up. Best keep yer eyes peeled case there's another dog out there. Watch them coulees and brushy fence lines fer movement."

They continued north.

"How long've you known this Cookie Monster character?" said Henderson.

Red looked at the skyline awhile before he spoke. "We been pards quite a while I s'pose."

"What's he do?"

"Well fer one thing, he kills folks that pisses 'em off. Aside from that, he's a fry cook at the Circle Café. Learned to cook while he was in the pen. That's where we met up actually. We was bunkies. Cookie's quite the badass—got sentenced fer murder. He joined up with the Aryan Brotherhood in there. 'Course the Brotherhood didn't want 'em to join—and they told 'em so. But he's so goddamn badass he just said he was joinin' the club regardless and that's exactly what he did. Pretty soon them White Power boys were payin' 'em cigarettes and ramen noodles and potato chips every day. He got all tatted up with swastikas, demons, SS skulls—shit like that. Cookie got paroled a few years back. Now he spends his time cookin', ropin' and trainin'."

"Trainin' fer what?"

"Fightin'. The kind o' fightin' they do in a caged ring—no holds barred. Blood baths basically. Last one standin' wins. Cookie'll beat the livin' shit out o' whoever he feels like. He'll take on anybody—big—or small." Red glanced at Davy through the rearview. "Like I said, he's one badass dude. You *don't* wanna make 'em mad."

"Why you call 'em 'Cookie Monster?'" said Henderson.

The runaway watched Red's eyes in the mirror.

"'Cause he's a cook. And 'cause he's a monster. When you see 'em you'll catch on real quick. Three hundred and fifty pounds o' ex-con Aryan Brotherhood badass—'The Cookie Monster'—as big and mean as the devil himself."

Davy donned his black headband.

9

THE COOKIE MONSTER

MONTANA
DECEMBER 18TH, 1999

THE THREE-QUARTER TON crested the windblown ridge then dropped into the frozen Redwater Valley. The little town of Circle lay ahead in the dimness, half-buried in wind-packed snow drifts.

"In the summer you can still see the teepee rings on that sagebrush bench overlookin' the town," said Red, "but the rocks are all sunk down flush with the ground now. See where them creeks come together? See that hill there? That's where the Indian village was. Then the fur trappers came and went. Then the wagon trains. Finally, a Confederate officer drove a herd o' Texas longhorns up here and turned the whole damn Valley into a cattle baron ranch. Opened a saloon and a store and pretty soon it was a regular cow town. Then those goddamned sheepmen moved in and pushed most of us cattlemen out. 'Stead o' huntin' buffalo, it seems the only Indians left 'round here now are flippin' burgers or herdin' sheep," said Red. He glanced in the rearview at Davy.

"When I first started workin' the Valley, the boss had me plantin' wheat up top in the spring, then workin' the bottoms there all summer—sprayin' and irrigatin', mowin' and bailin'—alfalfa and timothy hay. Then come fall he'd have all us hands do the big roundup and the brandin'. But lately, the Corporate Office has been phasin' out the cow-calf operation and puttin' more emphasis on the sheep enterprise."

At sundown, Red pulled to a stop in front of the café. The sign said 'closed,' but a light shown from inside.

"Grab yer bag Sheepherder—you might be beddin' down here tonight," said Red. "And I'm pro'bly bunkin' with Cookie as usual. His place is kinda small. So, Henderson, you'll have to fend fer yerself. You'll figger somethin' out."

A little brass bell sounded as they entered. At the back of the café sat a mountain of a man with his back to the visitors. His black felt hat was pulled low. Davy was shocked at the sheer enormity of the man. At the table with him were two young waitresses. One held an infant.

Red approached, while Davy and Henderson held back. "Hey Cookie. I got somethin' fer you." Red gave the coil of rope a flip and it landed on the table in front of the big man.

Cookie Monster grunted.

"And this is fer tonight," said Red. He set an unopened plastic jug of whiskey beside the lariat. Cookie Monster tapped it and grunted his approval.

"That ain't all Cookie. Looky here. Henderson and I drug this leppy sheepherder along with us."

"Goddamn sheepherders," grumbled Cookie.

"And guess what Cookie—he's a Indian. Apache Indian. What d'you say to that?"

Cookie Monster slowly lifted his head, then spoke. "Fuckin' Injuns."

Davy's blood ran cold. He felt under his coat for the knife handle.

Cookie Monster slowly turned around and peered straight into the runaway teen's eyes. A toothless grin spread across his broad brown face. Davy released his breath sharply and dropped his arms.

"Really gotcha there didn't I Kid? Sorry I rattled you like that," chuckled Cookie. "That's just my Indian humor comin' through. Natives like us—we gotta stick together, huh?"

"Sheepherder can't talk," said Red. "He's a mute—a hand talker. But you can figger out what his hands are sayin' some of the time. And when you can't, he writes it down fer you."

"I don't read too good," said Cookie. The big man paused. "Well Sheepherder, Red brought me whiskey and a rope. What do *you* got for me?"

Davy quickly retrieved the deerskin bundle from his duffel and set it on the table.

"What's this? Deer meat, huh? Fresh. I thought the season was over. Thanks. Hey, I was just kiddin' Kid—you don't owe me nothin'—but thanks. So did you cut yourself skinnin' it or what?"

Davy shook his head 'no.' He turned the bloody sock dressing over for the man to see.

Cookie beckoned one of the waitresses to examine Davy's hand, then he opened the bundle of meat. "Hey Sheepherder, I'll cook up the meat for you, but you keep the skin and guts—got it?" He laughed and handed hide and sinew and brain halves back to Davy.

Cookie draped the backstraps over his massive palm. "Well Boys, find your-selves a seat somewheres. I'm gonna work you up some loin steaks—butterflied and bacon-wrapped. Red, go get me a bag o' spuds and three onions from the back. And slice up them onions Red 'cause you're the one gonna be cryin' like a baby tonight—not me—got it?" he laughed.

"But what about them?" grumbled Red. He gestured toward the waitresses. "Can't one o' 'em do it 'stead o' me?"

The older waitress was feeding the baby and speaking with Henderson. The younger one had retrieved a first aid kit and was carefully unwrapping Davy's hand.

"The girls clocked-out already Red. B'sides, Brooke is trainin' at bein' a nurse's aide. Can't you see she's busy playin' doctor on Sheepherder's hand al-ready? That leaves you for the preppin' and me for the cookin'—got it?"

Undated Entry
from Hand Talker's Journal

One day these three pretty Mexican girls came to see their cousin who was a senior there at our all-boys school. These girls were from the San Luis Village in Colorado. All of us guys thought they were absolute foxes. I think they knew it too because they flirted with us. We were all there at the boarding school studying to be priests, but they flirted with us anyway. Us guys were giving them a tour and walking around the school with them. Their cousin left and pretty soon it was just three of us guys and those three girls. We all went behind the gym. It was almost dark and the other guys were talking and laughing and joshing with the girls. I was hand talking with this one girl fox who was really flirting with me. I think she liked me because I was quiet and different from the other guys. Her name was Gabby Sanchez. She talked a lot. I mean a lot. She was a couple years older than me, about 16 or 17. She was the most beautiful girl I had ever seen. The girls and us guys got into couples and got apart so we could be alone. Then Gabby stopped talking and showed me how to kiss. She opened her mouth and we put our tongues in each other's mouth and kissed that way for a while. Then she put her hand down my pants. She kissed my neck and ears and told me I was her savior priest and she was a devil woman there to tempt me. Then she undid my pants and used her mouth. It was very soft. I felt the electricity when Gabby did that to me. When I came it was like lightning. After that she taught me how to work her little beaver with my hand. I worked her little beaver for a long time and she got my hand all wet. When I was doing that Gabby did not talk at all. She just shivered and moaned. When we were done she said I was a beautiful guy and that was how girls wanted me to hand talk with them from then on. She said I was the best hand talker ever and it would be a shame if I ever did become a priest instead of a hand talker for girls like her. I never saw Gabby Sanchez again. After that happened with her behind the gym I thought a lot about whether or not I should stay at the boarding school and become a priest so I could help the Dené. I thought about it all the time.

10

THE SNAKE MAN
MONTANA
DECEMBER 19TH, 1999

IN THE EARLY DAWN LIGHT Davy leaned forward in his chair and methodically scraped the salvaged piece of deerskin with the back of his knife. Now and then he looked down at the sleeping golden-haired waitress breathing heavily near his feet. She was tucked halfway into his bedroll under the café table on the plum-colored carpet.

He watched Brooke's bare breast rise and fall—its curvature changing with each rapid breath. She was flushed and sweating. He stopped scraping and observed the tiny dust particles dancing and flying over her freckled nose and twitching lids and lashes for a while. He hoped that, when she awoke, Brooke would tell him more of her stories about Billy Gantry—the traveling faith healer she claimed was a Snake Man able to give people new tongues. 'Billy Gantry will fix your voice box tomorrow,' she said. 'I swear to God he will.'

Brooke mumbled something in her sleep. He couldn't quite make it out. Then she said it again louder—more urgently: "Hallelujah!" She arched her back and fluttered her eyelids wildly. She moaned and gasped for breath. Then Brooke opened her eyes and saw that he was watching her. She smiled and reached up to touch the fresh gauze on his hand. He continued scraping.

"What you makin' Davy?"

'Deerskin pouch,' he signed.

"I bet it'll be really cool when you're done."

Brooke yawned, then slipped out of the bedroll and into the john.

Davy stuffed the piece of deerskin and his bedding into the duffel. In the café kitchen he reheated some of yesterday's coffee and found some foil and made a packet of leftover venison and fried potatoes and onions for the road. Brooke joined him. They heated some food and ate while her car outside warmed-up and the windows defrosted.

Together they stepped out and she pulled the café door shut behind them, making sure it was locked. She kissed him and told him where to meet her later in the day. "You better be there Shy Guy. That Snake Man will make you talk. I promise."

Davy waved his bandaged hand at her, cut finger extended. Brooke laughed and flipped him off in return. He smiled. She drove away down the freshly plowed street.

On the west side of town Davy found the three-quarter ton parked in front of a small white house. The cowdog eyed him as he let himself in the front door. He heard loud snores coming from down the hallway. The living room smelled of wet dog and blood and whiskey. A game table was overturned. Cards and poker chips lay scattered about. Red lay unconscious on the green, ivy-patterned carpet. Except for a pair of bachelor-washed, pink-tinted underwear and a snake tattoo covering each scarred wrist, he was naked. Thick, half-dry blood crusted his face, neck and chest.

The blue heeler stared at Davy while the teen washed Red's swollen face with a dishrag and warm water. Red moaned. Pieces of the cowboy's broken nose gently scraped against one another beneath the bloody cloth while he worked. Davy carefully bandaged the man's nose and helped him onto the couch.

"Last night we got to drinkin'," explained Red. "Cookie overdid it again. Got totally wasted. I must've done somethin' or other that set 'em off. Don't really recall too much."

Davy nodded.

"Goddamn this fucked-up life," groaned Red. "So anyway, how'd it go with you and that young nurse gal last night? What's her name—Brooke?"

He shrugged.

"No kiss and tell, huh? Hell Boy, you truly are a sheepherder."

Davy back-trailed Red's blood drippings to a back room where Cookie lay sprawled on his bed, drunk and snoring. Atop a nightstand sat the empty plastic whiskey jug. He tried to rouse the slumbering giant, but it was no use, so he followed the blood trail back to the living room.

Red was busy contemplating a dead fly stuck in a crack in the ceiling plaster above the couch. The cowdog lapped at the little pool of blood on the floor. Against one wall leaned the half-dry coyote skin hooked to a wire stretcher.

Davy retrieved his cedar flute from his duffel. He cleaned the mouthpiece, then pulled a chair over next to Red. As he played, the blue heeler cocked its head and stared at him. After he finished four healing songs, he cleaned the mouthpiece again and put the instrument back in its otter skin pouch.

"Thanks—Hand Talker—best thing anyone's done fer me in quite a while. Have a safe trip up north, okay? Look me up if you ever make it back this way. You know yer welcome in my camp anytime."

Davy nodded.

"Hey, I seen you admirin' that songdog pelt. It's yers if you want it."

Davy shook his head 'no' and scribbled something.

"Bad luck, huh?" said Red. "Some kinda Indian taboo? Well it's pro'bly fer the best I s'pose 'cause I only own half of it anyway. Henderson and I were plannin' on sellin' it and splittin' the proceeds."

Davy waved 'goodbye.'

Stepping out onto the icy porch, he shouldered his duffel and headed into the glaring mid-morning sun. He picked his way along the plow line at the edge of the street. There was a high school off to his left. He spun right. A red brick church with large, jagged cracks in the mortar and tall stained-glass windows loomed to one side. A few people in heavy coats trundled up the steps, shook hands with a bespectacled elderly priest and filed through its arched doorway. The black-robed man noticed the boy and waved him over.

Davy stopped and stared at him. The priest flashed him a grin. Davy looked away and trudged sunward. He passed a Traveler's Inn and a Tastee Freeze nestled among the snow drifts. In the middle of town, he found Brooke's car in a parking lot next to a whitewashed cinderblock building. Gospel music resonated from within. A plastic banner over the entrance read: *'Revival Meeting—Billy Gantry—Faith Healer & Snake Man'*

A man at the door grabbed Davy's elbow and led him inside. The air was thick and warm and smelled of sweat. Mothers and fathers and siblings and cousins and grandparents stood at the pews, crowded together. They sang to the accompaniment of an electric organ played by a blind man in a too-tight yellow and black plaid suit. An old hound dog laid its head on one of the man's worn vinyl shoes.

Soon, Brooke spotted Davy. She gave him a hug and escorted him to a pew near the front platform. At the pulpit stood a wiry preacher with flaky skin and oil-slicked hair in a shimmering diamond-pattern polyester blazer. The preacher's body rocked while he sang. The members of the congregation smiled and sang along with him, swaying with arms held high and eyes closed tight. Brooke held up one of Davy's arms while the man beside him raised his other one. "I am your brother," the man yelled to him over the din.

When the song ended, the people took their seats. Preacher Man spoke, calmly at first, but then more and more excitedly. He told the people that they were all each other's brothers and sisters. Then he brandished a battered book and said 'amen' and everyone yelled 'amen.' Blind Man played a chord on the organ while his old dog howled. At the closing of the chord, Blind Man tossed the hound a dog biscuit. Preacher Man shouted 'hallelujah' and everyone yelled 'hallelujah.' Blind Man played another chord while the dog howled, then gulped down another biscuit. Preacher Man ranted about 'evildoers' and 'sinners' and some other kind of people called 'fornicators.'

"Amen," hollered golden-haired Brooke.

The brother beside Davy nodded approvingly at Sister Golden Hair.

Preacher Man told of a glorious heaven and a fiery hell and eternal damnation and the need to repent and to listen to Jesus's message of salvation so as to be saved by God's grace. He talked about God and the devil and trials and tribulations and a coming battle with a beast that would bring forth victory and a jubilee celebrating a New Kingdom. Then he told of a Holy Ghost who allows men like him to cast out devils and take up serpents and talk with new tongues. Preacher Man asked if any brothers or sisters needed to be healed.

Brother Man and Sister Golden Hair grasped Davy's arms and pulled him forward from his seat till they were standing with him on the platform in front of the pulpit. Preacher Man leaned forward. Brooke whispered something to him. Preacher Man nodded and placed a clammy hand over Davy's mouth and another over his bandaged hand.

"I've been told this poor boy cannot speak-uh. We pray today the Holy Ghost shall visit upon him the gift of tongues." Preacher Man begged and pleaded with God for the power to heal the teen. Then he thumped Davy's forehead with his palm. "Speak Boy."

Davy tried to say something, but was unable. Preacher Man thumped him harder and yelled, "You're healed. Now speak Boy—speak-uh."

Once more Davy tried to talk. Only an eerie hiss came forth.

Then Preacher Man thumped Sister Golden Hair on her forehead. Eyes closed, she fell into the waiting arms of Brother Man. He laid the babbling, shaking, quaking girl onto the platform where she lay, one shoe off, the hem of her dress riding up across her lap, a small triangular patch of white cotton exposed.

"Praise Gawd-uh," shouted Preacher Man.

"Praise God," yelled the people while Blind Man played a chord and flipped the dog a treat.

Davy went and carefully pulled Brooke's rumpled dress down to hide her underwear and thighs. He retrieved her loose shoe and held it.

Preacher Man bent low and placed his hands upon Sister Golden Hair. "As sure as Gawd-uh makes apples, he grants me the power to heal. Amen. Hallelujah!"

"Hallelujah," yelled the people to the accompaniment of Blind Man's organ and howling hound.

Then Preacher Man started to sweat. His body began to weave this way and that, back and forth, to and fro while he placed his hands here and there upon Sister Golden Hair. Soon, the babbling girl began convulsing. She grasped one of Preacher Man's hands and clasped it to her breast.

A buxom middle-aged woman in a wheelchair called out from the back pew. She quickly wheeled herself down the aisle to the platform and shrieked for Preacher Man's attention. He left the girl and went to the chair-bound woman and placed his hands upon her shoulders reassuringly.

"Now tell me Woman. How long have you been imprisoned by this chair-uh?"

"Twenty years," she stated.

"This woman has been bound to a wheelchair for twenty years-uh." He paused and looked into her sober eyes. "Woman, do you wish to be healed?"

"More than anything Billy Gantry. I want to walk again. I want to walk."

"Woman, do you see that boy over there? That gentile?"

"Yes. I see him."

Davy's face reddened. His muscles tensed.

"That boy cannot speak-uh because he lacks faith. He does not believe in the power and the glory of Gawd-uh. He does not believe in the power of healing-uh. Now tell me Woman. Do you truly believe? Do you believe that *He* gives *me* the power to heal *you*?"

"Yes. I do believe—I do believe Billy Gantry."

"If you truly believe, then I command you to walk-uh. Stand up Woman and walk-uh." Preacher Man thumped her forehead.

The woman closed her eyes, threw her head back and shivered her body. Then she opened her eyes and looked directly at Preacher Man. She placed her hands on the armrests and stood. The congregants gasped. She took a small, hesitant step—and then another—and soon she was walking and stepping lively and prancing and dancing with her hands held high.

"Praise God. Thank you Jesus," she said. Tears streamed down her cheeks.

"Thank you Jesus," shouted the wide-eyed onlookers.

Perspiring profusely, Preacher Man weaved and gyrated back and forth and leapt high in the air. Then he shuffled to the center of the platform and stood there. Still. Solemn.

He looked skyward and whispered, "Brethren, together let us pray: Heavenly Father, your mighty prophets have said that men who take up serpents in Your Name shall not be harmed. It is in Your Name then that I take up a most deadly serpent."

Brother Man stepped forward. In his hands was a large plywood box with a screened top. Preacher Man removed his sweat-soaked blazer and rolled up the sleeves of his white shirt. He unlatched the lid of the box and peered in.

"I am protected by His armor. Praise Gawd-uh."

"Praise God," echoed the people.

He reached in and lifted a large rattlesnake and held it aloft for all to see.

Blind Man began playing a rhythmic song on his organ while Preacher Man circled Sister Golden Hair with the snake in his outstretched arms. Brother Man kneeled beside the prostrate girl. He trembled his hands over her and quivered his body as she gibbered to him. Her eyes momentarily opened. Preacher Man leapt high over the babbling Brooke, displaying his snake to her. There was a sudden blur of motion. Something small landed on the platform beneath him. Preacher Man's foot landed on the girl's empty shoe. His ankle rolled. His knee buckled. And, for a brief moment, he glanced at Davy and beheld the fierceness in the runaway teen's piercing eyes.

The faith healer's body slammed into the platform. The snake bit into him at the base of his neck. He grunted in pain and jerked away, ripping its fangs from his flesh. Two bright crimson spots appeared on the man's white collar.

The people gasped.

Brother Man held the screened lid open as Preacher Man got up and returned the rattlesnake to its cage.

"Fear ye not Brethren," said Preacher Man, "for I am fine. Gawd-uh protects me." He rubbed his neck, then asked if there were any brothers or sisters in attendance who wished to be saved. Sister Golden Hair arose and kneeled there before him at the edge of the platform.

Preacher Man placed his sweaty palms on the girl's flushed face. She simultaneously laughed and cried and squealed her gibberish to him.

"Child, may you be washed in the blood of the lamb-uh."

He orated and gesticulated ever more feverishly while his reddening shoulder and neck and head swelled and his throat constricted. His speech thickened, his words slurred, and his tongue slurped in and out of his mouth. The girl gushed forth a soprano gibberish louder and louder and louder till she was screaming in a fit of ecstasy. His skinny neck now plump and purplish, Preacher Man croaked and coughed and hunched and thrust and sputtered and spat. Without warning, he lunged forward, slid off the platform, and collapsed on the floor. The woman-who-could-now-walk ran to his side. She comforted the gagging man. Foam squirted from his mouth while his jaw rhythmically flexed and slackened like a spent salmon at the end of its spawn-run.

It was high noon when Davy caught Brooke's attention. Upon seeing her shocked expression, he shyly waved farewell, then eased his way out the side door. A siren sounded from behind as he walked eastward with the duffel slung over his shoulder.

At the edge of town he reached a crossroads. He turned north and tramped along the plow line till the town was far behind.

II

Border Crossin'

Montana
December 19th, 1999

MERLE HAGGARD BELTED OUT a golden oldie big rig tune on the AM radio station while the 18-wheeler rumbled north on Highway 13.

The road sign said, *'Canadian Border 1/2 Mile Ahead'*

The driver lowered the volume. "Davy, get your passport ready. They'll wanna see it."

Davy shook head 'no.'

"What—you don't have one? Why not?"

He shrugged.

"Dammit Kid. I should've known. You're a runaway aren't you? From Fort Peck—right?"

He shook head 'no' again and scribbled.

Going to La Ronge

"La Ronge. That's in Saskatchewan?"

Davy nodded.

"Never heard of it. Your family lives there?"

My Auntie Millie

"Where are your folks?"

Dead—Car accident

The trucker was silent for a moment, then spoke again: "You're positive you don't have a passport?"

Davy shrugged again, head tilted.

The man pondered his options. "Just play along with me. Let me do all the talk—sorry. You know what I mean."

Davy shrunk into the door of the big rig and chewed his lip.

The trucker braked as he approached the border check station. He rolled down the window and displayed his driver's license to the uniformed agent below.

"How long were you in the States, Sir?"

"Two days." He handed him the manifest for the return load of cattle, along with some other papers.

"Vet certification—brand inspection report—looks to be in order. You can head on over to the scale. The ag inspector will meet you there. But wait. Before you go, open your door for me."

The trucker complied. The agent ascended the tractor step and locked eyes with Davy.

"What about him?" said the agent.

"Him?"

"Yeah him. You see anyone else sitting there next to you?"

"That's my kid."

"Well where's his driver's license?"

"Doesn't have one. He's not quite old enough to drive."

"How about a passport?"

"Sorry. We left it at home. But we travel together a lot. My boy Davy and I. Forgot it this time."

"Sir, I'm the one who checked you two days ago when you were south-bound—remember? You were alone then."

"Right. He—Davy—was staying with relatives in Billings. I'm bringing him back home."

The agent's brows narrowed. His brown eyes searched the White trucker's blue eyes for signs of deception.

"He's Indigenous," explained the trucker. "Adopted by me and my wife."

"What's your name Kid?" said the agent.

Davy shrugged and scrunched tighter against the door, focusing his eyes on the border agent's gold badge.

"My boy's mute. Like I said, his name's Davy."

"Is that right Kid? You're Davy—and he's your adoptive dad?"

Davy nodded vigorously.

The agent was suspicious. "No need to be so nervous Kid. You're not in trouble or anything. Now tell me exactly where you live in Canada? Which town?"

Davy thought back. What the heck was the name of that place the trucker mentioned to him when he was scrambling up into the cab earlier? His map showed the national border, but nothing beyond that. The teen scribbled, then showed the agent.

Vagina

The agent guffawed loudly. "Being a wise guy, huh?"

Davy shrugged and shot him a stupid grin.

"Seems there's a joker in every family. That's what my goofball brother used to call it too. Welcome home to Canada Davy. Just make sure to bring your passport next time. Now before I change my mind, you two jokers best be on your way back to Regina."

12

REUNION

LA RONGE, SASKATCHEWAN
DECEMBER 27TH, 1999

H E FOUND THE CABIN right where the letter carrier said it would be. Last house on the dead-end street. The yard was cluttered with broken-down, snow-draped machinery. An old brown sedan was parked in the driveway. A rusty truck sat propped on blocks to one side. Fresh bark and wood chips lay strewn about on the track-packed snow near a makeshift sawhorse. A nearby black spruce sheltered a massive pile of freshly split firewood. Tufts of hollow brown hair and bits of rawhide skittered in the breeze across the porch planks.

At his knock, an overweight Indigenous woman in a long gingham dress answered.

"Sheez—Hand Talker!" said Auntie Millie. "Get in here. Come inside where it's warm." Her strong hands gathered him in and slammed the heavy door. The woodstove behind her belched a puff of smoke.

Davy hugged her hard.

"I can't believe it," she said. "You came all that way alone. I could've come and got you, you know. You didn't have to run away Kiddo. I would've come for you."

He shrugged and grinned.

"Put your bag down. Rest awhile. You must be starving. You need a solid supper in that skinny thing you call a belly after such a long trip. Betcha could eat a whole moose, eh? Aoo'. Well that's just what you'll be eating then. There's moose loaf in the fridge. And I baked bread today." She put the tea kettle on the stove. "Sorry if I'm a little slow—my knees aren't doing too well. Sit down there while I get a plate ready for you. You like ketchup, right?"

He nodded.

"So tell me about your trip Hand Talker."

'Long story,' he signed.

She looked him over as she pushed back her faded flowing hair. "You don't seem too worse for wear."

'Where'd the moose meat come from?' he signed.

"Your cousin Nate got it. He usually comes home empty-handed. Only two days left in the season when he stumbled on a young bull and got off a good shot. It's real good and tender, eh? Half of it is hanging in the old school bus out back. Keeps it safe from the town dogs that wander by. Nate takes good care of me. Did you see that pile of firewood out front? That was him."

When he'd finished eating, Davy scribbled on his notepad and signed to his aunt, telling her the story of his journey from Denver to northern Saskatchewan.

"You could always go back to school you know," she said.

He shook his head 'no.'

"Then maybe next fall. Stay here awhile. Give it a rest. Then go back."

'I'm not going back,' he signed.

She saw the pain in his bright eyes. "Well, maybe you can enroll at the high school here—or study for the equivalency test."

He looked away.

"School's important Hand Talker. Education helps you get to where you want to be in life. Helps you do things you enjoy doing. It opens doors for you."

He scribbled on his notepad.

School sucks—I can't go back—My decision

"I know it is. Well, let's just think on it awhile, eh? No use deciding right away."

He shrugged.

"Come on Kiddo. Let me show you your room so you can get settled in. It seems you need a shower too."

He grabbed his duffel and followed Auntie Millie.

She motioned to the bed. "It's got brand new sheets. I washed them so they won't make you all itchy. You'll need to change them once a week. And I put a couple towels there on the dresser for you."

Davy noticed the letters 'HT' embroidered in the color of red ocher on the corner of the pillowcase. He touched one of the letters.

"I was hoping you won't mind if I keep calling you 'Hand Talker.' I never could get used to you calling yourself 'Davy' in your letters after you went away to that school in Denver. Anyway, after I got the call you were on your way here to La Ronge, I had some time on my hands—waiting. I wanted to do something special and embroider it all out for you, but the arthritis in my fingers got in the way. So I shortened it to 'HT.' Hope you don't mind."

He grinned and gave her another big hug.

"So, HT," she chuckled. "My joints are sore. Will you play me some songs on your ts'isǫǫ́s before you go to bed?"

THE NEXT MORNING HT heard noises coming from down the hallway. Pots and pans rattled. Soon the aroma of frying bacon reached his nostrils. He dressed and padded into the kitchen.

"You're up early, eh," said Auntie Millie. "Did you sleep well?"

He nodded.

"Sorry about yesterday. I don't mean to bug you about school, eh. It's just that education is my passion. Can't help it I guess—I'm on the Assembly's Education Committee. Anyway, I don't mean to be bossy or anything. It's your life to live as you see fit."

'It's okay,' he signed.

"This is your home now. And if there's anything you need to tell me, you know I'm always here to listen. Aoo'. I've heard some rumors about those residential schools. You'd tell me if any of it was true, eh?"

He shrugged and stuffed a big piece of bacon in his mouth.

She smiled and gave him a bear hug. "Teachers aren't perfect. But you can always count on them to protect you.

"Sit down Kiddo. You want some tea? How about some eggs to go with your bacon? Two or three?" He held up three fingers.

The wind flexed the outer pane of glass as he studied the gray sky beyond.

"Have you got any plans for today Hand Talker?"

He shrugged.

"Maybe you can drop by the Wellness Center and have them look at your hand. There might be something they can do to fix your finger."

HT held out his hand, middle finger extended. Auntie Millie examined the nasty looking scar at its base.

"Can you move it at all?"

He shook his head 'no.'

"Yeah. Having a stuck finger like this might cause you problems. Folks might think you're from California or something."

13

A VISITOR

LA RONGE, SASKATCHEWAN
JANUARY 1ST, 2000

HT CRACKED OPEN the cabin's heavy wooden door.

The young visitor smiled. "Hey there Hand Talker. Happy New Year!" HT studied the fur-framed face of the girl peeking out at him through her parka hood. His gaze quickly dropped to her winter boots.

"Well, are ya gonna let me in or what Cousin?" she laughed.

He opened the door wider.

"Millie told me you'd be here all alone." She looked around the empty room. "So anyway, I'm Macha. 'Member that time we visited you guys at the rez—and a skinwalker almost got us?"

He nodded, then shrugged.

"That was some crazy shit, eh? It still scares me to think about the door bustin' open like that."

HT studied her boots some more.

"Millie said you was even cuter now—and she's right."

He smiled.

"You got cool eyes Hand Talker. They're silver-like. Fuck!"

'Wait a minute,' he signed.

Then he got his notepad and scribbled something and showed her.

"Shut up! You're a funny guy. Well anyway, I came by to say 'hey' and welcome you to La Ronge. So I'll be seein' you around school, eh?"

He shook his head 'no.'

"You're graduated?"

No—Just not going

"Oh."

Long story—School sucks

"Yeah, it does. So when's Millie comin' back?"

He scribbled.

"She tell you why I moved out?"

He shook his head 'no.'

"Oh. Well it was 'cause she's always gettin' into my shit. Instead of lettin' me do stuff on my own. So, you wanna go catch a movie Hand Talker?"

He nodded.

"Got any pot?"

He shook his head 'no.'

"No worries. I'll share with you. So what do you think of La Ronge so far? It's a real shithole, eh? There's absolutely *nothin'* to do here. I get so friggin' bored out of my gourd."

He shrugged.

I like it here—Peaceful—Nice people

"For reals? What's your clan? I'm Whitefish Clan."

Born to Mud Clan—Born for One Walks Around Clan

"Mud Clan? Your mom was Mud Clan?"

He nodded.

"You got a protector, eh?"

He scribbled: *Porcupine*

"That's cool. Porkypines are cute—like you. C'mon Honey, let's go."

They walked downtown to the theater and went in. An action flick was playing. Macha chose seats in the back row. She put her arm around him. He stared at the rainbow of lights flickering across her brown skin.

"You don't gotta be so shy Hand Talker. If you stay shy it'll always just be coulda, woulda, shoulda for you."

She kissed him, then reached down and began kneading his lap.

"Good thing we're marriage cousins and not blood cousins, eh?" she whispered. "Otherwise, we couldn't do nothin' at all. Not even kiss."

After the movie they walked several blocks to a modular church building and went behind it. Macha produced a small canister of marijuana and a little soapstone pipe shaped like a fish. She lit up and offered him a hit.

'No thanks,' he signed.

"Why not?"

I promised someone

Macha tried the church door. It was unlocked, so they snuck inside and she locked it. They stood behind the altar. She put her arms around his neck and began rocking with him. Kissing him.

Then she stopped. "You got protection, right? Hey, you don't keep a porkypine in your undies do you?"

He smiled and shook his head 'no.'

"No worries. Just pull out beforehand so I don't get pregnant, eh Honey? I'll get you a box of rubbers from the Wellness Center for next time. They give 'em to us fuckin' kids for free."

14

THE FISHERMEN

LAC LA RONGE AREA, SASKATCHEWAN
JANUARY 15TH, 2000

NATE BAITED HT'S HOOK with a chunk of fish.

"Hey Cousin," he said, "Auntie Millie and me are signed up for *Introduction to Sign Language* at the Ed Center. Every Tuesday and Thursday evenin'. So we'll be better at talkin' with ya, eh?"

HT nodded. 'I need to pee,' he signed.

"Go ahead. Just step outside. But close the door to keep the heat in. And here, take the auger out as long as you're goin'.'"

HT etched his name in yellow on the lake ice. As the steam rose, he recalled how he and his twin Shash Yáázh made curving yellow crosses in the desert air when they urinated together outside. The north wind bit at HT's exposed neck.

Back inside the shanty he rubbed his hands together for warmth and gave a low whistle. 'It's damn cold,' he signed.

"Yah, she's a cold one out there," said Nate. "But this is whatcha gotta put up with if ya wanna catch fish in the winter, eh?"

HT nodded hesitantly.

Nate showed him how to jig the bait up and down to attract fish. They sat on their padded seats and waited.

"Hey Cousin," said Nate, "I can tell there's somethin' been botherin' ya. I've got a lot of personal stuff goin' on myself too. Do ya wanna talk about it?"

The short pole in HT's hand suddenly bent nearly in half.

"Ya got one there. Reel it in quick. Here—I got the gaff. Don't get too close to those teeth, eh. He's a northern pike and he can take a finger right off. Ya don't wanna lose that special finger of yours now do ya?"

HT displayed his finger to Nate.

"Just kidding. Those teeth are sharp, but ya wouldn't lose a finger or nothin'. Hey, that one's probably six or seven kilos. Good job there Cousin. Way to go. Club it—club it hard. eh."

HT was amazed at the size of the pike. 'You eat them?' he signed.

"Damn right we eat 'em. Why'd ya say that?"

HT pointed his chin south toward Navajoland.

He wrote: ***We don't eat fish***

"Ya probably ate fish every Friday at that residential school but thought it was chicken or somethin'. Bein' a rez kid, ya might not have even known it. Anyway, tonight you'll know it's a fish that you're eatin'. You'll find out what ya've been missin' all this time. We'll catch a few more maybe, then go back and cook some up fresh. Auntie Millie makes a special batter. We'll do a fish fry tonight, okay? She'll be glad ya got this one. Betcha she's gettin' tired of eatin' moose every day, eh? We need to filet it before it freezes. Watch how I do it, and then ya get to do the next one."

Nate ran the long thin blade along the fish's spine and showed him how to fold the flesh back and cut it free from the rows of bones.

"Look Cousin—ya got another one. You're quite a fisherman."

HT grinned.

15

DREAMS OF UNITY

SASKATOON, SASKATCHEWAN
FEBRUARY 3RD, 2000

WITH HT IN-TOW, Auntie Millie pushed through the group of chatting First Nations chiefs and elders. Together, they made their way to the far side of the meeting room. HT chose a chair against the wall behind his aunt's seat at the massive round table. Everyone stood while the Indigenous Honor Guard placed the flags. The previous Regional Chief offered a blessing, then he passed her an eagle wing.

"Márcı ją nuwe ghą núhdël," said Auntie Millie. "Thank you all for being here. Please go ahead and take your seats. Now I want to thank our outgoing chief—Billy—for all his hard work during this past term. Thank you very much Billy. And I want to extend my appreciation to everyone—no matter who you supported during the election. I'm thrilled to have been chosen to serve you. As the new Chief of Saskatchewan's Federation of Sovereign Indian Nations—representing all 74 of our First Nations—I want to assure you my door is always open. I'll do my best to keep the commitments I made to you all and make sure no one is left out.

"First, I'll focus on ensuring our youth can get the education they need to find good jobs. Education is, and always will be, number one in my book.

"Second, I'll continue working closely with the Housing Committee and Health Committee to ensure our people are adequately sheltered and cared for. This increasing homelessness problem we're experiencing is unacceptable. We need more affordable housing.

"Next, we need to make sure everyone—especially our young people—have the opportunity to get a job that pays a living wage.

"Hey there Sarah. Glad you could make it. This was quite a long trip for you, eh? There are still some empty seats here behind me along the wall. Come sit next to my nephew.

"Now where were we? Yes. Finally, I'll be working with our National Chief to expand the Assembly of First Nations to include all Métis, Inuit and First Nations people, including our neighbors in Alaska and the Lower 48 states—to make it a stronger organization—an international union of nations. Most of you here are Ojibwe-Cree and Dené. My late husband Petey Roberts was Lac La Ronge Woodland Cree. Dad was Buffalo River Dënesųłıné—that's how I became chairwoman of our Band. And of course Mom is Navajo-Apache. I am of the Mud People Clan.

"As someone who used to travel quite a bit, I can tell you the Dené are a pretty diverse group. Those of us here up north run traplines and hunt caribou and moose. Those of us along the coast are salmon eaters. And those of us in the desert raise sheep and corn. Although our languages are dying out in many places, we share many of the same words. And we are all family. Really, I think that goes for all Indigenous people, eh? We are all family. And family members need to help each other out.

"We owe it to our young people—youngsters like my nephew behind me here, Hand Talker Judd. Stand up so they can see you. Aoo'! Don't be shy Hand Talker. You're the reason we need to grow the National Assembly into an international group. And who knows? Maybe someday you'll be leading it, eh?" She chuckled and winked at him.

"Anyway, on behalf of the FSIN Executive, thank you all very much for the opportunity to represent and serve you this term."

16

THE WITCHERY WAY

LA RONGE, SASKATCHEWAN
FEBRUARY 5TH, 2000

OUTSIDE, THE AFTERNOON WIND HOWLED AND SCREECHED. The snow-blow was horizontal, creating near white-out conditions.

Auntie Millie settled her bulk onto the old Chesterfield sofa next to HT. She zipped up her thick gray Cowichan sweater. Together, they listened to the creak of the cabin timbers.

'Will you tell me?' he signed.

"You heard it all before when you were a little guy. But I suppose it's good to hear it again."

HT waited.

"There's a lot of superstition and magic in Diné [Navajo] culture, eh. Good magic is used for good things. Like when we women heal ourselves during the Blessing Way sing to reach hózhǫ́ [inner peace]. In the same way good magic can be used for good things, bad magic can be used if someone wants to be a witch and do bad things. People who decide to use bad magic are called 'ánt ii hnii. A witch is called 'adiłgashii. Witches follow the witchery way—a perversion of the healing and blessing ceremonies of our people. And when a witch disguises itself, usually at night, it's called yee naaldlooshii—a skinwalker. Witches become skin-walkers by shapeshifting into an animal or by disguising themselves with a skin, usually one from a big dog or a wolf. And if a witch needs to see farther or go on a journey or something, it may even shape-shift into a crow or raven."

He nodded.

He wrote: ***But how do you stop it—How do you kill it***

"When someone witches you, they might steal something you leave behind like chąą' [poop] or spit or hair or clothes—and they hide it away. As long as they possess it, they can use it to control you or make bad things happen to you. So, to break the curse, you have to get back the thing they got from you. Another way to witch someone is to sneak something inside their body when they're sleeping. To break the curse, the object must be removed by a trained person using good magic. Once it's removed, you can overpower the witch."

HT nodded. He stood and donned his heavy coat and mitts and bomber cap.

"You're going out in that storm, eh?"

'To walk around,' he signed. 'I'll be back in an hour.'

"Supper will be waiting. Are you visiting Macha again this evening?"

He nodded and left.

Auntie Millie stood at the frosted window and watched him disappear into the ground blizzard. She lingered there for a spell. After a while she couldn't hold herself back any longer and shuffled down the hallway and entered HT's room.

She fished around through the pile of dirty laundry beneath his bed, snagged a pair of his underwear, and stuffed it under her sweater. Then she began a systematic search. She went through his duffel bag. She lifted the corners of his mattress. Finally, in his top dresser drawer, she found it: a small half-empty white box that he'd placed there under some clean underwear.

The woman sat on the bed and withdrew a tin container from her sweater pocket, opened it, and peered inside. She sorted through the collection of sewing needles, chose the thinnest one and reached in the white box for a condom packet.

17

A NEW BEGINNIN'

LA RONGE, SASKATCHEWAN
MARCH 14TH, 2000

"I MISSED MY PERIOD AGAIN," said Macha.

'What?' signed HT.

"My monthly period you asshole—I missed it again. I'm pregnant. We're havin' a baby Dummy."

'How?'

"Don't ask *me*. You was the one wearin' the rubbers. Maybe you put 'em on the wrong way, eh?"

He stared at her in disbelief. 'Oh,' he signed.

"I'm gonna keep it. If it's a girl, I'll name it 'Sunshine.' And if it's a boy, I'll call it 'Sonny.'"

'Good names,' he signed. 'When are we getting married?'

"No. I don't wanna be married to you or nothin'. I'll raise the baby myself. There's lots of programs for that."

HT shrugged.

He wrote: ***I'll get a job—I can give baby $***

"Yeah. That'd be cool, eh. I could use the money Honey." Macha smiled at the thought of it.

He nodded.

"You can come visit the baby and stuff. And babysit."

'I'll visit a lot,' he signed.

"Cool."

'Where will you live?'

"With my mom—at first. I gotta finish high school, eh."

He nodded.

What's it feel like

"In my stomach? Like nothin' right now. It's too small. When it gets bigger it'll start movin' around in there. Girls say it feels weird then. Like a big fat bony worm or somethin'. But I can dress it up real pretty when it comes out, eh. I can practice my makeup on it."

HT grinned broadly.

I can't believe it—We're having a baby

"Yeah, with lots of shitty diapers."

PART 2

FAMILY TIME

18

Tradin' Post

La Ronge, Saskatchewan
March 16th, 2000

AUNTIE MILLIE SLID A PLATE of warm flapjacks and steaming moose sausage in front of him.

"So you're off to see Trader Bob today, eh?"

HT nodded.

"Right. Well tell him I said 'hi.' Eat up Kiddo. You'll need it for energy. If Bob decides to take you on, you've got a long day ahead of you. And remember: once he gets going it's hard to get him to shut up—kind of like you eh, Hand Talker?

He smiled at her joke.

THE FRONT OF THE BUILDING was nondescript—like any other modern store. But inside, Bob's Trading Post was museum-like. A step back in time. There were photographs of First Nations elders and portraits of them painted on drums and moose antlers. Taxidermy mounts and dozens of beaded leather shirts and other brain-tanned garments hung from the walls and rafters. Indigenous handcrafts from across northern Canada were on display—some with price tags—some boldly marked 'Not for Sale.' All manner of canned and boxed foods and trade goods were stacked on the store racks.

"Hey Bob, that kid is back," hollered the clerk over her shoulder. "You can go on back there. He's in the fur room. What's your name again?"

He scribbled: **Hand Talker Judd**

"You're Nate's cousin, right? Millie's nephew?"

He nodded.

HT found Trader Bob sorting through stacks of dried fox pelts. Gray, black, white, and orange ones.

"Good mornin' Hand Talker. Nate told me you might come by. I'm workin' on gettin' some parcels ready to ship for the April auction. Wanna help? I'll pay ya fair wages."

HT noticed a small stack of timber wolf skins against the wall. His eyes immediately blurred. The carotids in his neck thrummed. The familiar feeling of dread seized him. He shook his head 'no' and bid the man goodbye.

"Alright then. Take care Hand Talker—it was nice meetin' ya. Come back anytime."

He nodded at the trader and hastily re-entered the main part of the store. HT stopped to feel a pair of muskrat fur mittens on display. *Tábąąh mą'ii*, he thought, remembering the Navajo name for the animal. He examined some of the old photographs of Indigenous families hanging on the walls. Some of the images were of brown-skinned people like himself with strings of walleye, or pike, or whitefish, or fresh moose kills, or piles of winter furs ready to be traded. An antique birch bark canoe was suspended from the ceiling.

While wandering the store aisles, he stopped and picked up a tiny jar of creamed carrots. The label showed the smiling face of an infant. HT considered his options.

He returned to the fur room. Bob looked up from the stack he was sorting. "Changed your mind, eh? I can sure use the help. There's enough work to keep us busy all spring. Let's get to it."

Trader Bob spread his arms wide and gestured at the stacks of pelts around the room. "Most of these were caught by First Nations folks like yourself. Today, most people around the world are livin' in cities, right? But a lot of First Nations folks are still livin' life out in the bush with nature. Huntin', fishin' and trappin' is how they put clothes on their backs and beans and bannock in their bellies, eh. I've been tradin' with 'em all my life and I know a lot of 'em personally. Times are changin' fast though and it's been hard on 'em. I do what I can to help 'em out."

The trader showed HT how to grade and sort fur according to species, color, size, and quality and how to tally the information on each packing slip. He noticed that HT avoided the pile of wolf pelts, but didn't question him about it. Bob showed him examples of blue tinged rawhide on skins harvested too early, and the rubbed or springy or singed fur on fox, mink and otter taken too late. He taught HT to pack beaver belly-to-belly and back-to-back to help prevent the remaining grease from getting on the fur. They sorted and counted and bundled the various furs into separate lots all morning, readying them for the upcoming sale. The trader passed a wealth of backwoods lore and fur trade information along to him as he chatted non-stop.

FOR TWO WEEKS, HT worked with Trader Bob, gradually gaining the man's trust. As he became skilled in his job duties, he did more and more work independently, without supervision.

One morning when HT was carrying bags of trash out to the dumpster he spied Bob smoking his pipe by the outer door to the fur room. He tossed in the bags, then joined the man. The trader blew a smoke ring into the frigid air.

"You've been doin' great here Hand Talker. You're a quick learner and a hard worker. Ya do things the right way—which is not necessarily the quickest and easiest way. It's somethin' I really appreciate.

"I s'pose you're curious about Henry Yellow Bird's trapline. Your cousin Nate told ya it's up for sale, eh?"

He nodded.

"Well come on then. I'll show where it's at on the map. And if the weather holds, maybe we'll have time for a flyover this afternoon."

HT grinned broadly.

They went upstairs to Bob's office.

"All the traplines are registered and overseen by the provincial and federal governments. That way the animals don't get over-harvested and the trappers don't get to fightin' over territories. The traplines are mostly passed down through the families—and each family manages the animals in their territory in their own particular way. But once in a while a line comes up for sale.

"Some land is reserve land—set aside for Indigenous folks. And of course Indigenous folks have treaty rights for huntin, trappin', fishin' and so forth. But most land here in the north country is Crown land administered by the provincial and federal governments. So the registered traplines are mostly located on Crown land—like Henry Yellow Bird's line."

Trader Bob unrolled a topographical map and pointed. "Ya see that tiny black square there? That's where the main cabin used to be. It burnt down. You'd have to build yourself a new one this summer. But the cache and line shacks and trails should all still be in good workin' order. The traps are included in the deal. They're still out there hangin' in the trees. Ya think ya might be interested?"

HT nodded.

"The line's about twenty-five kilometers or so west of here. Close enough to walk in and out whenever ya need to so your Auntie Millie won't need to be worryin' about ya so much. Most traplines require a plane or snow machine for access, so gettin' an established line that's relatively close-in like this one is really quite a find."

"I'll be actin' as sales broker for the Yellow Bird family. They're reasonable folks. They'll just be glad to get it sold. The price is a fair one, with payments spread out over ten years. You'll be makin' annual payments each spring usin' part of your fur check.

"But you'll be needin' to get ready for the reality of winters around here Hand Talker. It can be dangerous bein' out there in the bush runnin' a line all by yourself, eh? Especially when it gets bitter cold. Men have died out there ya know. A mistake or two and that's it. But I know you'll do just fine.

"You'll be needin' enough food to get ya through the winter. That means gettin' a moose durin' the fall hunt. And stockin' up on town food. Someone can fly it in for ya. A few cheechákos die out here each year because they show up thinkin' they can just live off the land. But that's simply not possible. Ya gotta buy all the basics from town—flour and beans and rice and such—to survive the long cold winters. There's no roots or wild rice or berries in the wintertime, eh? So, the old-timers—First Nations folks like yourself—used to gather up those things all summer long and into the fall. They filled their food caches for winter-time use. But ya see Hand Talker, you'll be too busy buildin' your cabin to do that sort of thing this first year. And you'll probably need to keep workin' so ya can buy food and supplies.

"Betcha you're hungry by now, eh?"

They grabbed some burgers in town, then drove to Barber Field.

Bob uncovered the Cessna's windshield. HT watched the trader conduct the exterior safety check. Once they were harnessed, Bob turned the key and primed the throttle. The engine coughed and sputtered and caught and roared. He tested the wing flaps and tail rudder.

The trader showed HT how to change the headphone volume.

"Have ya ever flown?"

HT shook his head 'no.'

"Well you're in for quite a treat. Hang on. If ya get sick there's a bag right there for ya, okay?"

The bush plane taxied and lifted off, then headed west over the stark land caught-up in the spring thaw. HT scanned the surroundings. The low rocky hills and jack pine-dominated ridges were surrounded by patches of evergreen and deciduous trees and shrubs and abundant ice-choked creeks, sloughs and ponds. Swampy muskeg flats swept north.

The trader adjusted the trim, banked the Cessna and pointed out the still-leafless willow stringers and alder thickets below, telling HT those were places where snowshoe hares lived, and therefore good places to catch lynx. He showed HT how to identify marten crossings where the spruce stands narrowed and touched one another. When they reached the frozen expanse of Egg Lake, Bob quickly crossed to the far shore, then circled. At the edge of a meadow, HT saw a black square surrounded by melting snow—the burnt remains of a log structure.

"See? Just like I told ya. Nice location, eh? Just needs a new cabin. Everything else is there—cache, outhouse, smokehouse, a creek with good water, and plenty of trees for buildin' a cabin and makin' firewood."

HT grinned and nodded.

He scribbled: ***What happened to trapper***

"Henry Yellow Bird? The Mounties found the cabin burnt to the ground after his family asked for a mid-winter welfare check on 'em—stopped answerin' his radio. They sifted through the ashes, but they never did find any bones. There was a ground search after the spring thaw of course, but it was called off after a couple weeks. His family was pretty shook-up over the whole ordeal. That's why they're sellin'. It's been more than a year now. Because his body was never found, Henry's still listed as missin'. But everybody knows he's dead. If you happen to find his bones it'd bring his family some much needed closure, eh."

19

HELL RIDERS

WHITE ROCK, NEW MEXICO
APRIL 1ST, 2000

THE BIG BLACK LINCOLN sped west along State Road 4. Its headlights shone through the branches of the roadside piñons and junipers. Eerie shapes and shadows crawled across the broken basalt slopes and rock faces.

The driver quickly braked, then accelerated as he rounded another curve. Then he clicked on the overhead light to check his hair and slip-on collar in the rearview mirror. He plucked another one of those cream-colored worm-like things from his nostril and flicked it onto the vinyl floor mat.

"You smell that Pat? What *is* that?"

"It's probably your brakes Archbishop," said Valdez. "You've been riding them this whole trip. It's better to pump them gently instead of constantly stomping and holding them down. No offense—maybe try to baby them so the pads don't burn out, okay?"

"Good advice. Why didn't you say something sooner?"

"I figured you didn't want a backseat driver nagging you the whole way. Besides, we're almost there. When was the last time you visited?"

"November. They hosted our semi-annual retreat. The Jémez Hot Springs resort is operated by the townspeople. But the Via Coeli facility is run by the Servants of the Paraclete—the Church. It's for treatment and retraining. Clergy from all over North America get sent there to sort out their problems if you catch my drift."

The archbishop glanced at the full moon and alternately stomped the brake and gas pedals around each curve. The big sedan sailed past the Interagency Fire Center and Burnt Mesa toward Jémez Hairpin Curve.

"Say Pat, you've heard of the Jicarilla Apache Indians, right?"

"No."

"But you've heard of the Navajo."

"Sure."

"Well we're only a few miles from the Jicarilla Apache Reservation. It's just north of here. Anyway, the Apache and Navajo people believe that skinwalkers roam around on nights like this." He gestured at the moon. "They say a skinwalker looks sort of like a werewolf, except it wears a wolf skin the same way you and I wear clothes. And beneath the wolf skin is a demon-witch. They say skinwalkers do all kinds of evil things like snatching kids and impregnating young girls—the ones who happen to wander too far from home at night that is."

"Oh my God!" said Valdez.

The archbishop slammed on the brakes and powered through the hairpin turn. Dust and smoke billowed as the right rear tire spun-out on the narrow shoulder. He regained control and gunned the accelerator. The Lincoln whizzed westbound toward the Valles Caldera.

"Don't worry Pat. I've driven this road many a time. Believe me, I know every single curve."

"Glad to hear it Archbishop. I was worried there for a second."

"You just need to have a little faith Pat. Like me. God always watches over us, right? He wouldn't let anything happen to the guardians of His Church."

"Yeah, you're right of course." Valdez swallowed hard.

The two men were quiet for a minute or two.

"Archbishop?"

"Yes Pat?"

"I've been thinking about some of our activities. Our extra-curricular activities."

"You'll need to help me out here Pat. What's your problem? Spit it out."

"Well, I know we're helping the Church and all. But what about the other people involved? Isn't there a better way to do things—so the other people aren't left—hurting—so much?"

"Listen Pat. We have no choice in the matter. It's not debatable. Protecting the Church is our number one responsibility. Nothing can get in the way of that—even if—" The archbishop tapped his left breast pocket, rattling the gold-capped teeth inside his ever-present plastic vial. "—even if it goes against your training Pat. Do you understand me? Tell me you understand the importance of what I just said."

"Yes, I understand."

"Good. No more talk like that, okay? Now where was I? Right. I was telling you about skinwalkers."

Hubs smoking, the Lincoln passed over the mountain saddle and zipped down the grade toward the Valle Grande Overlook—the highway pull-off where daytime tourists often stopped to view the ancient volcanic crater below.

"Some of the local Indians are so scared of skinwalkers they think it's bad luck even to talk about them."

"Could you please slow down a little bit Archbishop? It's kinda steep."

"Relax. We're fine. Like I said Pat, I know this road well. Hell. Shut up already."

The Lincoln shot down the sinuous tree-lined corridor like a two-man bobsled.

"It's just that—"

"Just that what? Bawk-bawk-bawk. Don't be such a chicken. Like I said, you just need to have a little faith."

"What's that Arch—"

"What's what?"

"A skinwalker!"

The archbishop veered into the oncoming lane, barely missing the hairy figure hunched in the bright lights. He shoved hard on the brake pedal. Nothing. He pumped it over and over. The big black vehicle steadily gained speed. Dust flew as it rounded another bend.

"Pray for us Pat. Pray!"

"Bless us O Lord and these thy gifts which we are about to receive—"

"That's a mealtime prayer you damned idiot."

The archbishop deftly maneuvered the Lincoln to the center of the pavement.

"See Pat, we're already halfway down the mountain. We'll make it."

Valdez glanced over and read the speedometer: *'70 MPH.'* He grimly reflected on the life he'd lived and the sins he'd recently committed.

A warning sign for the approaching curve drew near: *'SLOW—35 MPH'*

"Archbishop?"

"Yes Pat?"

"You can go to hell."

"Fine. I'll see you there."

The archbishop repeatedly stomped the brake pedal. The vehicle careened around the sharp curve. Valdez reached for the wheel. The archbishop caught him with a solid left hook to the jaw. Valdez was temporarily knocked senseless. But he quickly recovered and grabbed the other man's groin in a crushing grip. He squeezed with every bit of strength he possessed. The archbishop shrieked like a banshee. Rubber left pavement. Sand sprayed. Gravel flew. The rugged slope fell away as the airborne Lincoln delivered its cargo of fighting, screaming men into the dark abyss. The fiery explosion was visible basin-wide.

In the roadway above, the hairy figure—a coyote—squatted, then defecated. It vigorously raked its hind claws on the asphalt.

The flames below gradually diminished.

In the past, the coyote had discovered uneaten food remains in the abandoned fire rings of local campers and hunters. It let out four barks and a howl. Faraway, an acquaintance howled a response. The trickster barked again. It farted and grinned, then descended toward the smoldering wreckage in search of a freshly cooked meal.

20

MEDICINE BUNDLE

LA RONGE, SASKATCHEWAN
APRIL 10TH, 2000

"TAKE IT," SAID AUNTIE MILLIE. She handed HT a faded tan oblong object. "It's called a jish. I was saving it for when you started your own family. And now it looks like you and Macha have decided to do that. I'm so happy for the two of you. With Petey gone, it gets lonely around here. I've always dreamed of having a bigger family."

He nodded, then examined it. The medicine bundle was wrapped in some sort of thin animal skin—perhaps from a sheep. The jish looked familiar to him. Yet he couldn't remember exactly when or where he'd seen it.

"It belonged to your dad. I know he wanted you to have it someday. It ended up with me after the truck accident," she explained. "Shimá [my mother] gave it to me. It's very important for the family. Just remember that it's meant to be *used* by the family—not just stored away in a closet or something."

HT nodded.

'Thanks,' he signed.

"I'm not sure what it's for Hand Talker. Maybe you can figure it out, eh?"

'I'll try.'

21

CABIN BUILDIN' TIME

LA RONGE, SASKATCHEWAN
EARLY MAY 2000

THE RIVER AND LAKE ICE BROKE UP and gradually melted. Honking geese returned to their northern nesting grounds.

One morning, HT bid farewell to his aunt, donned his new packbasket and headed out on the trail the trader showed him during the flyover. The well-worn meandering path took him deep into the taiga. Eventually, it brought him to the western shore of Egg Lake to the small clearing and scorched remains of the Yellow Bird family's trapline cabin.

Behind the clearing were low hills blanketed with jack pine. The swamps and drainages held patches of black spruce and alder. Near the former cabin site, he found a protected hollow in the land with a broad earthen mound. *This is the place*, he thought.

The cool air was thick with mosquitoes, so he donned a headnet and smeared mud on the back of his hands as advised by Trader Bob. He knelt by the mound and emptied the packbasket. He'd brought along an immense supply of dried food, his bedroll and coat, some mosquito netting, a rain tarp, a sharpened axe head, a shovel blade, a drawknife, and his otter skin and deerskin pouches.

HT got out his flute and played the *Beginning Song*, for it was time to build his new home. *But how do I begin?* he thought.

A chickadee landed nearby and tilted its black cap at the newcomer.

HT emptied his deerskin pouch and studied its contents: kits for firemaking, fishing and first aid; a smaller pouch that held his mother's broken crucifix and his father's ring; and the jish—the carefully wrapped sacred bundle—given to him by Auntie Millie. He examined the bundle again, more closely this time, and decided its covering was indeed fashioned from an ancient sheepskin. It appeared fragile, so he took his time unwrapping it. Secreted inside were packets of herbs and raw minerals, several stone fetishes, a tiny stone bowl and a knotted black cord wound around six small silver spikes. Traces of red earth adhered to several of the tarnished spikes.

He stared for a long time at the ancient cord and spikes. *I need to remember what they're for.*

HT sorted through the other items. Eventually, he fixed his gaze on his father's silver ring. In its center was the six-sided inlaid piece of turquoise. He delved deep into his earliest memories, trying to recall its meaning. Then, the design for the cabin became clear. It was so obvious. He would lay out its walls in the manner he'd watched his father do long ago when he and his brother and father helped a neighbor construct a new home. HT would build a traditional Diné winter lodge.

He unrolled the cord and drew it taut from east to west, tapping a spike into the soft earth through knotted loops in the center and at each end. Then he slipped the loop off one outside spike and scratched a complete circle on the ground. Next he pulled out the center spike and used it to trace an arc on each side of the circle, like two drawn bows facing one another. HT tapped the remaining spikes in the ground where the arcs met the circle. Then he gouged shallow trenches along each line between the spikes. He stood back to admire the large hexagonal design he'd created atop the mound. The trenches would serve as guides when he dug the floor and installed the lowest logs.

Using lengths of peeled green ash, he fitted the shovel blade and axe head with handles. The rest of the day he excavated the floor to a depth of about half a meter and pitched the black soil outwards. Unbeknownst to HT, the freshly dug earth held burnt bone bits and siliceous stone slivers from long-ago peoples. The mound was an ancient Indigenous habitation site—a place where others dwelt perhaps hundreds of years before his own arrival.

That evening, while he chewed pieces of smoke-sweetened 'ałk'iniilaizh [jerky], his eyes rested on the results of the day's work. He felt good—proud in fact. Proud he'd remembered the purpose of the silver spikes and wool cord. Proud of the progress he was making in building the lodge. Proud to continue on in the way of his ancestors.

Morning came quickly. He was roused by sore muscles and the raucous calls of two whiskeyjacks that flitted about in the tree canopy above his bush camp. Excited, he gulped down his breakfast of oatmeal and dried fruit.

Taking up the axe, HT surveyed the surrounding swamps and chose the straightest trees. After three days, he'd felled forty and chopped them into shorter lengths. He skidded them to his new homesite and skinned bark from them with the drawknife. He chose the thickest, heaviest logs for the lower runs of the structure and the lighter logs for the upper runs. By the end of the week, every log laid peeled and piled by the edge of the pit.

Tier by tier, he raised the six walls, notching the logs together and chinking them with moss as he went, levering more logs higher on temporary pole ramps. It was in this way he built the framework of the lodge, the walls rising straight six feet, then arching upward and inward toward a central smoke hole, forming a corbelled roof.

HT tossed a thick layer of bark peelings over the log framework and blanketed it with soil. Atop the bark and soil he laid chunks of meadow sod, creating a living roof. Finally, he fitted the entrance with a sturdy door pegged together from hand-hewn planks—a door strong enough to withstand the brutal northern winters. Four weeks had passed. The completed earth-covered lodge was six-sided with an east-facing window and door. At some later time, he planned to hire a charter plane to fly in his winter food supply, a glass window and a cast iron stove.

Like he'd done since the work began, that evening HT went to the creek pool and braved the mosquito swarms so as to rinse off the caked-on wood chips, dirt and sweat.

Afterward, he gathered an armload of dry wood, then kindled the first kǫ' [fire] in the center of the lodge floor with a Bic lighter. He knelt by the open hearth and focused his gaze on his mother's crucifix now hung in its new place over the doorway. His thoughts wandered here and there. And then, for a reason not clear to him, HT was overcome by a profound loneliness—nearly as deep as that which he'd experienced after the wreck that killed his family.

Outside, summer rain began to sprinkle the sod roof. Droplets slanted through the smokehole and sizzled in the flames. Lightning split the sky. The bright white bolts flashed and flew, illuminating the peeled logs around him. And as thunder spoke, its mighty roar reverberated through the open door. The gentle rain became a squall, and then a torrential downpour until, finally, the thunderheads opened and hailstones pounded his new home. The windstorm within him raged. Tears streamed down his face.

22

KIDS WITH KIDS

LA RONGE, SASKATCHEWAN
OCTOBER 15TH, 2000

"HERE," SAID MACHA. She passed him the infant. "Sonny just shit himself again. You change 'em, eh."

'Sure. I don't mind,' signed HT.

"Well I do, Asshole. You're always off workin' on your cabin or scoutin' your new trapline and I get stuck doin' everything. It ain't cool."

After he changed Sonny's diaper, HT took out his notepad and pencil.

I said we could get married—We still could—Then I could be here more often

"Whatever."

Macha grabbed the TV remote and plopped down on the Chesterfield.

"I'm takin' a break from my nurse's aide training. I need to rest up. Sonny doesn't let me sleep. So you'll need to stay in town and watch 'em for a couple weeks."

Moose season starts next weekend—I need a moose for winter meat

"You're useless. I should kick you out right now."

I'll trap this winter and give you $ after fur sale

"You mean all winter long I won't be gettin' nothin' from you? You been spendin' all your money on supplies. And what if you don't *catch* nothin', eh? You expect me to keep livin' on government programs and per cap payments with just my mom's help? And nothin' at all from you?"

'I'm trying,' he signed.

HT scooped up the squalling baby. Sonny quieted as his teen father rocked him.

23

Northern Ghosts

Egg Lake Region, Saskatchewan
January 9th, 2001

IT WAS DEEP WINTER in the taiga. On the lookout for signs of a catch, HT cautiously approached his trap set. The conibear was closed tight. In its square wire grip was a marten—an American sable. The rigid wires had snapped its spine, killing it instantly. He removed the frozen animal from the trap and remade the set. He marveled at the brilliant orange blaze on the marten's chest and rubbed its silky fur against his half-numb cheek. *Enough to buy a three-week supply of food for Sonny*, he thought. He grinned.

The teen trapper took to the trail again. As he wound his way through the surrounding stands of spruce, he reflected on all that transpired since he finished the lodge. This first season on his trapline was unusual. Only shallow skiffs of snow came and went—less than typical. It made for easier travel because he didn't need to wear the clumsy snowshoes loaned to him by Trader Bob. Afoot, he'd explored the long looping bush trails used for generations by the Yellow Bird family.

Having no experience, he initially had difficulty catching furbearers. Bob taught him how to safely set the powerful, more dangerous traps such as the 330 body-grippers and Number 4 footholds. Those were traps that could easily injure a careless trapper. And the trader explained which of the various kinds of lures and baits to use and where to find furbearers along his line. But Bob neglected to mention the need to cover his bait to avoid non-target catches like birds and snowshoe hares. Through trial and error, HT discovered on his own how to prevent such unwanted captures. It dawned on him one day that his cubby sets, where the bait was hidden, caught no birds and hares, while his other sets did. After that, unless he needed a hare for a meal, he'd regularly cover his baits.

What puzzled him most during those early days on his line was when he'd arrive at a sprung, but empty trap. He would observe hairs stuck to its jaws, indicating he'd caught a hare or some other animal, but for some strange reason his catch was missing. HT searched for tracks on the hard frozen ground—signs of the thief—yet found none.

Bizarre things happened too in and near his lodge. After returning from a long day on the trapline, his axe would be in a different place than where he'd left it. Items on his makeshift table were rearranged. One day, HT returned home and a silver fox was missing from his small collection of furs. But even more concerning than that, his winter food stores were disappearing. They were somehow slowly being depleted by a ghostly thief.

And then there were those eerie sounds: strange moans and mutters and chants from the shadows behind the old cabin site. The haunting noises filled him with dread. So he'd get out his cedar flute and play a song in that direction. Only then would the sounds cease.

HT rigged a sturdy lock on the lodge door and began to tie the cache ladder to a tree prior to leaving to check his traps. That seemed to solve the thievery problem. But he was still hearing those eerie noises out in the woods. That very morning, in fact, before leaving the lodge, he'd again heard moans and mutters out among the dark conifers.

He continued checking traps. Most were empty. But a frozen lynx awaited him in his last set of the day. It'd become entangled in the willows and succumbed in the cold night air—a quick death in this land of extremes. HT removed the trap from its foot and put the animal in his packbasket alongside the marten.

Daylight was fading. He tramped along the trail, looping back toward the warmth and comfort of the lodge. It wasn't far now—one or two kilometers. Initially, the lynx catch lifted his mood. Yet the feeling of dread soon returned. Something didn't seem right out there in the dimness.

HT glanced behind him down the tree-lined trail. A low, gray, ghostly figure suddenly crossed the trail and disappeared into the adjacent shadows. Then it happened again, but closer to him this time. The third time the figure crossed the trail, he turned and broke into a full run and headed for the safety of his lodge.

As he entered the clearing he glimpsed a gaunt gray figure as it slipped into the black timber on the far side. When HT reached the lodge, a horrible sight met his eyes. His axe lay on the ground among fresh wood chunks and splinters. The makeshift lock was destroyed. His door had been hacked open.

24

GRAY MATTER

EGG LAKE REGION, SASKATCHEWAN
JANUARY 9TH, 2001

HT ALTERNATELY FOCUSED his attention on the open doorway of his lodge and the axe on the ground in front of it. In his angst, he was unsure what to do. He'd seen the gray thing retreat into the trees, but was it safe to enter? Finally, he shed his pack and, with knife drawn, poked his head inside. Everything seemed to be in order. None of his furs or other things were missing. Then he noticed that the leftovers of his breakfast were gone from the skillet on the table. And, once more, his big bag of smoked moose meat showed signs of tampering.

That night HT lay awake. The day's events replayed over and over in his mind. He thought about that gray creature that damaged his door. It didn't seem to fit the description of any kind of skinwalker he'd heard of. Why would a skinwalker break down a door and steal fried potatoes and smoked meat from a trapper? And those skinwalkers that followed him on the trail—what did *they* want? To scare him? Or something worse? Nothing made sense.

AFTER BREAKFAST, he skinned the thawed lynx and marten and tacked the pelts on wooden stretchers. He donned his black headband, strapped his fighting knife to his waist and slipped into the harness of his packbasket.

At the far side of the clearing HT entered the thick tree cover. On the forest floor were remnant patches of crusted snow. Here, for the first time, he found tracks of the skinwalker. The impressions were oval—long and wide with pointed toes—both man-like and animal-like.

HT cautiously followed the tracks, losing them on the hard frozen ground where snow was absent, but then finding them again when he circled ahead to the next patch. He tracked the thief through a saddle and descended into an unexplored part of his territory—a treacherous place of broken jagged boulders and bedrock—a labyrinth of sharp escarpments with myriad cracks and crags and faults and fissures.

In this stark, treeless terrain, the snow was gone. So too were the tracks. HT stood still. A light breeze ghosted across his face as he scanned—and waited.

He pressed forward. He searched every crevice, hunting the gray thing. Under a massive chunk of rock he found what he sought: a well-used trail. Here the ground was soft and dry, not frozen like it was elsewhere. The strange tracks in the sand were clear now—and fairly fresh.

Following the path, HT rounded another boulder and spotted a cavern entrance ahead. A faint wisp of smoke escaped through the narrow, blackened cleft above it. Then he heard chant-like sounds from the thieving skinwalker within. And as he listened, the chants and mutters grew louder.

A disheveled First Nations man with long, matted hair emerged. The man stopped and peered into the morning sunlight, shading his hollow darting eyes under a grunge-encrusted hand. He wore a patchwork outfit of half-tanned furs and filthy rags. Bulky, makeshift fur boots enveloped his feet. Atop his head was the missing silver fox fur—now made into a hat. HT estimated him to be in his twenties.

The man looked past HT and spoke out. Then he turned and muttered something unintelligible in a different direction. HT realized the man was speaking to non-existent people. He was diigis [mentally touched]. And just as quickly it dawned on him who this man was: Henry Yellow Bird—the missing trapper.

Deep in thought, HT watched the other trapper for a while.

Then he took the flute from his packbasket and faced the man. Seeing HT's movements, Henry shouted, then retreated into the cavern, ranting indecipherable words.

HT sat against a rock and began playing a healing song. The rantings and ravings subsided. Henry re-emerged. He looked at HT and smiled. Henry sat down and stared directly at HT, listening. HT played several more songs. When he'd finished, they continued looking at one another.

After a while, HT waved 'hello.'

Henry remained silent, smiling.

'Are you hungry?' signed HT.

Henry nodded.

'Follow me.'

Together, HT and Henry returned to the lodge. HT baked a batch of biscuits and stewed some dried potatoes, onions, tomatoes and lynx meat in a skillet of gravy. Henry gorged himself. When they'd finished eating, they sat for a while. HT ignored Henry's sickening stench. He handed Henry a strip of smoked moose meat and got out his notepad and pencil.

'Good food?' signaled HT.

Henry nodded and smiled and fidgeted with the piece of meat in his grubby fingers.

HT wrote: ***Your family is sad***

Henry read the note and stopped chewing. His smile vanished.

Will you come to town with me to tell them you're alive

"Sure," muttered Henry.

Undated Entry from Hand Talker's Journal

My first few winters at the cabin were pretty tough going. I could not handle being around people, so I ended up alone out in the bush. But I could not handle being alone either.

Skinwalkers and bloody demons visited my dreams, so it was hard to let myself fall asleep. Many nights I did not sleep a wink. Those were very long nights. Sometimes after a dream I would sit for hours with my gun in my hand. Sometimes the gun barrel rested on my lips. I could taste the burnt gunpowder at the end of it. Sometimes my finger was on the trigger. It would only have taken a little squeeze.

I do not know why I had those thoughts about ending it all. I only know those thoughts would not go away. Except when I thought about Sonny and Auntie Millie and Cousin Nate and Shimásání [my grandmother] *then I would not feel so lonely and I would put away my gun for a while. Eventually those dreams and thoughts became fewer. Things became more peaceful for me.*

25

CALLIN' UP THE SPIRITS

EGG LAKE REGION, SASKATCHEWAN
OCTOBER 24TH, 2010

THE SMALL FAMILY busied itself around Auntie Millie's old red Formica-top kitchen table. HT was deboning a shoulder from Nate's fall moose. Auntie Millie cut the chunks he gave her into cubes to be fed into the grinder. Nate took half the pile of ground and mixed in pork fat and spices. Meanwhile, Sonny tore strips of masking tape and labeled the white butcher paper-wrapped packages in large letters: *'Sausage 2010'*

"Sonny, what did you think of this morning's service?" said Auntie Millie.

"What?"

"The church service?"

He shrugged. "It was okay I guess. I didn't understand a lot of the words though."

"What words?"

"'Eucharist.'"

"That's the part of the service where they served us bread and wine. The Eucharist is a re-creation of Jesus's last supper. What other words didn't you understand?"

"'Fornication.'"

"Nate, you explain that one to him, eh?"

"Auntie, what makes you think *I* know what it means," scoffed Nate.

She turned to Sonny: "It means people having sexual intercourse before they get married—when they're too young to have it—something like that I guess."

"Oh," said Sonny. "What's intercourse?"

"Hand Talker, haven't you taught him anything about sex yet?"

HT shrugged. 'How?' he signed. 'By drawing pictures for him? He's only ten.'

"Then I guess I'll have to have a talk with Macha. She'll need to handle this one."

"Dad, where's my DS Lite?" said Sonny.

'In my jacket,' he signed. 'By the door. You can play for one hour.' HT turned to Nate. 'I wish Macha hadn't given that to him. It's all he does now.'

Sonny went to the coat rack and felt around in his father's pockets. He pulled out a short cylindrical wooden object about the width of his palm and read the label: ***'Burnham Brothers Predator Call.'*** One end looked a bit like the end of his father's cedar flute. The boy returned to the kitchen doorway and touched it to his lips.

Waaahhh—waaahhh—waaahhh!

"Good Lord," said Auntie Millie, "what in hell's bells *is* that thing?"

'My call for lynx and fox,' signed HT.

"Real funny Sonny," said Auntie Mille. She stuffed another fistful of cubed meat into the hopper. "Blow it outside please—not in here. It sounds so creepy—like you're calling up the spirits or something."

Sonny set the predator call on the kitchen counter next to his father's silver and turquoise yoostsah. He powered on his Nintendo, intending to play *Mario* yet again.

HT tossed the de-fleshed bones in a bag. He washed and dried his hands and slid his yoostsah back on, the knotted scar on his paralyzed finger holding it securely in place. He rubbed the sky-blue stone on the ring, then stretched his sore shoulders and leaned against the counter awhile.

"Hand Talker, why didn't you come to church with the rest of us?" said Auntie Millie.

He gestured at trees beyond the window. 'My church is out there,' he signed.

"That's no excuse. You missed out on seeing everybody."

'Maybe next time.'

"'Aoo'," she said. "You know there are some nice young ladies who attend All Saints every Sunday. You might meet one of them, eh?"

Sonny snickered. "Yeah Dad, you might meet a nice young lady."

Nate laughed.

'What's so funny?' signed HT.

"Cousin, if you're so good at callin' in things, maybe ya oughta try callin' in a nice young lady, eh?" Nate winked at Sonny and flung a look at the predator call on the counter beside him.

Sonny complied: *waaahhh—waaahhh—waaahhh!*

26

THE TEACHER

MELBOURNE, VICTORIA, AUSTRALIA
APRIL 25ᵀᴴ, 2014

THE STIFLING HEAT AND MUGGINESS dizzied the professor. He took a deep breath and removed his spectacles. With his damp 'kerchief. He swabbed his forehead, the back of his neck and the fat folds under his chin. Although his legs were cramped and swollen—almost ready to give out—it made him smile to know that his nearby Education Department students had endeavored to persevere and had finally earned their teaching credentials under his tutelage. *Perhaps all this suffering is worth it*, he thought.

He shot a suspicious glance at the nearby group of paparazzi with their assorted cameras and contraptions, then followed their gaze to the prince standing with his daughter Beth and a group of her fellow students. The prince glanced at his cell phone, pecked Beth's forehead and rushed away. Most of the paparazzi followed.

The professor shuffled over to the cheerful cluster of graduates. He tentatively nudged Beth's elbow. "Are the shutterbugs behaving themselves? We can always ask security to remove them. After all, this is not a public event."

"They seem to be keeping their distance for now. Besides, with those monstrous lenses, I think they already captured whatever fresh meat they came for tonight Professor."

"I'm sorry he couldn't stay longer. At least he was here for the ceremony. Can I get you a drink Beth?"

"Father said there is an emergency of some sort at the Consulate." Beth gestured toward the remaining photographers. "Anyway, it is probably best that he left early, or there would be even more of them still lurking here. And yes Professor, I'll take one of those bottles from that cart over there—a full one," she laughed. "Oh, and please do get me a pack of herbal cancer sticks while you're at it."

"Well you'd certainly deserve it—a celebratory smoke I mean—not cancer." He chuckled and blushed. Then he recalled Beth was a non-drinker. He suspected it might have to do with the tragic loss of her environmental activist mother. After the single-car accident, the tabloids reported that alcohol intoxication was to blame.

Beth's boyfriend Sean had been listening to their conversation. "How about iced tea?" he suggested.

"Yes, of course," said Beth.

Sean motioned to a passing waiter.

"Beth, you know you've been my star student ever since you entered the program," said the professor.

"Aye, teacher's pet princess," said Sean as he wrapped his arm around her waist.

The group of graduates laughed. She was hardly a teacher's pet. Beth was far too opinionated to endear herself to any of her professors for long. She always seemed to piss them off in one way or another, even including the University Chancellor. No. She'd gotten her high marks and a begrudging respect from her professors not through her connection to the Royal Family, but rather, through hard work and determination—blood, sweat, and tears to be sure. Though she could have graduated summa cum laude, her spirited spats and showdowns with virtually every professor prevented her from earning that honor.

"Just think of it," said the professor, "soon you'll be flying off to that faraway exotic land for your first assignment." He handed her an umbrella-crowned iced tea.

"I'd hardly call it exotic Professor—babysitting a bunch of ankle biters in some backwater town in Saskatchewan. Were it not for all these bloody photographers, I'd be staying right here with all of you instead."

The professor's brows narrowed. He gulped the remainder of his champagne and wondered once more if she was cut-out to be an instructor. *She should be thankful the Canadian and Australian provinces have the teacher exchange program,* he thought. He congratulated the group one last time, then left.

Sean leaned over and kissed Beth.

"Don't Sean. Not in public. I don't want to be on the front page tomorrow. You know how I feel about it."

"Aye Lovie," he whispered. "By the way, we need to talk about our plans. Today I received an offer to interview with that school in Saskatoon—not too far from where you'll be at—Backwoods Beth."

"Backwoods Beth is it now? Why you little prick. Well, if I'm a backwoods woman, then you must be Sean the Lowly Sheepherder."

Beth punched his belly and gave him a quick kiss and a squeeze. She leaned in and whispered mischievously, "Speaking of little pricks Sean, when this is all over tonight, maybe we can do more than just *talk* about our plans."

He covered her mouth. The two of them laughed as each checked to see if anyone had overheard.

A photographer approached the couple.

She glared at him.

"May I?" he asked.

She turned her back to the man. After a while he wandered away.

"I absolutely *hate* cameras!" she told Sean.

"Aren't you used to them after all these years?"

Powwwp!

Beth jerked and clutched Sean's arm. "What in the bloody—"

Champagne gushed from the bottle in the nearby waiter's hand.

"Crikey," she said. "I thought for sure someone was shooting at us."

Her phone vibrated. "Oh, hello Granny-mum—you remembered! Yes, I received it today. Thank you so much. It was so thoughtful of you."

Undated Entry from Hand Talker's Journal

Yesterday I went to town and visited with Auntie Millie. She told me that Shimásání died. Auntie was crying when she told me that. When I was walking back to the cabin afterwards I was just in a total daze like my body was moving but my mind was no longer inside it. I know Shimásání was very old and would die someday. But it is hard to believe she is no longer rocking in her chair there in the hogan. She is the one who buried my umbilical cord. She was so good to me. She understood me and took care of me. She taught me about nature. She taught me so many of the Diné traditions and legends. Why do the people I love keep dying?

27

FATHER AND SON

EGG LAKE REGION, SASKATCHEWAN
MAY 6TH, 2014

HT PLAYFULLY TUGGED on Sonny's long Dene-style ponytail as they walked side-by-side on the trail from La Ronge to the lodge.

"Knock it off Dad."

'Where did you get those pants?' he signed.

"From school. My cross-country coach issued 'em to us."

'Grade 9 has a track team?'

"Of course we got a team. We came in 4th at the Provincial tourney."

HT grinned.

'Take those off so I can see you better,' he signed. He gestured at Sonny's fly-eye sunshades.

"I want 'em on. My eyes are sensitive."

HT clicked his tongue, signaling for them to stop. They slipped out of their packs.

"What Dad?"

'Spruce grouse. By those chokecherries. Wait.'

HT broke a branch to the proper size. He walked toward the small family of birds at an angle to prevent them from flushing. When he was within range, HT flung the stick. It spun parallel to the ground toward the edge of the thicket. As it passed through the cluster of scuttling grouse, two young ones dropped and flopped.

"Great shot," said Sonny.

HT wrung their necks and brought them back to the trail. Sonny plucked some of the richly striped feathers and put them in his and HT's hair while his father eviscerated the grouse.

'Guess what's for supper?' signed HT.

"Can't we have mooseburgers instead? Todd always gets me burgers."

'There's no moose meat this time of year. Who is Todd?'

"One of Mom's boyfriends. He's stayin' in the back room."

'He treats you okay?'

"Yeah, he's a happenin' dude. He even gives me beers sometimes when Mom's not lookin'."

'Does he let you smoke too?'

"He don't give 'em to me or nothin' like that. But he don't mind if I smoke my cigs out back when my buds come around. And he don't say nothin' when I bring a girl over neither, eh."

'And your mom—is he good to her?'

"Pretty much. They fight once in a while I guess. Todd only smacks her around a bit when she really deserves it."

HT's brow furrowed. 'Make sure he treats your mom right,' he signed. 'That's your job. And make sure you treat your girlfriends right.'

They continued down the trail.

'Want me to play my flute after supper?' signed HT.

"Maybe only one or two songs Dad. This time I brought my own tunes." He held up the iPod pouch around his neck for HT to see.

AFTER THEY FINISHED THEIR HOTCAKES, HT scrubbed the dishes. He loaded a few things in his packbasket, then they set out on the trail uplake.

"Where're we goin'?" said Sonny.

'Fishing.'

"But where's the fishin' poles?"

'You'll see.'

HT pointed at the various tracks along the shoreline.

'What's that?' he signed.

"Moose tracks and moose shit of course. That's super easy."

'And that one?'

"Black bear. Back left foot. On top of its front left foot."

'How do you know it's not grizzly?' signed HT.

"Just look at those little front claws Dad. It's black bear."

'Look *inside* the bear track Sonny.'

"Oh, I see it now. That's from a fox."

'Pretty good Sonny. Okay. What plant is that?'

"Dad, you ask me that every summer. It's cow parsnip. The shoots come up right when the snow is meltin'. Best spring green around—unless you find fire-weed shoots. But stingin' nettle's even better."

'Great. Maybe you could live here someday too,' he signed.

Sonny shrugged.

HT let Sonny take the lead. The trail brought them to a marshy area where a creek widened, then entered the lake.

'It's shallow here,' signed HT. 'The water is warmer. Come on. Let's swim.'

They stripped and dove in.

"Dammit Dad! You said it'd be warm."

'Warmer. Not warm,' he signed.

Suddenly Sonny dunked HT. They wrestled and splashed each other, long black hair whipping.

Tired, the two of them sprawled on sand beds next to their clothes, the sun and breeze drying their skin. Sonny brushed out his hair and re-tied his ponytail. He stuck in his earbuds and queued up a tune on his iPod. They both fell asleep.

A little while later, HT awoke to the sensation of something bumping against his foot. Then it happened again. It felt like a dog just licked him. An animal huffed loudly and sneezed, spraying his foot with snot.

HT slowly opened his eyes and lifted his head. A full-grown boar grizzly was sniffing his bare foot. He froze. The bear slathered and slurped his toes. The grizzly raised its head for a moment, then turned and continued its casual walk along the edge of the marsh.

HT reached over and nudged Sonny's arm. Sonny pushed him away.

"Let me sleep Dad."

He trilled his tongue and patted Sonny vigorously until the pissed-off teen finally sat up.

"What? I was sleepin' so good."

HT pointed at the massive grizzly tracks in the sand by their feet.

'My brother Shashtsoh tickled my foot,' he signed.

"Shit Dad—why didn't you wake me up?"

'I didn't want to scare you—or him.'

HT was exhilarated over the close encounter. 'Come on, Sonny. Time to fish.'

Together, they walked up the flowing creek bed. It became narrower and rockier. More shaded. Livelier. This part of the waterway contained myriad large and small rocks, sand and gravel beds, logs, overhanging banks, root wads, small pools, eddies and tiny waterfalls.

"There's fish in here?"

Just then several pan-size trout zipped by and disappeared under a cutbank.

"Okay Dad. So there's fish. But how are we s'posed to catch 'em, eh? We don't have hooks or poles or fishin' line or nothin' 'cause *you* didn't think we needed 'em."

'You want fish for lunch?' he signed.

"Sure."

'Follow me.'

His father dipped low in the cold water and eased his way over to one end of the bank. He probed the wall of mud and rocks, searching for hollows and holes and crevices—suitable hiding places. HT found a hole between two large rocks stuck in the overhanging bank. After a few seconds, he held up a fat flapping trout, his thumb and index finger linked through its mouth and gill openings.

"Dad—you gotta be kiddin' me! Where'd you learn that?"

'From no one. One day I got pretty hungry for fish.'

HT bit down hard on the back of the fish's head and tossed it onto the bank, then spit out the bitter slime.

'Come here,' he signed. 'Put your hand in there. Go slow.'

Sonny felt the two rocks. Then he realized there was a sort of underwater chamber below the point they touched one another. As his hand entered the opening, several soft and slippery bodies bumped into it. He jerked back, eyes rapt.

"Wow. I felt a couple. They feel weird, like snakes. They're soft and warm-like."

'They feel like trout,' signed HT. 'Snakes are rougher. Not so slippery. Try again. Don't pull away this time.'

Sonny reached back in. His hand carefully explored the fish's hideout. Several darted back and forth, occasionally hitting his hand. At first, he instinctively jerked away. But then he forced himself to gently touch them—feel their shape— feel them stop and swim in-place.

'Now do like I did,' signed his father, looping his thumb and forefinger together.

Sonny tried grabbing a fish, but it escaped his grip. He tried several more times, but the fish kept slipping away.

'Go slow. First trap it against the side. Be patient. Use both hands. Then force your fingers in.'

The boy became frustrated. "It's not workin' Dad. I'm freezin' here. The mosquitoes are drivin' me crazy. C'mon, let's go."

'Sonny, we still need lunch.' HT knelt and reached in. After a minute, he pulled out a holdout trout, bit into its head and threw it next to the first fish. From a hollow further down the bank he caught four more. With his fingers, he pinched each one behind the gills and pulled out the viscera. He hooped his catch on a willow switch, then nodded at Sonny. Together, they scaled the bank and walked back to the cached packbasket and clothing.

HT built a cooking fire.

Sonny turned on his iPod. "Shit Dad"

'What?'

"My iPod's dead. The battery needs chargin'. You got a generator back at the cabin, right?"

He shook his head 'no.'

When the coals were ready, HT and Sonny spitted and slow-roasted the fish. Juice dripped and sputtered. Soon, they gorged themselves on the flavorful greasy trout. HT sucked out the eyes and rescued the cheek meat and crunchy tails from Sonny's picked-over skeletons.

With bellies bulging, both leaned back and relaxed while the discarded bones sizzled and smoked in the embers.

THE SCENT OF APPROACHING RAIN was heavy. They sheltered under the canopy of some nearby conifers. Soon, the clouds let loose. HT played an old healing song on his flute while Sonny stared eastward through the gray rain. While they waited for the storm end, he brooded.

When it finally let up, they emerged. The forest behind them quietly dripped.

The meadows and marshes on each side glistened clean and green in the afternoon light. And before them, eastward, the mirror of the now-calm lake surface met the brilliant multicolored arc in the nearly black firmament beyond, creating a dazzling full-circle display.

With outstretched arms, HT faced the brilliantly banded rain ring. He turned to Sonny. 'Isn't this amazing?' his hands whispered.

"It's kinda cool I guess."

THE BLACK FLIES BEGAN TO STIR. HT scrubbed their breakfast dishes with a handful of horsetail shoots. When he'd finished, he stood and stretched. He squinted at the sun's reflection in the surface of the creek. *What can we do today?* he wondered. *It seems like nothing interests him.*

Sonny called out to him from the direction of the lodge. When HT reached the edge of the clearing, the boy stood in the doorway leaning against his backpack with his ever-present sunglasses on.

HT approached him, smiling. 'Ready for another hike?'

"No. I wanna go back home."

HT stared at Sonny's muddy white high tops for a time. 'You used to like coming out here,' he signed.

Sonny looked toward town and shrugged, avoiding his father's eyes. "I like different things now Dad. I'm not a little kid no more. Besides, I need my electronics. There ain't shit to do out here at your place. How can you live all alone like this? You don't even have a dog to play with."

'It is true I'm the only man out here Sonny. But I am not alone.' HT motioned toward the plants and animals and land and sky and water. 'Don't you see my friends?'

28

SUCKED

BRISBANE, QUEENSLAND, AUSTRALIA
JUNE 8TH, 2014

BETH FIDGETED ON THE VINYL SEAT in the waiting room. She smoothed the blouse over her belly. She thought about the fetus inside of her. She wanted a baby someday of course, but not with Sean. They'd broken up shortly after graduation. Without consulting him, she'd scheduled the procedure at a clinic far from the usual prying eyes and cameras. After that, upon approval of her Canadian work visa, she'd be able to start her teaching job. The school administrators, parents and students at La Ronge, Saskatchewan were all expecting her to show up—*without* a bun in the oven.

A nurse poked her head into the room, chart in hand. "Elizabeth? Elizabeth Winsley?"

"That's me. I go by 'Beth.'"

"Oh—oh it's you! I'm so sorry My Lady. I'm just surprised seeing you in person like this. Everything here at the clinic is confidential of course. Shall we begin?"

Strangely, while the nurse reviewed the paperwork and medical risks with her, Beth's thoughts turned to memories of her mother. She recalled walking to the park as a child with her, holding hands, both of them wearing their matching lime green 'People for the Ethical Treatment of Animals' t-shirts. She remembered how her mother visited with the other mothers at the playground and complimented the newborns in their strollers.

The procedure went pretty much like they'd explained it to her. When it was over the doctor turned his back to her while an orderly accidentally pushed aside the white curtain covering the machine. She glimpsed tiny pink body parts suspended in translucent reddish fluid in the holding jar attached to the evacuation pump. And, as if frozen mid-wave, a miniature hand bid her farewell through the glass while the nurse wheeled her away.

In the recovery room Beth gazed out the fly-specked window at the gray clouds and the manicured garden. She thought again about her mother. A tear trailed down her cheek on its way to the vinyl floor beneath the stainless-steel gurney. Beth softly sang a song her mother used to sing to her.

Then something at the edge of the garden moved. One of the hedges didn't look quite right to her. She spotted what looked like an enormous snake eye peering at her through the foliage.

"Help," she screamed. "God—no—please."

A nurse rushed in as the photographer hiding outside bolted away. Beth thrashed on the floor in a jumble of white sheets and plastic tubes.

"Why won't they leave me alone?" she sobbed.

29

MAKIN' MEAT

EGG LAKE REGION, SASKATCHEWAN
OCTOBER 20TH, 2014

NATE SQUATTED BY THE CAMPFIRE and stirred the thick bed of coals with a stick. The wind gently blew wood ash about. "Hey Cousin, I've been comin' out here fishin' and moose huntin' with ya goin' on fourteen, maybe fifteen years."

HT shifted position on his mossy bed, then nodded.

"Things around the world are changin' for the worse Cousin. Maybe ya don't see it 'cause you're out here so much of the time and it's happenin' gradually. But every time I come back here to the lake I see how it's so different."

'You're right,' signed HT. 'Certain animals and plants are disappearing. A third of the trees out here have died. There's more rain and less snow. I've read a lot about it—climate change. People close to the land like you and me see it. Any hunter or trapper or farmer knows it's happening faster and faster.'

Nate poked at a big coal. "A lot of people are puttin' the economy ahead of the changes needin' to be made. Don't they understand that without a world, there's no economy? No need at all for food or rent or hydro bill money? How many times do the politicians need to be told somethin' before they act, eh?"

Ash blew in a whirlwind above their bush camp. 'There's your answer,' signed HT. He motioned at the swirling mass.

Nate continued, "A lot of the First Nations bands west of here are keepin' quiet 'cause they want the tar sands money to keep comin' in. And the federal and provincial governments seem to be movin' about as slow as a turtle, eh. Have ya thought about gettin' into politics like Auntie Millie maybe? To make things happen quicker? Your dad was a chapter president at the rez, wasn't he?"

HT nodded, then shrugged. 'My family said I'd make a good politician,' he signed. 'But I never thought so. Instead, I thought about becoming a priest so I could help the Dené that way. I wanted to help calm the ones with broken spirits.'

"But Cousin, what about helpin' people in other ways? There's still time. If ya don't like the way history is headin', ya need to try to change it."

'Not when my own spirit is messed up. I can't help my people when I'm the one who needs help.' HT relayed to Nate his history of nightmares with giant yellow-haired demons. He told him of his visions of gray things and skinwalkers and how the visions were fewer now, but still happened from time to time.

'Some of my dreams are real,' signed HT. 'It's hard to know what is real and what is just in my head.'

Then he confessed to Nate about holding the revolver in his mouth.

"What was it that was botherin' ya so much Cousin?"

'I don't know. It started when I ran away.'

The two men stared into the glowing coals for a time.

HT noticed Nate looked nervous. He was trembling in fact.

"I've never told ya this before Cousin. I never told anyone. Maybe ya already know it, eh?"

'Know what?'

Nate got up and looked around as if searching for a place to run. He hesitated, then blurted: "I never told ya I'm gay."

'I sort of guessed that,' signed HT.

"It tears me up inside bein' gay and not bein' able to talk about it and live it, eh. If I ever tell anyone other than you, I know my life is over."

HT shook his head 'no.'

"Yes it will be Cousin. I'll be a laughin' stock. I'll lose half my buddies and most of my family. Ya know what my dad says about gay people. What would it do to 'em if I came out with it, eh?"

'You have to live for yourself, not your father. You need to be true to yourself Nate.'

"At church I've tried to pray the gay away. But it doesn't work. I've been this way since I was five years old. Maybe younger. My thoughts and feelings and urges—no matter what I do—they won't stop. The people at church will kick me out if they ever find out."

'You can find a different church. One where they accept the way you are.'

"And I've thought a lot about it too. Like when ya put a gun in your mouth, eh? I've thought about suicide for years. For years Cousin." Nate's shoulders spasmed as he fought to control his sobs.

HT's cheeks were wet. He got up.

'You're going to be okay Nate.' he signed.

They hugged one another beside the dying coals. Above them the northern lights danced.

IT WAS A CRISP MORNING. Fog was lifting from the surface of the nearby slough.

HT rose ever so slowly from his crouched position. In a single motion he drew back, aimed and released the bowstring. The razor-tipped arrow sailed low and disappeared into the chest of the young bull moose. The animal crashed away through the frosted willows. After a bit, the noise stopped. He waited a minute, then waved Nate over.

"Did ya get 'em Cousin?"

HT grinned and nodded. 'Winter meat,' he signed. 'But now the work begins.'

They followed the blood trail. After fifty meters or so, they found where the massive moose piled up. HT dipped his fingers red and tasted them. Nate propped one long hind leg behind him while HT opened its bulging belly to gut it. The thick odor of steaming offal and blood hung in the air.

"Ya hit 'em right in the lungs Cousin. Don't ya ever miss?"

'Sometimes. But a moose is a big target. Hard to miss.'

"Why didn't ya use your rifle?"

'Because you've been using it,' he signed.

"I mean today. Ya could've hunted with it today, eh? My moose has been hangin' on the meat pole for three days."

HT shrugged. 'I like my bow. It's quieter. More peaceful. It's the way we used to hunt.'

Together, the two men quickly skinned and quartered the animal. HT set aside the kidneys, heart and tongue for himself while Nate kept the liver. They trimmed the remaining meat from the pelvis, spine and ribs and packed the white cotton bags and hide bundle down to shore.

After the canoe was brought around from camp, they loaded the craft and ferried the heavy load downlake closer to the lodge. They packed the bags and bundle to the foot of the cache where HT sorted the pieces. Some were hoisted high and hung on the cross-pole so they could cool quickly and be out of reach of the local bears. The rest would be processed into jerky.

The two men sliced meat well into the afternoon. When the racks were full, they fired up the smokehouse. After a time, cool white vapors filled the tiny shack and wafted from the cracks and the smokestack. The hunters made beds in the nearby moss. Sleep came quickly.

HT dreamt of a long-ago time and place. Gabby Sanchez was there with him behind the school gym talking away while she gazed into his silvery eyes. She examined his injured finger and told him what a great hand talker he was. Gabby unbuttoned her denims and placed his hand down there on her warm little beaver fur. She told him she wanted him to talk with her again. Then she wrapped her brown arms around his neck. Her lips were just like before. Warm. Wet. Wonderful! He devoured her delicious kisses and massaged below her fur patch in gentle, rhythmic circles like she'd taught him. But Gabby's hands gradually became rough on his skin—sharp even.

As he slowly opened his eyes, HT was slammed with adrenaline. He was mouth-on-mouth and hand-on-fur with a skinwalker. The witch-wolf pawed his chest and continued licking his tongue and teeth. Terrified, he threw off the heavy gray thing. It tumbled across the moss, then rose on its haunches. It hunched there, surveying him, seemingly out of curiosity. Was it smiling?

HT crouched there in horror with his hands clutched to his broken voice box.

Nate awoke. "What's wrong Cousin?"

"Nothin'," said the bush pilot. He set down a big bag of dog food. "I think he just got a little scared is all Nate. Don't worry Hand Talker. She won't bite. She likes ya. You two boys were sleepin' like a couple of fat winter bears when we got here. Can't believe ya didn't hear us fly in. Ya must be pretty darn tired, eh?"

Shocked, confused, HT looked at the pilot then back at the wolfish dog. Trickster-like, the animal grinned at him again, leaned a bit to one side and broke wind. Its curled tail wagged.

"She's a husky-mix," said the pilot. "Doesn't have a name yet. Hey, Nate. Is that your moose hangin' there? There's two of 'em. Hand Talker got one too, eh?"

The pilot turned to HT. "Your boy Sonny told me ya needed a companion. I found her at the end of Stunt Man Road when she was a little bitty pup. She was one of the ones left there by that dog dumper Ronny. He's a professional breeder. Lives just off Highway 2 down south of La Ronge with his girl Pearl. Ronny does that anytime his own breeds accidentally cross, or if a stray gets in one of his dog yards and there's mixin' goin' on. It messes with his financial bottom line as a purebred breeder. So he takes the mixed breed pups north of town and dumps 'em out by Barber Field close to where Martha and I hangar the plane. That damned fool doesn't give a shit about the dogs. At the end of the day, all he cares about is their genetics and his paycheck. Anyway, this one needs a home 'cause last week that idiot went and dumped another litter of pups. I need to make room for all the new arrivals. So will ya help me out here Hand Talker? Will ya take her in?"

HT hesitated, then slowly nodded. 'She can eat moose scraps and fish,' he signed. 'And other things I catch.'

"What'd he say?"

"He says he'll take the dog. And he's got food for it."

"I brought along a half-dozen bags of dog chow too," said the pilot. "Well boys, let's get Nate's moose loaded in the plane. We're losin' daylight."

30

ANKLE BITERS

THE PRINCIPAL MET HER at the office door. The two of them briefly exchanged smiles. He offered Beth a seat. She was immediately drawn to his good looks. She tried to focus on the swirling snowflakes outside the window behind him—to not be so obvious about it. But she found it difficult to take her eyes off her new boss.

"Don't worry Beth. No one here knows who you are—yet. We'll try to keep your presence low profile until you get settled in like we talked about on the phone. But it's a small community and soon *everyone* will know you're a member of the Family."

Just look at that crooked nose, she thought. *He's too cute.*

"We try to keep it informal here, so please just call me Yuri. I think you'll really like it here. There's time before First Period for a quick tour of the facility. But first, let's review the school mission statement and policies together, eh?"

Boring, she said to herself as she gazed into his beautiful hazel eyes.

Thankfully for Beth, Yuri's bureaucratic orientation ended quickly. He recounted the story of his childhood move from Ukraine to Manitoba with his parents. He was an only child growing up. Eventually he entered the university in Saskatoon and earned a degree in business administration. But, after graduating, his interest turned to boxing. He became a professional fighter, he told her. Then Yuri retired from that career and tried his hand at TV sportscasting. And then he switched careers yet again to become a school administrator at La Ronge.

Yuri was fascinated by Beth's exquisite face and captivating blue eyes. And, while he couldn't help but notice the curve of her hips and the fullness of her breasts, what absolutely mesmerized him was the young Aussie woman's accent. They talked non-stop and ended up postponing the school tour he'd planned for her.

YURI AND BETH ARRIVED LATE. He opened the classroom door and winced. They were met with chaos as they stepped in.

"They're all yours Beth," shouted her grinning boss. "You're the one who's trained to teach them—not me."

"Babysit don't you mean? Thanks a lot Yuri."

He waved 'goodbye' and shut the door.

She went to the front and wrote on the whiteboard in big letters.

'Miss Winsley'

'Absolutely no telephones or cameras allowed'

Beth began tapping the table. "Alright now. Please take your seats."

The kids ignored her.

She spoke more loudly: "I said please take your seats."

They looked at her, then continued roughhousing.

She stopped tapping. "Then I suppose there won't be any lunch today."

The room quickly became quiet as the students took their assigned seats.

"That's better. Now that it is quiet, I want you each to know that things are going to be different around here from now on. It won't be like it was before. I am not a substitute teacher like the others you have had so far this year. I will be your instructor every day for the remainder of the school year.

"I would like to introduce myself to you. Then I will ask each one of you to introduce yourself to me and tell me what your favorite hobby is and the reason you like to do it, alright? I am Miss Winsley. I am your new Grade 9 instructor. One of my favorite pastimes is to visit zoos and nature preserves because my mum and I used to do that together. If it sounds funny to you when I speak, that is because I am from Melbourne, Australia—a different part of the Common- wealth of Nations—much different than northern Saskatchewan I assure you. There we have kindly little koala bears. And I am told that here you have giant grizzly bears!"

The kids laughed.

"Alright then. Now what are *your* names? We will begin with you Miss. Yes, you in the flannel shirt. Please stand when you introduce yourself."

"I'm Darcey. My hobby is reading science magazines from the library. I like it because they're interesting and I'm always learning amazing things."

Darcey sat down. The girl next to her stood.

"My name is Candace. My favorite thing is drawing dresses and other kinds of clothes. I'm going to be a fashion designer."

AT THE END OF THE DAY, the kids lined up and waited for the bell to ring. Beth walked down the line of students and spoke to each of them in turn, making sure to call them by name.

"And you Miss Darcey, what are you doing wearing those mittens young lady? They are made of real fur aren't they? Caught by some bloody evil trapper."

"My uncle made them for me for Christmas last year Miss Winsley. He's a First Nations trapper."

"Well, we can't have that now can we?"

"No, we can't have that," echoed Candace.

The bell rang and the students began filing out.

"Remember to dress nicely for the school yearbook photos tomorrow," announced Beth. *Great, just what I need,* she thought. *Picture Day. Maybe I should call in sick.*

Candace stayed behind.

"Miss Winsley, tomorrow I'm going to be wearing an outfit I put together myself. It's a red and white evening gown with long red gloves."

"That sounds wonderful Miss Candace. I want you to tell me all about it."

SHE FOUND YURI still at work in his office.

"So how did it go Beth?"

"Lovely. The kids are behind in some subjects—but we should be able to get caught-up soon. And I do think there will need to be some changes made around here."

Yuri grinned. "I'd like to hear your ideas. We could talk about them over a drink maybe, but it might be a little awkward being seen together at a bar in town, eh? What do you think about discussions over a drink at my place instead? I could cook dinner for the two of us."

"I don't drink, Yuri," she said, focusing once more on his hazel eyes and crooked nose. "But yes, I *will* take you up on your dinner offer. I would like the opportunity to discuss my ideas with you. And I suspect that this situation may get a little awkward no matter how we approach it."

BETH SOON FELL into a routine: she rose early; breakfasted; arrived at the teacher's lounge to prepare for class; taught Grade 9 till 3 p.m.; returned to her small apartment to grade papers; and then went to Yuri's house where they discussed school policies, student needs and the day's events while she watched him mix a drink for himself and prepare their dinner.

One evening after dinner, Beth planted herself on the Chesterfield in his living room. Yuri took his usual place at his desk in the corner.

"Yuri, why don't you sit here with me."

"Are you sure?"

"Yes. I'm sure."

SHE PEELED BACK THE SATIN SHEET, exposing Yuri's face. He grinned and continued kissing her foot.

"You know that practice is reserved for kings and queens don't you?"

"Really? Then I won't kiss you, My Lady—I'll bite you instead."

"Just what I need—another ankle biter nibbling away at me," she laughed.

31

TROUBLE BREWIN'

LA RONGE, SASKATCHEWAN
FEBRUARY 17TH, 2015

THE STUDENTS LINED UP by the door and waited for the bell.

"Still wearing those real fur mittens Miss Darcey?" said Beth with raised eyebrows. "You know I don't approve."

Beth sighed, then changed the subject. "You did very well in chemistry today. Maybe you have a future in that field. Have you thought of attending university? When you get to that point, I will be happy to write a letter of recommendation for you."

"I'll just be happy to graduate high school Miss Winsley. Besides, there aren't any jobs in Saskatchewan for chemists except maybe at the tar sands facilities. I wouldn't want to work for them. Have you heard about the damage they're doing?"

"Yes, I've heard. Well I'm sure we can find a way to use your many talents locally. I volunteer Thursday evenings at the Ed Center. There, we provide access to a variety of scholarships, internships and apprenticeships—you don't *have* to go to university."

"Miss Winsley, *I* plan to attend university," said Candace.

The bell rang.

Once outside, Candace confronted Darcey. "Hey Bitch Girl, why you keep wearin' those ugly beaver mittens?" Darcey shoved her hands deep into the pockets of her faux fur parka.

"Because it's winter—it's cold out—and they were a gift. I think they're beautiful."

"All the fashion designers use *faux* fur. They don't use *real* fur anymore."

"Fine. That's their choice."

"But that beaver was caught in a trap."

"Yes, by my uncle. He tanned the fur. He's the one who made them for me."

"Why can't you wear *faux* fur like Miss Winsley and me?"

"I like mine better. It's all natural. Your parka's made from *plastic* fibers—

plastic that probably came from the tar sands."

"Your uncle just trapped that poor beaver for its fur and threw the rest away. He didn't even eat it."

"He *did so* eat it. Our whole family ate it."

"Liar."

"Freak of nature."

"Trappers are bloody evil!" Candace yanked a one-liter plastic bag from her coat pocket and flung it at Darcey like a water balloon. The bag burst.

Shocked, Darcey stared at her mittens and coat. They were drenched in sticky red liquid.

"I'VE GOT SOMETHING FOR YOU My Lady," said Yuri. "It's a surprise, eh."

"Really?" said Beth. "I love surprises—good ones that is."

Wrapped in a satin sheet, she scooted herself upright and leaned against the headboard of his bed.

"I think you'll like this one."

Yuri opened the top of his blue backpack which was propped in the corner and withdrew a gift-wrapped box he'd hidden inside. He stood at attention and made an exaggerated bow.

"Your Highness, may I present to you—a gift—a most wondrous gift—from Sir Yuri the Bold."

They laughed.

"Yes, you certainly are bold—and completely naked I might add. And let me guess, Sir Yuri, is this gift of yours *another* pair of shoes for me? Or perhaps a pair of slippers for me this time? Tell me, are they glass slippers or ruby red slippers?"

"Open it and see."

Beth tore back the wrapping and lifted the shoebox lid.

"Why Sir Yuri, they're not slippers at all. They're heels—a love pair of golden high heels. Why am I not surprised?" she laughed. "And they happen to be in my exact size—again. I think that makes five or six pairs you've given me now. You sure like lady's shoes don't you Lovie?"

"Indeed I do. Aren't you going to try them on My Lady?"

Beth slipped on her golden heels, while Yuri queued up a romantic Ukrainian song and dimmed the lights a bit. They slow-danced beside the bed, kissing.

YURI SAT ON THE EDGE of the bed and began putting on his socks and work slacks.

"Beth, I need to speak seriously with you for a minute, okay?"

"Sure Lovie. What is it?" "You realize things will have to change, eh? You've been bringing too much attention to yourself lately."

"No Yuri. I haven't. The Royal Family has been getting more and more threats. I've done everything I can to keep my head low while living here—to stay *out* of the spotlight. Believe me, it's so much quieter here for me than it was living in Melbourne. It's like I have a whole new life here in La Ronge—away from the paparazzi."

"No. It's got nothing to do with your royal relatives and all of that craziness. I'm talking about your students Beth. What I'm trying to say is that many of these kids come from traditional First Nations families. You're criticizing the way the families live. They've lived this way for hundreds of years. You shouldn't be telling them that the way they live is wrong."

"Well they *are* wrong—and I'm right."

"Are you sure about that?"

"If you don't want me at your school Yuri, maybe I should apply to be a criminal investigator trainee with the Mounties. You've seen their recruitment announcement haven't you? They certainly pay better than you do."

"I think you'd make a great investigator Beth. But I don't want to lose you. The kids need you. I need you."

"I need you too, Yuri."

"Why don't you take off an extra week or two over spring break, eh? Make it an extended holiday—to think about it. Maybe go camping or something. Don't you dare enlist with the Mounties Beth!"

32

PASSIN' THROUGH

EGG LAKE REGION, SASKATCHEWAN
FEBRUARY 26TH, 2015

DURING HIS MANY YEARS at Egg Lake, he'd seen signs left by a series of different intruders. Now he'd intercepted tracks in the snow of yet another interloper passing through the bounds of his registered trapline—big tracks—man tracks. HT decided to find out what this particular man was doing infringing on the territory for which he'd paid the Yellow Bird family in full. The stranger appeared to have circled the lake and was now headed around the north shore back toward La Ronge on a part of the trail that crossed a network of sloughs.

HT shed his pack and strapped on his holster. He summited the nearby brushy slope and followed the windswept ridgetop at a run in an effort to cut-off the intruder. He sprinted along the ridge till he thought he was well ahead of the man. Then he dropped down into the frozen lake basin and rejoined the trail. HT crept along the path as he searched for a place to lie low. He skirted a ring of dead trees around an area of thawed, soggy, rust-stained soil. At its center was a large cauldron of boiling, steaming water—a natural hot spring encircled by a screen of half-dead brush.

Further down the beaten track he encountered a wide stagnant pond covered in black ice. At its edge was an upturned root wad from a fallen snag. HT slipped into the natural blind. His eyes scrutinized the shadows among the black spruce surrounding the water.

A gunshot sounded, catching HT by surprise. It came from perhaps a kilometer away

Crouched there, concealed behind the twisted roots, he waited. An hour passed. Then he noticed movement ahead on the snowy trail—the encroacher. A large chubby man in camouflage overalls trudged toward him balancing a massive moosehide-wrapped bundle over his shoulders—a high-power rifle with scope slung across his chest—a black cowboy hat in-hand. The man grunted under his heavy load and coughed water vapor into the dry taiga air.

HT remembered the gunshot and concluded that the intruder—a poacher—

killed a moose outside the legal season. The stranger drew ever closer. HT's vision blurred. His cheek began to twitch and his neck muscles grew as taut as a hangman's rope. He steadied the barrel of his revolver over a bare root and took aim.

33

THE BODY

EGG LAKE REGION, SASKATCHEWAN
MARCH 23RD, 2015

*B*EAR SHIT! thought Beth. *Bloody hell, I'm kneeling in bear shit.*

All the while she'd been crouching in a bear toilet, oblivious to the shivering and quivering of her half-numb body and the dark frozen lumps on the matted grass beneath her. She broke off a willow twig and scraped the thawed feces from her navy-blue trousers.

When she looked up he was there—the killer—seemingly from out of nowhere. That bloody lowlife was approaching the scene she'd been surveilling. Through the veil of her brush blind she warily watched him, unblinking. The man glided across the flatwater in his battered canoe, its wake rippling toward her. Sunrays stabbed at the tangle of branches encircling her. Tightness gripped her throat. Edge-ice shattered like glass as the dark-haired man slid the slim craft onto the shore of the grassy spit. He panther-padded up the brushy bank and headed her way, slinking along the trail. And like before, the hard-frozen mud captured no impressions, leaving no evidence of his—or anyone's—passing.

From his behavior it was now clear to Beth this man was the murderer whose return she'd awaited. A renewed sense of fury seethed within her. She observed his methodical approach. Soon she'd get her chance to confront him about the body she'd discovered nearby. *Returning to the scene of the crime*, she thought. *But I doubt he'll confess.*

Through the screen of willows she witnessed his long black hair and the sparse sickled bristles on his face. She noted his stained leather britches and footwear. Shirtless in the morning frost, from the waist up he wore nothing but a crude pack of woven wooden strips. Sunlight highlighted his swarthy complexion and well-toned physique.

Beth scoffed at his arrogance. *This scumbag decides to show up half-naked after I have been freezing my bum off out here waiting for him all morning.*

HT slipped out of his packbasket and set it on the flattened blades of yellow sedge beside her blind. He went to the water's edge, then stooped and peered into its murk. While he was distracted, she leaned out, unsnapped the holster on the pack's rim and shoved his revolver into her jacket.

A raven swooped low, then croaked and veered away. Startled, he turned and faced her. He squinted against the sun's glare.

She stood her ground—challenging him.

Baffled, he just stared at her, wondering how he could have missed the signs. He should have noticed she was hiding there—lying in wait. *Must be losing my edge.* he thought. *Is she one of those new recruits the Mounties hired on?*

"Are you *the one*?" she asked.

He nodded and wondered how in the heck she'd managed to find him.

There, she thought. *I got my confession.*

It was time she lay down the law: "I know what you have been doing out here. I'm here to put an end to it."

HT snorted and abruptly turned his back to her. He raked around in the water with a stick, hooked a line obscured below the surface, and tugged. The body slowly drifted toward him. He grabbed a leg, grunted and heaved the slippery bloated-looking thing up onto the bank.

She grimaced in disgust. "Enough of that. Stop—turn around—now!"

Without looking, he waved a hand in her general direction, middle finger extended.

"It's over," she barked. "This time you won't be getting away with it."

His lean body tensed. Yet he remained kneeling there over the waterlogged body as if to admire the morbid beauty of his handiwork. Then he arose and circled back across the spit to the canoe, giving a wide berth to the tough blue-eyed woman blocking the trail. She hollered at him.

HT ignored her.

I caught him with the evidence red-handed. Does he think he can just haul it off and dispose of it? If I don't stop him now, he is sure to kill again.

She followed him, staying back a bit in case he tried something. Once more she ordered him to stop and once more HT refused to comply. He prepared to board the canoe and shove-off. She decided it was now or never and drew the weapon and aimed at his vitals.

"You murdering bastard. I said turn around *now*!" She pulled back the hammer to make her position clear.

Hearing the all-too-familiar clicks, HT realized he'd misjudged the young woman. Wild-eyed, he jerked upright and spun. His cat-quick reaction caught her off guard. Beth's grip on the gun tightened as she lurched back. The morning stillness exploded.

Kpoomf!

34

WOODEN CHALICE

EGG LAKE REGION, SASKATCHEWAN
MARCH 23RD, 2015

ACRID SMOKE DRIFTED from the muzzle of the old revolver in Beth's hands. Her ears rang. HT was hunched across the side of the canoe, legs dangling in the dark water, head cocked sideways looking back. His bright gray eyes penetrated her like those of some tortured animal—not those of the killer she knew him to be.

"Oh my God—I am so sorry. Shit—bloody shit. I did not mean for that to happen."

A sickening knot formed deep within Beth's gut. *What the bloody hell have I done? I only meant to talk—to make him come to his senses.*

She grabbed the gunnel to keep the canoe from slipping away.

"Are you hurt badly?"

Stunned, HT stared at the blood escaping between his fingers. He nodded in disbelief. With his free hand, he yanked out his notepad and pencil stub from a satchel in the canoe and scribbled a message in large letters and thrust it at her. He pointed to his mouth and shook his head 'no.'

"What are you saying—you are unable to speak? Is that it?" She read the note.

Put down gun—Stow under bow deck—Help me

"You need a stow? What is a stow?"

HT grimaced in pain and scribbled again, nodding at a crate resting in the canoe's forward hold.

Put gun in box

She placed his antique .32 caliber revolver in the box, then read his new note.

Help me get in canoe—Bring pack & beaver

Beth hesitated. In her mind, she quickly milled over her available options.

"Do it now," screamed his eyes.

She wanted to flee this nightmare she'd created. Yet she stayed there and forced herself to face the First Nations trapper she'd shot.

"Do it!" his eyes pleaded.

She was determined to help. "Okay—yes." Plunging her own legs into the icy water beside him, she helped him roll his body up into the craft.

He lay there in a fetal position like a colicky child clutching his side. His crimson lifeblood dripped steadily onto the cedar planks beneath him.

"You'll be alright," she said, not sure if it was true or not. "I'll be right back."

Beth sprinted back down the moose trail to the blind, gathered her belongings and crammed them into the man's packbasket and hefted the load back to the canoe. She clambered across the stricken man and stowed it behind him. Then she returned along the treeline on the faint path to her hidden bush camp. She ripped out the tent stakes, gathered the bulging mass and stuffed the tiny tent and all of its contents into her backpack. Abandoning the cookware and small campstove, she ran for the canoe, pitched in her pack and prepared to launch.

HT rapped on the side of the canoe to get her attention. He pointed across the grassy spit at the beaver lodge.

She protested.

Frustrated, he pounded even harder. His eyes bored into her.

Beth rushed to the spot near the beaver lodge where she'd awaited his return. The drowned animal was lying there atop the matted sedge. Its weight was at least a third of her own. She tried depressing the trap's springs, but they seemed too powerful. She unwrapped the slide-wire and freed it.

The young woman grasped the paddle-tail and swung the sodden animal over her back, but lost her grip. The fat beaver *thwomped* onto the bank and rolled into the pond. She seized the disappearing trap chain just in time. She grabbed the webbed feet, lurched upright and slogged back to the canoe. With a heave, the drowned beaver slid into the space between HT's legs. The water from its fur intermingled with his small but growing pool of blood.

Once more she delved into his haunting silvery eyes. A new rush of adrenaline jolted her to action. She launched the slim watercraft and attempted to raise herself high on the yoke pads. The canoe rocked wildly. He gestured for her to kneel low on the duffel amidships instead.

Beth lifted the carved wooden paddle. "Which way?" she demanded.

HT jerked his head toward the southwest. Beth spied a lone weathered snag on the far side of the pond and used it as her waypoint. She stabbed the water with the pointed blade and the craft cut a tight arc stern-first. It was gliding across the water backwards, but it didn't much matter. He slapped the canoe and motioned for her to take three strokes, switch sides and then take three more strokes.

"Got it."

She continued toward the snag. Her course across the pond soon straightened. Three strokes—switch—three strokes—switch. Then Beth modified her stroke pattern further: three right—four left—three right—four left. Now she was getting the hang of it.

Looking over his shoulder, HT pointed to a dark horizontal line at the far end of the pond. She made for it. The canoe eventually bumped into the mud-plastered dam.

"What now?"

He gestured for her to portage the canoe. She climbed over him and hopped out. It took every bit of her strength to drag the loaded craft with its injured occupant onto the narrow dam. She balanced the keel atop the dam, aimed for the muddy chute below, and heaved. The canoe slid slowly at first, then suddenly careened down the beaver slide, dragging Beth with it while she clung to the prow.

It hit with a huge splash. The momentum carried them forward into the narrow creek channel. Beth was now chin-deep in icy water, stunned and choking. The craft bobbed and drifted between willow-stubbed hummocks. She hurriedly scaled one and managed to re-board, nearly swamping the canoe as it rocked wildly.

Nauseous and dizzy, HT stared in fascination at the drenched, sunlit woman who knelt there before him. She was sucking air and shivering in her dripping garments like a freshly baptized neophyte. Everything around him seemed large and slow-moving. Burgundy blood-water sloshed across his body as if he was being swirled about in a wooden chalice by some giant high priest of old.

Beth interrupted his shock-induced vision: "Hey you. Look at me. Are you doing okay?"

HT thought about it and shrugged. *We need a fire to dry-off and get warm—but there's no time*, he decided matter-of-factly.

He bailed with an empty tin while she guided the slim craft downcreek, maneuvering the gentle bends, steering it onward. Although shivering, the northern sun and toil of paddling kept the cold at bay for her. Soon, Beth's prior doubts gave way to confidence. But her aching arms were heavy with fatigue. Her shoulders burned.

The meandering channel widened. The bank-scrub was now shorter and the grass tussocks and sedges more abundant as the nearby slopes merged with the muskeg flats and feeder sloughs. The winding creek grew shallow, braided into a lacework of channels, then spat the cedar canoe into Egg Lake.

35

TO BUILD A FIRE

EGG LAKE REGION, SASKATCHEWAN
MARCH 23RD, 2015

BETH SCANNED THE COLD, open gray water. Low waves licked and lapped the hull. She rested the paddle for a moment. Her muscles spasmed. Violent shivers shook her as the strong breeze brushed across her wet clothing, whisking away the heat generated moments before from the effort of paddling. The fire within her could no longer resist the demands of the steady wind. It stole what little warmth remained within her.

"Where do I g-go?" she asked.

There was no response.

She flailed HT hard with the paddle.

"Which way?"

He opened his eyes and flung a look backwards toward the western shore. With one hand, he outlined the shape of two hills and indicated to go there. Fingers now numb, mind sluggish, he jotted a final note.

Aim between hills—Cabin is by clearing—Put on coat & mitts

HT gestured at the canvas duffel upon which she knelt. She opened it and withdrew a thick caribou skin parka and began draping it robe-like over him. He shook his head 'no' and indicated for her to wear it instead.

Beth's numb fingers barely functioned as she donned the oversized garment and struggled with the fur mittens. Convulsions racked her body and coursed along her spine. She commenced a jerky side-to-side sway-dance with the paddle like some drugged alley woman of ancient Magdala. Her eyes remained focused on the faraway hills in her desire for deliverance—salvation from this damned predicament she'd put the two of them in. HT prodded her with his foot and motioned her onward.

"Faster," screamed his piercing eyes.

In a primal burst of effort, she frantically paddled through the waves—three right—four left—three right—four left, as she fought to save the life of the man she'd shot. The pain in her upper body gave way to utter exhaustion. The numbing wind continued to drain her body heat, pushing her closer to death. Three right—four left—between the hills—to the cabin—three right—four left.

The Indigenous trapper in front of her gestured to her. She tried to answer, but her words were slurred—not coming out right. *Those hills are so far away.* Life became a blur.

⟫◇⟪

WHEN THE WATERCRAFT RASPED to a halt on the gravel beach, Beth continued methodically sweeping the paddle blade—stabbing, heaving—stabbing, heaving. She was deep in the drunken stupor of hypothermia, no longer shivering. HT drummed the side of the canoe and prodded her with his foot. But it was useless. Her core temperature was perilously low and she'd lost the ability to communicate or even to reason. Her organs were slowly shutting down. Somewhere nearby a dog barked.

The wound in his side reopened and flowed when he pulled Beth from the canoe and dragged her to the lodge. He was stiff and cold and suddenly thirsty. The intense pain brought on another bout of nausea. He retched, but maintained his hold on the stumbling woman.

Inside it was cool and dark. He lost hold of the antique revolver tucked under his armpit and it skittered across the wooden floor. Now the brash woman was mumbling and wandering about the lodge grunting, bumping into things, acting out some cold-spawned hallucination.

The fire he'd banked the previous evening was gone except for a few coals deep in its ashen remains. HT's numb hands and feet were more like frozen clubs than living flesh and bone. With such useless appendages, it was only his experience that enabled him to use his wrists and cold-deadened fingers pincer-like to rekindle the fire. He dug a couple coals from the bottom of the firebox, arranged birch bark strips and a few pitch sticks atop them, then breathed them to life. The fatwood splinters snapped and screeched. Tiny flames flared high. He nourished the small fire with thumb-thick pieces of kindling. After it burned for a bit he added larger sticks, then stoked the crackling stove with hefty log chunks. He latched the door and left the damper and vents wide open.

The woman who'd shot him was slumped on the floor—unconscious—on the verge of flatlining. HT stepped outside and whistled. At first it refused to break the rule—to enter the lodge—but the dog came in when it perceived his sense of urgency. It licked Beth, then whined and paced. HT tugged hard with the crook of his arm and wrenched off both of her packboots and liners. He stripped her of the skin parka. Unable to grip her frozen pants, he rolled her onto her belly and retrieved a hunting knife from the table. With the gut-hook clenched between his club-hands, he skillfully split her pants down the rear. He grabbed a fabric flap with his teeth and yanked hard, pressing the instep of his mukluk into Beth's armpit. The dog seized the other flap in its jaws and tugged violently. Together, using their teeth and brute strength, HT and the dog jerked and wrestled the frozen garments from the unconscious woman's body. The dog barked and licked her face.

HT shoved the bedding aside and spread out a rabbit skin robe. He lifted Beth onto it and signaled the dog to lay atop her, then placed a second robe over the two of them.

Finally, he attended to his own needs. He released the slip knots on his frozen mukluks and leather pants, doffed them and hung them to dry. In the brightness of the roaring fire, he held his side and stared at his pale, wrinkled, blood-water-smeared feet. The thaw-pain would come soon enough. He'd known it before, having made mistakes a time or two out there in the bush which resulted in the near freezing of his hands or feet. It was a memorable pain—like a thousand thorns piercing him while the nerves in those appendages thawed and resurrected from the death-hold of the Northwoods' brutal cold.

HT braced himself and waited. In the flickering firelight, the jabbing pain hit him hard. He hung his head and moaned and gnashed his teeth. He endured immeasurable agony while the blood circulation to his extremities slowly returned. By and by, the pain subsided and he regained full feeling and movement in his aching fingers and toes. Yet the burning from the bullet hole in his side persisted and tormented him.

He retrieved a bottle of Seagram's and doused the oozing wound. Then he dried the area around it and set about cutting pieces from a hank of linen. He took a few swigs, then secured a whiskey-soaked dressing over the area.

Then it dawned on him: *No exit hole. It's still in there—stuck in my liver.*

The kettle whistled. HT steeped two big mugs of tea, then stirred a shot of

Seagram's, a glob of honey and a dash of salt into each one. He pulled back the fur robe from the young woman's face and saw she was shivering once more—a good sign. He propped her up and deftly dribbled some of the bush medicine into the corner of her mouth. The soothing vapors crept into her nostrils. She opened her eyes and responded vigorously. He saw she was dazed. Trembling even. But she seemed to recognize him. She emptied her mug of warm elixir and half of his own.

He re-draped her, dampered the stove, then took a few more pulls on the bottle to take the edge off his pain.

HT noticed the dog was now halfway out of the robe, overheated and panting heavily. He directed the dog to lay on her feet. Then, ignoring the pain, he slipped under the covers between the wall and the woman. He laid on his uninjured side and faced the peeled logs.

Feeling the warmth of his backside, Beth curled against him, ignoring his nakedness. She clutched HT—absolutely savoring his delicious body heat. Exhausted and wrapped up in the euphoria of being alive and almost warm again, she'd completely forgotten the bullet wound in his side. Together, the strangers slept.

36

REFUGE

EGG LAKE REGION, SASKATCHEWAN
MARCH 23RD, 2015

BETH SAT UPRIGHT AMONG THE FURS and blankets. It was nighttime. The fire had gone to embers. The lodge was now cool. An orange glow shone from the bed of coals through the tempered glass window of the woodstove. The dim light waxed and waned while the outside breeze brushed against the curve of the lodge and suckled the stove pipe. She examined her surroundings. The heavily furred dog was asleep against the door, twitching in a dream-run below an old crucifix mounted on the lintel. Moonlight spilled from the window onto the faded tapestry rug and pooled on the hand-hewn floorboards.

The lodge was rustic, its furnishings eclectic. It smelled of woodsmoke and spices. And there were other fragrances too, reminding her of the sweet musk of the spring beaver she'd carried to the canoe that morning and the scent of a hard-working man. She counted six walls. The stove was centered in the room beneath corbelled beams from which hung dozens of bundles of dried herbs. A high shelf filled with books spanned most of the walls. There was a handcrafted table and two chairs along one wall. An antique highboy chest stood against the nearest wall, an old roll-top desk against the farthest. One wall close to the door held a row of wooden pegs from which hung an assortment of clothes and articles of primitive gear made of hide and wood. Beneath it was a storage bench and some footwear and animal traps.

Beth was amazed at the beauty and simplicity of the dome-shaped log dwelling. Sheltered there in the cozy lodge, she recalled a dream she had while attending the university—a vivid dream of brown people in small round houses like this one—the children speaking to her in muffled words. In the dream she desperately wanted to communicate with them—to tell them things—to teach them. Though she couldn't understand them, she felt at home there with the cinnamon-colored children.

She became aware of the Indigenous trapper curled beside her. His breathing was deep. Peaceful. The strong odor of whiskey permeated his bedspace. *Is he an alcoholic?* she wondered.

She contemplated the incident at the beaver pond. *It was an accident, right?* Now she wasn't so sure. She mentally retraced the day's events and concluded that somehow, together, they'd managed to reach the safety of the man's lodge. She vaguely recalled waking up and drinking tea. The hot liquid and warmth of the dog brought her back from the brink of death. Her body ached from the hours of paddling. But this Indigenous trapper suffered more than she did during the day's ordeal. He was the victim of a shooting—she being the shooter who'd recklessly brandished and discharged a weapon she didn't even know how to use. *If only I had been more clear-headed this morning,* she thought.

Beth noticed HT's pile of fur robes at the foot of the bed. The only thing he had on was a silver ring on one particularly straight finger. She re-covered him.

And now, feeling the chill, she needed to pee. Beth rose and sorted through the pile of soggy clothes. The heavily furred dog lifted its head and wagged its tail. It padded over and nuzzled its cold nose on her leg.

She held up her wet pants and knickers and saw where HT sliced them open. *Bloody hell,* she thought.

Shivering, she pulled on her soppy boots and donned the damp parka. When she cracked open the door, the dog wrenched through and bolted outside. It ran around for a minute, making its familiar rounds. Then it urinated and disappeared up a ramp into what looked like a miniature cabin.

The air had calmed. She listened to the burbling, gurgling creek as it supped at the rocks and crept along the edge of the bank. A great gray owl hooted in the distance. Starlight reflected from the shimmering lake.

There was a trail leading to a narrow shack set in an opening amongst the trees and shadows. *The privy.* She cautiously opened the door. Inside it was pitch black, so she stepped to the side and relieved herself there on the frosty ground, warm steam rising.

Back in the cabin, Beth stuffed wood chunks into the stove. She searched the dresser and the assorted garments hung from pegs for some sort of pajamas— anything dry to wear—to cover herself. She remembered the clothes in her backpack she'd loaded into the canoe earlier. Surely the craft was somewhere nearby. But at that moment she was too tired and cold to search for it. *It will have to wait till the 'morrow,* she thought.

She slipped out of the wet boots and parka and eased her way under the fur robes beside the stranger, wishing for a way to hide her bareness—not that it mattered, for he was deep in slumber, still reeking of whiskey.

37

BEAVER ON THE BARBIE

EGG LAKE REGION, SASKATCHEWAN
MARCH 23RD, 2015

DAYLIGHT POURED THROUGH THE WINDOW, yellowing the interior of the lodge. Outside a whiskeyjack called for handouts.

Beth bolted upright out of bed. The Indigenous man beside her was quietly grunting and snorting. His breathing grew raspy and irregular as he got jerked about by whatever tall demon it was that once more invaded his dreams. The anesthetic effect of the Seagram's had long since worn off. He was feverish. Unbeknownst to Beth, he'd pushed off the fur robes and blankets again during his nighttime thrashings. She noticed his right side was bruised and a bit distended. The dressing he'd taped across the wound was stained black and red and ringed yellow-brown with whiskey. She re-covered him, then began a methodical search of the lodge for medicine—drugs—anything to stop those godawful noises he was making.

BETH NUDGED HT. He woke to the smell of baking-gone-wrong. She handed him some Tylenol caplets and a mug of cool water. "These are all I could find. I hope they help with the pain. Are you hungry? I made us some biccies."

He looked at the plate of burnt unleavened biscuits in her hand and shook his head 'no.'

"Can I do anything to help you?"

He shrugged and thought about it. He signaled for his notepad and pencil:

Tell them I got shot

"Do you have a cell phone out here—or maybe a two-way radio?"

He shook his head 'no.'

"I'm not sure how to get back to La Ronge from here. I'll just get lost if I try. I think we should stay here for now—at least until you heal some."

He grimaced and nodded.

"My name is Beth Winsley. What is yours?"

He scribbled: ***Hand Talker Judd***

"I am terribly sorry that I hurt you Mister Judd. I did not mean to do it. It was so stupid of me. I had never even held a gun before—before I shot you."

He shrugged and looked away.

"I have never really cooked before, but I can try to make you something. You need to eat. What else is there for food?"

Powdered milk—Flour—Beans—Beaver

"Crikey. You must be joking. You expect me to cook and serve you your own murder victim?"

HT stared at her, unblinking.

"You really are serious aren't you?" She thought for a moment. "Then I suppose it will be beaver on the barbie for you. And hopefully some biccies that are not so black this time. Your dog must be hungry too. What do you feed her?"

He pointed at the note.

"She eats that?"

He nodded.

"And what do you call her?"

He wrote: ***Dog***

"No. I mean what is her *name*?"

He pointed at the note.

They continued to stare at one another.

Flustered, she grabbed the knife from the table and went outside in search of the beaver.

38

THE SNOOP

EGG LAKE REGION, SASKATCHEWAN
MARCH 28TH, 2015

HT's GUNSHOT WOUND was on the mend. She had helped him suture the .32 caliber bullet hole with a sterilized curved needle and thread.

Today, while he slept, Beth took it upon herself to explore the lodge. She analyzed the old crucifix hanging above the door. With its sharp broken base, the heavy plastic cross seemed dagger-like. Its silver Christ figure was worn smooth in places, like the surface of a much-handled antique coin. *Is he religious?* she wondered.

She perused the titles of his books neatly arranged on the high shelves and on top of his old roll-top desk. They encompassed a wide variety of subjects: history; science; nature; art; music; literature; environmental topics and Indigenous crafts and lifeways. She took down one of them about a topic close to her own heart—wildlife conservation—and thumbed through it. She noticed he'd made notations on some of the page margins in his distinctive script. *Who the bloody hell is this wild man?*

Her curiosity now piqued, Beth thumbed through a few of the magazines atop four tall stacks of them along one wall. There were issues of *National Geographic, Newsweek, Time Life, Navajo Times, Mother Earth News, Fur, Fish & Game* and many others. Some were stamped 'library discard.' Others bore labels with Auntie Millie's or Nate's name and mailing address.

She opened a drawer in the back of the desk. Inside was a well-worn leather-bound book. On its cover he'd penned the words, *'Poems & Chants.'*

Beth turned to check on him. HT was asleep. *What could it hurt?* she thought. The young woman opened the book toward the back and read one of his more recent entries.

MY SAD EARTH

*I hum ancient hymns
to my sad Earth.
I chant old rhythms
learned before birth.
In the desert—dead,
in the gray rain,
my tears touch the mud,
soothing Her pain.
The trees have all died.
Fish belly-up.
White brothers have lied.
Poison—corrupt.
From charcoal-choked skies
foul waters fall.
More cities rise,
burying all.
What can I do? I'm
one man, no more,
my voiceless whisper
against the roar?
I sign in sorrow:
"Let live, why slay?"
"Maybe tomorrow—
progress!" they bray.
Dismissing the ancient
wisdom ways,
denying the climate
weirding days,
oil and coal nourish
their selfish gains,
politicos flourish
and ignorance reigns.
Chaos, mayhem,
economy crash,
disease, riots, famine,
artillery smash.
Now thirsting and dying,
they starve, they bloat.*

The spoiled are crying,
*   no more to gloat.*
Their sickening moans
*   echo, then falter—*
entombed in false stones—
*   their concrete altar.*
I eat roaches, mice,
*   rats and stale seeds,*
*   the resistant lice,*
*   mutated weeds.*
Their world is ending,
*   yet life goes on.*
Mine is the mending
for time—long—long.

HT slapped the log wall beside the bed. 'What's that?' he signed.

Unnerved, Beth quickly closed his book and put it back. "I was just curious."

'That's my stuff.'

He rolled over and went back to sleep.

39

BROTHERS

EGG LAKE REGION, SASKATCHEWAN
MAY 5TH, 2015

ACCOMPANIED BY DOG, Beth wandered here and there sampling the early summer wild plants around the lodge. She reflected on the happenings of the past few months. The swelling in HT's wound gradually subsided, but the 100-grain wadcutter bullet remained permanently embedded inside him. With his explicit instructions and a map he sketched, Beth had made her way back to La Ronge and, when the school break ended, returned to teaching her Grade 9 students. She never reported the shooting incident—or HT's injury—to the Mounties.

Beth and Yuri continued their relationship through the spring. She adored him more than ever. Yet her thoughts returned time and again to the strikingly good-looking Indigenous man called 'Hand Talker Judd' living in his six-sided sod-covered cabin by the lake. Somehow, he'd forged a life out there in that stark land. He must have overcome incredible odds in life, she concluded—being mute—and alone—a récluse. *Maybe he needs help.* She sensed he must have retreated there to the wilderness for some reason. Yet, at the same time he seemed worldly, having that diverse collection of books and magazines.

That haunting, apocalyptic poem he'd written intrigued her. *How can he feel so strongly about the environment, yet be so cruel to animals?* She wanted to learn more about this man of contradictions. She was determined to see him again. *That rich brown skin of his—those silvery eyes—crikey!*

Without mentioning HT, she told Yuri of her plans to return to the remote cabin where she planned to spend her summer break.

Beth continued plucking and tasting the fresh shoots, leafy greens and wildflower buds as she and Dog explored the vegetation near the western lakeshore. Dog barked and chased a red squirrel to a tree. They watched it chitter at them from its high perch.

"Come on Girl. Time to move along. Let it be, okay?"

But when she turned to leave, Beth spied something small and yellowish-tan in the short, lush grass at the tree's dripline. There were several of them: mushrooms with long thin stems and bell-shaped caps. The largest one had been nibbled. *Well, if the squirrels can eat them, they must be safe*, she thought. Beth plucked several of the unblemished ones, then took a small bite just in case. *Well it tastes perfectly fine to me.*

She took another small bite, then continued her journey along the pebbled shoreline. As she explored, Beth kept munching on various plant tidbits. She stopped and drank from a brook where it entered the lake. But when she started to stand, she got woozy and quickly sat down beside the water. Her head pounded. Then, for some reason, she suddenly became light-hearted and giddy. Everything around her seemed absolutely hilarious—especially that goofy Dog. She couldn't stop laughing at the silly looking creature. Her vision blurred and her head spun. Dog tugged on her arm, but she couldn't get up. Everything went black.

BETH'S HEAD HURT when she awoke. She felt a bit nauseous. HT handed her a small bowl of black powder and a mug of cold tea.

"What happened?" she said.

Dog got me—I found you by lake—You ate mushrooms

Then she recalled finding and nibbling the yellowish mushrooms. HT took down a book from one of his shelves, turned to a page, and showed her.

"Liberty caps—is that what they are called?"

He nodded, then gestured for her to swallow the powder.

"Charcoal? For poisoning, right?"

He nodded.

And willow bark tea for headache

As she swallowed the powder a pinch at a time with tea, HT removed a different book.

My brother Little Bear gave it to me the year he died

She read the title on its worn cover: *Edible Native Plants of the Rocky Mountains* by H.D. Harrington.

He tapped the book and gestured to the others on the shelf. 'You need to learn,' he signed. He handed her a blank notebook and a book about Northern

Saskatchewan plants. 'Come with me.'

Together, they examined the vegetation near the lodge. HT showed her the delicate male and female parts on the flowers they encountered. Only a few types of plants grew in the moss carpet beneath the trees, but the meadows and marshes had many. He pointed out the different shapes and numbers of petals and bracts. With his guidance, Beth began to notice patterns that allowed her to distinguish the plants from one another by their flowers and leaves and other characteristics. He showed her how to find each one in the book. It listed the common and Latin names. In the empty notebook she sketched each plant and wrote its name. HT penciled the Native names beside the ones she'd written. As he communicated to her how the local Indigenous people used them, Beth made lists of plants having edible greens, roots, and fruits, and medicinal and handcraft uses.

"Where did you learn all of this?" she said.

From my Dené family & books—And local Woodland Cree Natives—Like my trapper friend Eleanor—We get together sometimes when I go to town

"Crikey. That's a lot to learn."

I've had lots of time—I've been here 15 years—Eleanor taught me how to treat plants well—To respect them & not pick too many—She has much ikanisha [wisdom]

"And you know all the ones that are poisonous or taste bad?"

He nodded.

Just because animals eat them doesn't mean you can—People don't eat willows—Moose eat willows

HT had opened the door to a part of the natural world completely new to Beth. She was an eager student, and he was a patient teacher. He showed her how to dig edible roots using a gish [digging stick] and taught her the Indigenous words he knew for rock [tsé] and water [tó]. Eventually they entered a big meadow with a stream running through the middle. As they crossed, HT pointed to the various plants. Beth repeated their names and uses. When they reached the streambank, he pointed at a nearby thicket.

"Willow," she said. "Known by botanists as Salix. And known by Wild Man Hand Talker as K'ai'. It is used to make tea to relieve headaches. And willow is also an excellent food."

HT raised his eyebrows.

"For moose," she snickered.

He gripped her arm and put a finger to his lips. Then Beth saw it too—a large brown creature emerged from the edge of the thicket and made a beeline toward them. Beth turned to run. HT stopped her. She tried dropping to the ground, but he held her up and indicated for her to stand and face the oncoming grizzly.

Beth's heart raced. She alternately focused on the bear and scanned sideways and behind, searching for a way to escape. But they were in an open meadow with nowhere to go. The bear stopped and excavated a root with its long ivory-colored claws. It chewed and swallowed the root. Drool dripped from its powerful jaws. Then it continued its slow shuffle toward them.

HT scribbled a quick note and showed her.

Shash won't hurt you—He is my brother—We protect each other

The yearling boar grizzly stood on its hind legs and tested the air. Its small brown eyes scrutinized HT and Beth. The bruin raised its paws, then lowered its bulk to the ground, huffed, turned, and waddled back into the willows.

HT grinned at the yellow-haired young woman. She trembled against him like an aspen. He hugged her hard.

40

PROVOKED

EGG LAKE REGION, SASKATCHEWAN
MAY 10TH, 2015

BETH SAT IN SEMI-DARKNESS minding her own business. But she kept hearing strange sounds outside the cramped wooden shack: the snap of a twig; the shuffle of feet.

Crikey. What is that wild man up to this time? she thought.

"Hand Talker, a little privacy please."

There was no answer, not that he *could have* voiced a response to her complaint.

When she'd finished, she dropped the piece of moss into the dark hole and exited the privy. And there, not ten meters away was a moose calf staring at her. Beth was entranced by its large brown eyes and droopy nose.

"Why hello there Little Fellow," she whispered.

The curious young animal watched her for a time. It lowered its head and plucked the head of the nearest flower, chewed a few times, then swallowed. It took a step toward her as it browsed.

"Aren't you the loveliest little creature?" Beth took a step forward. And then another. And yet another.

A branch broke. She turned in time to see the charging cow. The young woman shrieked and ducked behind the privy. Its ears pinned back, the mother moose spun and went after her. Dog streaked in and bit the animal's hock. The cow kicked hard, sending the yelping animal flying, then continued its pursuit of the woman. Beth turned. The cow rose high and struck. The sharp black hoof grazed her forearm. She backpedaled, then tripped. The mad mother rushed in, preparing to stomp her to death.

A shot rang out. The cow hunched and turned. HT took aim once more. He squeezed, but the antique cartridge misfired. He tossed the revolver aside and leapt atop the tall animal. The cow bucked. His knife flashed. HT reached low and plunged deep. Her severed carotid spewed blood with each heartbeat as the cow bucked and lunged and spun. The gangly animal collapsed, landing partly atop Beth.

HT quickly levered the heavy legs aside and extricated the stricken woman. Sobbing and shaking, she wrapped herself around him.

"Ahéhee' [thank you]," she stuttered.

HOLDING HER BRUISED FOREARM, Beth and Dog watched HT gut, skin and butcher the dead cow moose. He sliced the massive muscles into thin strips and began hanging them in the smokehouse to dry and cure.

After a time, the calf reappeared and stood nearby watching. It called out for its mother. Beth began to cry again.

HT disappeared into the lodge. A short time later he emerged and handed Beth something warm and smooth. It was a glass bottle with a makeshift nipple of perforated soft leather. Inside was a mixture of powdered milk and warm water.

'Go ahead,' he gestured.

Beth approached the orphaned calf. She knelt and held out the bottle. The curious babe walked forward, sniffing. She petted its neck and touched the nipple to its nose. The calf licked the dribble of milk, then began suckling. Her tears became joy-tears. She quietly sang a lullaby to the orphaned animal.

Limping, Dog joined Beth and proceeded to lick spilled milk from the nursing calf's face.

"I will call you Melvin," she stated. "Hello, Melvin the moose."

HT clicked his tongue to get her attention. 'It's a female,' he signed.

"Well in that case I shall call her 'Gertie.' That is short for Gertrude."

She smiled at HT.

41

POACHED

EGG LAKE REGION, SASKATCHEWAN
SUMMER 2015

H T HEARD THE GUNSHOT just before his splitting maul cleaved the upright round of seasoned spruce. Were it a fraction of a second later, the distant sound would have merged with the sound of metal-on-wood and he'd have completely missed it. He leaned the maul against the block and listened. A second shot sounded.

The hunting seasons are closed, he thought. *Better check it out.*

HT clicked his tongue at Dog and poked his head inside the lodge and signaled to Beth.

He loaded his packbasket. Together, they set off in the direction of the shots. They hiked upcountry and scaled a low ridge. From their vantage point, HT scanned easterward. He pointed at a family of ravens circling the beach near a series of alder and willow patches. The corvids dropped to the ground. They squawked and tussled with each other.

The trio slowly descended the ridge and snaked forward through the shrubland mosaic. They rounded an alder thicket. The ravens flushed. Beth and Dog stayed back while HT warily approached. *What the heck are they fighting over?* he wondered.

HT abruptly snorted and hissed. He grabbed a piece of driftwood and thrashed the ground and nearby alders. In his rage, he flailed everything within reach. The driftwood broke. With the remaining piece he stabbed the earth over and over.

Not knowing what happened, Beth stayed back. She'd never observed anyone behave this way—so distressed—so angry. Ferocious even.

After a time, HT calmed somewhat and she felt it was safe to approach. But what she observed lying there on the ground beside him was beyond belief. A bloody fly-covered corpse. A skinned, decapitated, muscle-bound man. *Who would kill someone and skin him?* she thought. *And remove his head and hands and feet? God—who would mutilate someone like this?* It seemed like some horrible dream. Yet it was real—the body was right in front of her.

"Who is he?" she said.

'Shash,' he signed. 'My brother.'

At first Beth couldn't accept his answer. Surely this was a man, not a bear—not the yearling grizzly they'd observed together by the creek a couple weeks previous. The body looked like a skinned football player. She examined the bloody carcass more closely. It dawned on her she'd never seen a human quite this large. And although the arms were the right length, what would have been the man's legs seem a bit too short to be human.

HT scribbled a note.

Shash was poached—His meat was left to rot

He showed Beth the boot scuffs in the gravel. The tracks were headed north toward the trail to La Ronge.

'Go back to the lodge with Dog,' he signed.

HT took to the trail, intending to find out who'd killed Shash. The meat was unprotected from flies—abandoned. It was obvious the poacher only wanted the skull, hide, and claws for sale on the black market. Although HT didn't check, it was likely too that the bear's gallbladder was missing. The hide and head and paws comprised a heavy load, making the bear killer's boot tracks deep and easy to follow. HT observed where the tracks rounded the lakeshore and joined the main trail.

Soon the trail forked. The poacher took the right one which was flatter—easier to traverse with a heavy load. HT chose the left fork—a hillier, shorter route. He jogged along, climbing and descending the low hills, skirting the boulders and swamps and ponds. Upon arriving at the trail juncture, HT shed his pack, strapped on his holster and began running.

Suddenly, HT halted. Trudging toward him was the chubby man in camouflage overalls, a rifle slung across his chest, black cowboy hat in-hand. Once more the man balanced a bulky bundle atop his head and shoulders. It was the same man HT had watched before over the years, but never confronted. Today would be different. HT spread his arms wide and stood in the middle of the trail to block the man's way. Irritated, the poacher came to a stop. He was drenched in sweat—breathing hard—and glowering. The man set the bear hide bundle on the rust-colored ground and stood there facing HT, wiping his forehead with a bandana. He donned his hat and planted his feet widely. Upon eying HT's holster, he tightened his grip on the rifle.

'You killed my brother,' signed HT. He snorted and hissed in anger.

"What? I can't understand you. Speak up Man."

HT pointed to his mouth and shook his head 'no.'

"Are you dumb, or just stupid? Get outta my way."

HT wrung his hands and waved his fists at the poacher in frustration, damaged finger extended.

"Well fuck you too!"

HT lunged at the heavyset man. The poacher started to lower the muzzle of his rifle, but the gun discharged prematurely. He tossed it aside and sprang sideways through the trailside wall of brush, plunging headlong into the waiting deathtrap. HT landed on the empty path, regained his footing, then turned toward the hidden pool.

The man resurfaced, red-faced, screeching: "Help meee—Gaaawwwd!" He dog paddled madly in a desperate attempt to escape the hot spring. He whirled and swirled and splashed and spun about in the geothermal cauldron, treading water to no avail. And while his blistering burns deepened from first to second to third degree, he screamed in agony and terror, spiraling ever closer to the boiling center. Soon, the plump poacher passed out and rolled onto his belly.

Through a gap in the brush, HT watched in horror as the man's bloated body slowly rotated onto its back like a giant cooked pig. Its scalded white eyes blindly faced skyward as if searching in vain for salvation.

42

THE BATH

EGG LAKE REGION, SASKATCHEWAN
SUMMER 2015

FLASHING DROPLETS FLEW when the Aussie woman—the exotic Beth—sheila from Down Under—stripped sparkling creek water from her corn tassel strands then twirled and spun them over her head like a beguiling Magdalenian dancer of old. As she bathed, the young woman sang an ancient canticle—a *Song of Songs*—to herself. Vixen-like, she stepped from the pool and laid there dripping, her soft supple belly against the warm altar-like stone slab, legs pointed eastward. The midmorning sun shower fell upon her pink flesh and iridescent hair. Soon, her goosebumps melted away. The breeze tingled her body like the touch of a lover. Time passed.

And from his vantage point upslope, deep in the shadows, the Indigenous trapper surreptitiously held her in his steel gaze—like he'd done before—while she bathed. In time, the sun and breeze dried her backside. The young woman then turned and offered her face, breasts, belly, mons and thighs to the sky.

Beth's natural splendor was intoxicating. To HT, she was a gift of nature—a delicious fruit of the Earth like the multitude of women before her from time immemorial—woman begetting woman begetting woman, each to be admired and craved and fought over and relished by starving men. She was beautiful, ravishing, ripe, unblemished, begging to be plucked. Her tanginess to be tasted. Her nectar to be savored. For what seemed an eternity he remained hidden—spellbound—watching her—unable to turn away while she laid there by the pool in all her glory—singing her *Song of Songs*.

Finally, HT went to the slab and stood over her. Beth was thinking of him. She opened her turquoise and jet eyes and smiled. Her pink-flint lips parted, exposing exquisite rows of polished white shell. She drew him down beside her onto the warm stone. They kissed and embraced. Trembling, he breathed the wonderfully rich scent of the Earth Woman. And then, touched by sun and water, they became one in flesh.

43

MUCKED

EGG LAKE REGION, SASKATCHEWAN
SUMMER 2015

HER MONTHLIES HAD CEASED. And now the sickness gripped Beth each morning.

How can I tell him? she thought. She wrestled with indecision.

She got a piece of paper from HT's old roll-top desk and began to write. But in the end, she just folded the unfinished letter and left it between the pages of one of his books.

HT noticed she wasn't eating much in the mornings. He'd seen her sneak off into the trees after breakfast.

She was down at the creek scrubbing her clothes one day when HT noticed one of his books was out of place. He found her half-written letter.

For several days he thought about it. Dark, ugly thoughts. Horrible thoughts.

One morning at breakfast, HT let her know he'd be gone for a few days in order to clear trail and scout for furbearer activity.

"So, you decided to wear a shirt today. Maybe there is hope for you yet you bloody wild man. Have fun out there among all your plant and animal friends."

As he headed out the door, HT smiled and gave his usual flippant wave. He trekked west with his freshly honed axe hung in its sheath from his waist-strap. After a while he circled back and took the well-worn trail toward La Ronge. At first he walked fast. Then he began to jog. In the end, he broke into a full run, ducking limbs, leaping brooks and roots, coursing like a wolf on its prey-trail.

At midday he stopped at a massive serpentine boulder jutting from the ground beside the trail. HT scaled it. As he surveyed the surroundings, his gaze followed a faint line on the land—a fox trail—that led to a dark hill about a three-hour walk to the north—a three-hour walk after freeze-up to be sure. The hill was known locally by its Woodland Cree name meaning 'Bosom of the Taiga.' *This is the place*, he thought.

HT descended his perch. He went to a nearby opening and rigged and baited an Ojibwe bird snare. Then he continued toward La Ronge and climbed the mound of rocks he'd occasionally used in the past as a lookout. From its top, he had a clear view of La Ronge and the various trails leading away from it. He descended the rocky mound and headed into town.

When he approached the Post Office, a half-inebriated Indigenous man was slouched against the corner of the building. They eyed one another. The man was silent. HT knew him from his previous trips to town. As always, the man just sat there waiting—not asking. HT usually gave him a piece of smoked jerky to eat and perhaps some extra stamps to sell to the other patrons when they came by to collect their mail. Today he ignored the man.

Inside, HT purchased an envelope. At the counter, he thumbed through the local directory and found the address he sought, then went and sat on the bench outside. He withdrew Beth's unfinished letter and scrawled a few words at the bottom. Then he took out a different paper from his pocket, placed Beth's letter atop it and traced something. When he'd finished, he folded her letter and a map he'd sketched on a paper towel and slipped both of them into the envelope. He glanced over at the man once more, turned his back and walked away.

At the edge of town HT entered an alder thicket. He found a hollow place to recline and waited for nightfall. Eventually, stars appeared.

He emerged from his hideout. The aurora borealis blazed overhead. Its blue and green and yellow light illuminated his path as he made his way into town along the backstreets. After a bit of searching, he found the address. Faint TV flickers streamed from inside the small house. He crept to a side window and peered in. Yuri was propped up on the headboard of his bed in his underwear watching porn. Spread around him on the satin sheets were shoes of many colors—women's high heel shoes.

HT set the envelope on the welcome mat, then rang the doorbell.

Yuri emerged in his white boxer's robe. He called into the darkness, but his late-night visitor was already halfway down the block. The ex-fighter picked up the envelope and closed the door.

THAT NIGHT, HT BIVOUACKED in the open air atop the rocky mound. For a time, he watched the glittering lights of La Ronge where his rival, Yuri, prepared for the coming battle.

Above HT, the brilliant aurora streamed from horizon to horizon across the star-studded sky. He lay still and listened to the sounds of the night: a lone mosquito whined; bats swooped and squeaked; a pair of owls called out; a lone wolf howled faraway. Long into the night, he mentally reviewed the ugly plan he'd devised. It was past midnight when he finally allowed himself to sleep.

IN THE MORNING HT rose early and went to the opening to check his snare. Raven wings flapped wildly. The trickster bird was held by a single foot. He removed the trap string, then ripped the bird open, crushed its heart and liver, and smeared the red mess on the back of each hand.

HT returned to his vantage point atop the rocky mound and sat there, ignoring the hungry flies. After a time, he noticed a faraway speck moving along the trail toward him. It disappeared now and then as it tunneled through the scattered alder thickets. Moving quickly despite his heavy load, the man-speck lumbered ever closer beneath his towering blue backpack.

It was time. HT slipped down the backside of his lookout and hurried to the base of the boulder. It was there that he crossed the main trail and followed a different trail: the faint fox trail leading north across the muskeg to a low mound with black spruce twisted by decades of winter wind, then further north to the Bosom of the Taiga. He stepped gingerly from hummock to hummock along the trail till he'd nearly reached the tree-covered mound.

The trapper stopped, looked around, then suddenly leapt sideways into the water. He writhed from side-to-side and thrashed his legs, soaking himself to the waist. HT pulled himself onto a nearby hummock and slogged back to the boulder. Dripping, he leaned against the huge stone for support, gasping for breath and appearing half-spent.

Yuri's blue pack came into view around the bend in the trail. It swayed from side-to-side as he trudged closer. At his approach, HT looked up in surprise, as if he hadn't expected to see anyone. The muscular man drew abreast and smiled broadly. He breathed hard and wiped sweat from his forehead.

"Hello there. You're a local fella, eh? I'm on my way to see Beth Winsley.

Do you know her?"

HT's brow furrowed. He shook his head 'no,' pointed to his mouth and indicated 'no' again. He fumbled in his shirt pocket for his notepad and pencil stub, scrawled some words and shoved the pad at Yuri.

Beth is very sick—Did you bring the medical supplies

Yuri was taken aback. "God, she just asked for 'supplies' in her message—not 'medical supplies.'" He yanked out the letter and gave it to HT. "I thought she meant food and batteries and stuff. Shit man, is she okay?"

HT shook his head 'no' and breathed heavily, as if to catch his breath. He scribbled more words and thrust them at Yuri.

She needs you now—I'll bring doctor—Go help her—The bleeding won't stop

"Bleeding?"

HT nodded.

"From where?"

HT squeezed his own groin. He showed the man the dried bird blood on the back of his hands.

"That's hers?"

HT nodded.

Yuri looked frantically about.

"Jesus. My God. Where is she?"

HT grabbed the man's arm and tried to calm him. But it was useless. Yuri was hysterical. He jerked his arm free.

"Where's the cabin?" he screamed.

Cabin is on that hill—Go north

HT pointed at the Bosom of the Taiga.

"That hill way out there?" gasped Yuri. "Past those trees, right?"

HT nodded.

Follow trail—Head straight to trees, then straight to hill—You can't miss it

"Go to town. Get a doctor. They'll need a bush plane or copter. Run dammit!"

Yuri, the cheecháko, rushed north on the fox trail toward the dark patch of trees, jogging, then slogging and straining under his heavy pack.

HT sprinted east along the main trail toward La Ronge. When he rounded the stony hill, he stopped. He squatted and studied the streaks and flakes of dried black blood crust on his hands. In a nearby brook he scrubbed them with clumps of yellow moss. He sat at the water's edge picking at the creases around his nails.

After a while HT returned to the serpentine boulder and scrambled up. He donned his black headband and stood there warrior-like and callously watched while his naïve opponent, an insect-like speck of a man, traveled deep into the barren boreal bogland. Godforsaken. A walking dead man, unknowingly delivering his spirit to his Earth Mother.

A heaviness hung in the air. Now, far from the main trail, Yuri approached the low mound with stunted, twisted black spruce. He pressed forward along the fox trail as the gel-like ground below grew less stable and the pools between the hummocks grew deeper.

Were he a woodsman or just a calm townsman, he'd have noticed then that HT's tracks had stopped and doubled back. But he was neither. In his haste, Yuri missed the signs. Unattuned to the hazards of the northland, the ex-fighter doggedly fought-on toward the phantom cabin on the dark breast of land. He continued on toward his fate, plunging himself forward to reach Beth before it was too late—before she bled out. But it *was* too late. For him. He slipped between two narrow hummocks at the base of the mound. He was mud-stuck—bogged to his waist—mired deep in the pungent muskeg muck—surrounded by a seemingly endless landscape of muddy pools and moss-covered lumps of peat blanketed in miniature willows.

Tired, desperate, Yuri dug into the depths of his pocket for his iPhone. Over and over he tried to power it on, but the screen remained black. Empty. The gadget was now wet and worthless to him—just a sodden chunk of plastic and metal junk. Yet he refused to admit defeat.

Throughout the morning and afternoon, HT squatted atop his perch, a vulture-like witness to the feeble thrashings of his love rival. Yuri had clearly lost the battle. His energy now depleted, there was no way to release himself from the clutch of the trapper's treacherous trap. The breeze picked up, taking with it the last of the black flies. Finally, HT descended the gray boulder and kindled a small fire on its backside.

He removed his headband and unfolded the letter Yuri had handed him.

My dearest Yuri,

I miss you so much Lovie. I hope you are doing well and enjoying your summer break as much as I am enjoying mine. As for me, I am very happy here at the cabin I told you about. I apologize for not writing sooner.

Lovie, there is no easy way to tell you about my problem.

Beth's letter ended there, unfinished.

Below her note HT had written more words.

Yuri, please come quick and bring supplies. Follow the map. I need you here now! I'll explain when you get here.

Beth

While going through Beth's backpack, HT had discovered her love notes from Yuri. Later, outside the Post Office, he traced over one of Beth's other papers to make the fake signature.

HT watched the fire for a while. Then he wadded the letter and tossed it in the flames. His deceptive words slowly charred and curled. A bit of breeze scattered the remaining ash, erasing all evidence of his crime.

IT WAS LATE IN THE AFTERNOON. Far out on the muskeg flat, Yuri continued struggling to free himself from the bottomless black crap. But no matter what he did, it squeezed-in on him, holding him fast, sapping what meager strength remained, pressing in on his chest. With each grueling movement, the slick sludge only gripped him tighter, steadily drawing him deeper into its stagnant womb. The baffled man tried again and again, pumping his hips, thrusting and pulling, thrusting and pulling, thrusting and pulling, battling for each breath against the ancient force of the slurping, queefing gunk. Now he was up to his neck in this no-man's-land—still sinking. And in the end, from his blue lips the goo drew a cold and broken, dispiriting wail: "Haaarrrlllaaayyyllloooeeeaaahhh…"

After he blacked out, Yuri's head tilted back and his mouth and crooked nose gradually filled with swamp slurry. Tiny bubbles gargled and gurgled up and whirled and swirled about and broke in the eddy over his pale submerged face. The top of his blue pack slowly sank. The iPhone in his outstretched hand eventually disappeared in the muck as the Earth sucked him into oblivion.

44

CHECKIN' OUT

LA RONGE, SASKATCHEWAN
SEPTEMBER 3RD, 2015

MACHA'S PER CAPITA CHECK was not in the mail. Normally, it arrived on the first workday of the month. The First Nations Band would receive its share of payments from the various mining and timber companies in the Province, then divvy-up them among households with enrolled members. But Macha and Sonny's monthly check was missing. At first she thought little of it. Maybe the finance lady was late returning from holiday—the postmaster was sick—something along those lines—a rare but understandable delay. But when the check failed to appear that third afternoon, she began calling around. The Band's Finance Office told her all the checks had been signed and delivered to the Post on time. So, on impulse she called an old high school chum who now worked at the bank.

"Yes, I cashed it for him Mach. Of course I did. Gave it to him in cash like he wanted."

"You cashed it for who?"

"For Sonny. He came in here on Monday around 2 o'clock. I figured you knew about it, so I cashed it. Why Mach? Something wrong?"

"Yeah, it's my money, eh. I need it to pay bills and stuff. He was s'posed to be in school Monday, but he didn't go. And he didn't come home last night neither. The little shit probably spent it on drugs or somethin'."

"Well I thought he was cashing it for you Mach. Sorry. He's a good kid, eh? You really think he'd spend it on drugs?"

"Yeah. He started usin' last year I think. Him and his buddies. Last week Angie broke up with 'em 'cause of drugs. Anyway, that's what her mom told me. Sonny was s'posedly doing pot and crystal and liquor—mild stuff like that. Sandy said Angie gave 'em chances but he kept usin' the stuff. So Angie finally told Sonny 'no more, that was it.' And he always steals my change too. Once in a while he sneaks a bottle or a twenty from me—kid's stuff like that. But he never stole my whole damn per cap check before. That little shit better pay me back ev'ry loonie. Oh my God. How am I s'posed to pay the hydro bill this month—and buy food?"

"Crystal meth is not mild stuff Mach. You know that. It's tearing us First Nations people apart, eh. When he gets home you should get him some help. Counseling or something. Meth is what Shannah was hooked on. Remember what happened to her?"

"Yeah, Shannah the Tweaker Girl. Maybe you're right. Maybe it's time someone gives Sonny a little help."

"Why don't you call the school? They've got a counselor on staff, right?"

"Yeah, that's something I could do maybe."

45

SWALLOWED

LA RONGE, SASKATCHEWAN
SEPTEMBER 3RD, 2015

BETH OPENED THE DOOR for the two officers.

"Hello. Miss Winsley? Miss, aren't you—?"

She nodded.

"My Lady—the Royalty Protection Command emailed me a while back. They said you'd be coming to town and that you wanted your presence here to be confidential. But they didn't include an address or other details. Just your photo."

"No titles please Officer. Just call me 'Miss' or 'Beth' as you wish."

"I'm sorry Miss, I didn't make the connection. I'm Staff Sergeant Watts—F Division—Lac La Ronge Detachment. And this is Constable Simpson of our General Investigation Section."

"Thank you both for coming."

"I'm honored to meet you Miss," said the staff sergeant. "So this is his residence, eh?"

She nodded.

"Does he have any roommates?"

"No. But I have a key. Here's a copy of the flyer I'm having printed. It has his information and his photograph from the school yearbook."

"This helps a lot. Is that his car in the driveway?"

She nodded.

"So first things first. Why is it you think Yuri is missing and not just away somewhere on summer holiday?"

"Well his car is here. His suitcases are here. And he would have left a note or told friends if he was going on holiday, right? I've checked with all the school staff and all his local acquaintances. But no one has heard from him in over a week."

"When did you last see him Miss Winsley?"

"Early June. About the sixth."

"But that was three months ago. You said he's been missing for about a week."

"Right. You see, I was on summer holiday—staying at a cabin at Egg Lake. I just returned yesterday. When I couldn't find Yuri, I called all his friends. And then I started calling school employees. That's when I realized he has not been seen by anyone for quite a while."

"Why didn't one of them report him missing?"

"I think that I'm the first one who realized he is missing. I contacted his parents in Manitoba, but they have not heard from him lately either. I'm really worried."

"Do you mind if we take a look around?"

"No, not at all. That is why I called you here. We need to find him."

The officers scoured the house for clues. They went through documents in Yuri's office area and flipped through his unopened mail. Then they entered the bedroom.

"Have you moved anything Miss Winsley?"

"I don't think so. Yesterday I just went through all the rooms like we are doing now. The only thing missing is his big blue backpack. He keeps it over there in the corner."

The staff sergeant gestured toward the bed. "And those—are they yours?"

"The shoes? Oh, no, mine are at home. The lady's shoe collection is his."

"So it appears that Yuri and his wallet, cell phone and backpack are missing, eh?"

"Yes."

"To your knowledge there's nothing else missing or out of place?"

"Correct."

"Constable Simpson will be in charge of this case," he said, gesturing toward the other officer. "He'll check with all the local drivers, charter plane pilots and charter boat operators to see if one of them might have ferried him somewhere for a campout. Well Simpson, do you think you have everything you need?"

"Miss Winsley, I will need to include your phone number, your address and your relationship to him in the report."

"Yes. I can provide all of those to you. He is my supervisor at the school where I teach Grade 9. We are also lovers. I need that to remain confidential of course."

"Our reports are strictly confidential Miss. However, if we do find evidence of a crime, that sort of information is usually released during court proceedings."

"Very well. Yuri and I are in a relationship."

"And I'll be needing to get the names, phone numbers and addresses of Yuri's friends, the school staff and his parents if you could please provide those. Can I use the photo and the information from the flyer you made?"

"Certainly."

"Don't you worry now Miss Winsley," said Watts. "We do get a lot of missing persons reports. Mostly for Indigenous women. They're the ones who never seem to be found, eh. Yuri's a white male, so he'll undoubtedly turn up. Of course we'll add him to the database: 'Canada's Missing.' And we'll notify the Ranger Patrol in case they run across any leads. But unfortunately, they need an area to focus on before they can mount any sort of ground search. Northern Saskatchewan is a mighty big place as you know. Occasionally we have cheechákos show up here and head out into the bush alone. And sometimes they do get swallowed up out there in the wilderness. But that wouldn't happen to Yuri because he's been around a few years and knows better. Who's to say he didn't put on his backpack and hitchhike south on Highway 2, eh? Either way, he likely left town of his own accord and just forgot to tell somebody. He could be anywhere really. Adults are free to come and go as they please, Miss. Unless we find evidence of a possible crime, there's not a whole lot more we can do."

"I SAW YOU WALK PAST outside earlier," said Beth. "Why didn't you come in when the Mounties were here? You could have."

HT shrugged.

"Well, thank you for being here now. For moral support. I know this must be awkward for you." She motioned at the room around them. "This is his place. Everything looks the same as before he disappeared. It's hard to believe Yuri's missing. I hope they are able to find him. I don't know what I would do if something bad happened. I'm having these terrible thoughts Lovie, and they won't go away. I just have this horrible feeling he won't be coming home."

He hugged her.

"Will you sit with me?" she said. "I have something very important to tell you."

Their eyes met.

"You know Yuri is my lover too—that we have talked of getting married, right? And having children together?"

He nodded.

"There is something else you need to know. I'm pregnant. I'm pregnant Lovie. And it's yours. Not his. I'm going to have your child. I want you to know I plan to keep it and raise it. It's going to get complicated. I'm sorry, but I cannot change that. You and Yuri and I—the three of us—will work it out somehow. And I don't regret our relationship. You are incredibly special to me." She pulled him close. "I miss him so much Lovie. I'm so bloody worried and scared. Will you be with me? Stay with me—just for a while?"

He nodded.

Beth got up and led him into the dead man's bedroom. HT's bright eyes narrowed. His head swam. She pulled off his shirt. He glanced at the colorful shoe collection spread on the bed in the shape of an animal trap. She guided him onto the satin sheets. HT lay on his back and thought about what he'd done—about his treachery against her other lover—about how he'd caused the man to sink to his death out there in the muskeg muck. Tears overflowed and flooded his twitching temples.

"Are you happy you are going to be a father? Is that it, Lovie? Please tell me you're happy."

HT nodded.

He stared at Yuri's Eastern Orthodox crucifix hanging above the bedroom doorway. *Why the hell didn't you stop me from doing it God?* he thought.

Beth unfastened his pants and slid them from his hips. She slowly stripped, then straddled him. She covered his nose and mouth with kisses, smothered him with shame, gagged him with guilt, and drowned him with dread. And, although he couldn't say it, in his mind he thought it as her lips drew from him his victim's final word, *"Haaarrrlllaaayyyllloooeeeaaahhh…"*

HT's face tilted back. Beth's moist lips slowly crept down his body, strangling, then squeezing, then finally crushing the life from him. Silently sobbing, he sank deeper and deeper into the bedsheets—breathless—as the beautiful young woman swallowed him into oblivion.

46

PISSED

DUMP ROAD, LA RONGE, SASKATCHEWAN
SEPTEMBER 8TH, 2015

THE PUNY YELLOW MUTT followed Sonny askew through the tunnel of dripping alders to his hideout. The teen had given up taking care of his long black hair. He whipped back the tangled mess, spun and plopped onto the old Chesterfield. His matted mongrel piddled pink urine on a moldy discarded girlie magazine near his feet.

"Piss somewhere else you little shit." The tail-tucked dog slunk away.

Sonny unzipped his knapsack and spread his stash on the stained upholstery. He glared at the gray sky from under the blue tarp. The flies were nowhere to be seen—hiding somewhere out there under the jagged alder leaves. But in the steady drizzle, the mosquitoes were out in force hunting for a blood meal. The boy removed his dark shades, shoved his earbuds in and queued-up a favorite Stones tune on his phone: *Angie*.

With a small stick, he hollowed out a stolen Granny Smith apple and lined the bowl with tin foil. Using an even scrawnier stick, he poked another hole completely through it, forming a makeshift pipe. Then, pissed-off and crying, wallowing in his post-dump misery, Sonny smoked a bowl of 'BC Gold' as he listened to Mick Jagger croon about the failing romance with his own Angie.

Earlier in the day, a local drug dealer provided the stash: three forty-pounders of cheap vodka and a dozen or so little 'Joe Bob Brown' methamphetamine and crack cocaine rocks. The dealer sold it to him cheap, trying to get him well-hooked so Sonny would buy from him from-then-on-out like the local addicts and inebriates did. The vodka alone was enough to get Sonny piss-drunk six times over.

After finishing the bowl of pot, he got out the glass pipes the dealer gave him. He chose the largest of the brown meth chunks and, with cupped hands, lit-up and huffed the harsh vapors. Euphoria kicked in quick and strong. Sonny's heart raced like a Harley and he got a hard-on. The mongrel saw the teen's change in temperament and approached. Sonny gave-in and began petting it. Soon, he was stuffing the bony, worm-infected thing plumb-full of jerked moose meat and fluorescent orange cheezies from his knapsack till the engorged mutt finally wandered off to find a safe place to digest the rare feast.

Sonny smoked another brown rock then leaned back and watched the rivulets of rainwater run together and drip over the edge of the tarp. His thoughts raced as his focus jerked here and there while he mentally rehashed the happenings of the past couple weeks.

Yeah, he cashed that damned per cap check. Of course he did. It was his money too, right? Like his mom Macha, he was a First Nations member, so he figured half the household check was his. Sonny never held so much cash-in-hand as when he left the bank earlier that day.

The trouble started when his mom cursed him out. He'd helped himself to a twenty from her pocketbook. That was one thing. The other thing was what he and his buddies did to the trailer after she went off again with that on-again-off-again boyfriend of hers for the weekend. Sonny had the place to himself, so he thought, *why not throw a party, eh*? But when she got back midday Sunday the place was pretty-well trashed and he and his buddies were all shit-faced and high. She kicked out his buddies and proceeded to rag on him and curse him till he slammed his bedroom door in her face.

Well to hell with her, he thought.

After the big blow-up he'd scraped together a bunch of loonies and coins—mere chump change really—and went straight to the trailer of the town's main drug peddler. Sonny bought a nice-looking brown rock. Afterwards, he went to Angie's double-wide and told her about the fight with his mom. Angie sympathized and agreed to hang out awhile.

That evening he took her to his hideout under the blue tarp. They drank pops and each ate a burger. Angie gave a third burger to the skinny dog while Sonny griped about how he'd planned on eating that one too. They sat and smoked cigarettes and talked about their dreams: Sonny to be a long-haul trucker; Angie to maybe be a nurse at the Woodland Wellness Center like her favorite auntie.

Sonny melted the rock and offered her a hit. He told her it'd make having sex with him feel even better, but she refused. It hurt her a bit when Sonny rammed his way inside over and over.

"Pull out! Oh my God, pull out before you cu—"

"Shut up."

"Sonny—get off me." Angie hollered and struggled and knocked off his sunglasses. She yanked his ponytail. He slapped her hard till she let go. She forced him out and clamped her thighs tight. She stayed rigid while he tried to re-enter. He tried flipping her over, but she was having none of it.

"Get off me Sonny—please."

Sonny pressed his palm tight over her mouth. She tasted blood and gave-in to his demands a bit. She cried while he jerked-off to her. He grunted and drooled till he finally spilt his seed on her belly. Afterward, they laid there on the old Chesterfield, each of them panting.

"You said it wouldn't hurt."

"Shut up Bitch."

"You said you'd pull it out so I won't get pregnant. What were you thinking Sonny?"

"Shut up. *You* was the one who said you wanted to do it. You gotta finish what you start. You can't just change your mind like that."

Angie gazed down the trail toward the road. "I'm not a whore."

Sonny ignored her.

"And I'm not your bitch neither."

"Angie, you're my bitch till I find a new one. Don't you *ever* leave me hangin' like that again, eh?"

Sonny thought things were still okay with Angie. But the next day at school she broke up with him. Her friends were there with her when she told him in case he decided to get mean or violent again.

After school that day the yellow mutt did something or other that pissed-off Sonny. In the heat of the moment he beat it mercilessly. Kicked it till it couldn't walk and till it peed pink in fact.

Afterward, twinged with guilt, he fed the injured dog better than it'd been fed in months—fed it well for a couple days anyway. When it was well enough to be up and moving around again, the scrawny mutt trotted at a perverse angle, coursing along behind him at a distance like a four-legged sidewinder. The crooked dog was much more wary of him than before. Now at the slightest change in the teen's demeanor it would immediately cower and rollover, display its belly and privates, and grin up at him like some crazy carnival clown.

The rain ended. The mosquitoes and no-see-ums beneath the blue tarp became voracious. But at this point Sonny didn't give a shit. *Let 'em drink their fill,* he thought.

He remained seated there on the old sofa, ruminating on the recent events in his life. His long hair was still hung-up in the overhanging branch he'd been too lazy to cut-back. With darkness falling, the troubled teen took his fly-eye shades from the armrest and put them back on. His mind grew more and more jumbled while his negative thoughts rolled and tumbled. The two meth rocks hadn't done quite what he'd hoped. So he took a long pull of vodka from one of the plastic jugs. He began fingering the misshapen little hunks of Joe Bob Brown and crack. Already tripping, Sonny decided to get even higher—higher than he'd ever flown. He loaded the crack pipe the way the drug dealer taught him.

47

ABSALOM: PLAYIN' TUG-O'-WAR

EGG LAKE REGION, SASKATCHEWAN
SEPTEMBER 13TH, 2015

THE BUSH PLANE BUZZED THE LODGE, white wings wagging. It circled wide, dive-bombed the nearby beach, then banked and headed back toward La Ronge. HT made his way to the gravel shore.

A yellow pine board with a note scrawled in black marker was waiting for him. It read, *'Go to town now—Urgent'*

HT loaded a few essentials into his pack and set out on the trail downlake to La Ronge.

In town, he went straight to Auntie Millie's place. The frazzled woman fretted and shuffled about, then relayed the news to him. "It's Sonny. He's gone missing. Macha said he stole her *per cap* check, then cashed it and disappeared. She said Angie broke-up with him a couple weeks ago, so she figures he's off somewhere feeling sorry for himself and drinking it off. But Macha checked with all his buddies. Nobody's seen hide nor hair of him in days."

NOTEPAD-IN-HAND, HT knocked on the door of Angie's double-wide.

Can you help me find Sonny

"I don't know where he's at neither."

Did he ever talk of running away

"No. I know he wants to be a long-haul trucker someday. But he never talked about where he'd drive to. He just likes big trucks I guess."

HT studied the scab on her split lip.

Were you here or at his mom's place when he hurt you

"No, not the trailer. We was at his bush pad hideaway over off the dump road. It's just a tarp and an old couch he and the boys hauled back in the bush. I was there just the one time."

Angie told him how to find Sonny's hideout.

It was mid-afternoon when HT spied the crooked cur sidewinding toward him on the gravel road. He recognized it as the dog he'd given Sonny when it was just a pup. He recalled how thrilled Sonny was when he'd first gotten it. The pair of them—boy and dog—were inseparable. At first, Macha was angry about the gift dog. But she got over it soon enough. Mostly she just ignored the mutt.

HT watched the yellow dog abruptly turn and slip into an opening in the roadside brush. He went to the opening and entered the alder tunnel. When he drew near Sonny's hideout, he saw the blue tarp and the soggy trash scattered about. A rancid odor hung in the stale air and lingered there in the afternoon haze. The sickening smell made him lightheaded.

Then he heard it—the thrum of black flies. The hum grew steadily louder. And, as he drew closer still, HT observed his son sitting on the old Chesterfield. He looked pale and weak. His loose hair was tangled in the overhanging limb. Sonny sat and stared at his father through his ever-present dark shades. His arm and shoulder jerked while he scratched the belly of his tagalong pooch—the two of them playing another game of tug-of-war. The boy was facing HT, mouthing words, but unable to vocalize them. In his drug-induced stupor, he'd apparently vomited. Brown liquid covered his chin and shirt. And it was obvious the miserable looking kid had pissed his track pants.

HT clicked his tongue and signed a greeting. Sonny's swollen face moved grotesquely and formed strange expressions the likes of which HT had never seen. Frankly, it was scaring the bejesus out of him.

'Sonny?' he signed.

HT stepped closer and stood there, relieved to have found the boy. When he couldn't bear it any longer, he grabbed his son and held him tight. But something wasn't right—the cool sloppy feel of him—the overwhelming stench—the pallor of his face.

'What is it Sonny?' HT signed frantically. 'Answer me!'

Then his eyes saw what his mind was refusing to register: a few at first, then hundreds—thousands of creamy maggots twisting and heaving in a singular writhing mass beneath the translucent peel of Sonny's face—mocking life itself. The buzz of flies and rasping of their offspring grew to a deafening roar. The larvae pulsated in a gluttonous orgy, sheathed in the dead boy's slick skin, rhythmical thrusting again and again and again till his father nearly fainted. The stench was disgusting—unbearable.

HT knelt there and retched till there was nothing to bring forth but phlegm and bile.

Shiye'—shiye'—shiye' [my son, my son, my son].

He wept uncontrollably and gnashed his teeth.

HT stayed there under the blue tarp with the stinking, putrid remains of his only child for what seemed an eternity, silently rocking. He had no voice. He had no flute. But in his mind he chanted the *End Song*.

The shadows lengthened.

Unable to look at the ghastly corpse hanging from the branch, its arm still jerking, he focused his gaze instead on the spoiled foiled apple. Over the past few days, the Granny apple inside had changed from plump green, to yellow, to slimy brown. Then, in the shadow of the apple, he saw them—the scorched glass meth and crack pipes—and realized why Sonny died. The drugs hyped the teen's heart till it couldn't keep pace. It simply seized-up like a hot engine out of oil.

I have to tell Macha, he thought. *And then the Mounties*.

HT stood. He clicked his tongue. The gaunt dog ceased its tugging and ripping of tainted meat from the flesh-hole it'd gnawed in Sonny's forearm and followed the man back to the road.

HT started toward Macha's trailer. Then he abruptly spun on his heel and headed in a different direction. Together, they went to seek out the drug peddler, the dog snaking aslant beside the fuming father. The crooked cur was still grinning—and still hungry.

48

THE TOWN DRUNK

LA RONGE, SASKATCHEWAN
SEPTEMBER 30TH, 2015

IN THE DRIZZLING RAIN BETH FOUND HIM. HT was digging through the dumpster behind Eddie's Restaurant searching for discarded bottles with drips and dregs able to be drained.

"There you are."

Dazed and glassy-eyed, he looked her way, then resumed rummaging.

"Lovie, I looked everywhere for you—for days. Your Aunt Millie told me what happened. Look at you, you are absolutely filthy."

A bottle flew and landed in the mud. HT hefted himself over the lip of the trash bin, balanced there for a moment, then collapsed in a puddle near her feet. He reached for the bottle.

She helped him prop himself up against the metal container.

"Hand Talker, what in the bloody hell do you think you are doing?"

'What do you think?' he signed.

"You don't have to do this. It won't help anything."

'You don't know.'

"I know you *were* a good father to him Lovie. I know that you tried. You did everything you could for him. It's not your fault he overdosed."

HT got out his soggy notepad and scribbled.

Sonny came to lake every summer—All summer at first—Then only for a month—Then only for a week—Then he didn't want to come at all—I should have known about the drug use—I failed him

"But it was up to Sonny, not you. Hand Talker, you need to come home with me—now."

You deserve better—I've done terrible things

"It's okay. We have all done terrible things we later wish we had not. It's not like you are a murderer or anything, right Lovie? We can talk about it when you are washed up and sober again. Come on. Give me your other hand."

BETH HELPED HIM out of the hot shower. She dried him off and led him to bed. "I put your ring on the nightstand here Lovie. You're dehydrated. You'd better drink some water and try to eat just a little before you go to sleep."

HT slowly sipped water from the mug she gave him.

"Try one of these. I eat them when *my* stomach is upset."

He took the cracker from her fingers. A wave of dizziness washed over him. He closed his eyes and chewed. He ate several more, then laid back on the pillow.

Beth turned off the lamp and got into bed beside him. She wanted to say something, but decided it could wait till morning.

HT stared at the ceiling. He thought of Sonny. And of Yuri. And of his and Beth's baby growing within her womb. His head throbbed. He was profoundly tired. But when he closed his eyes, his head immediately became a whirlwind. The room spun faster and faster, till he was overcome with nausea and forced to open his eyes again. He tried putting his foot on the floor, but the spinning resumed each time he closed his eyes. Drunk, exhausted, he laid there with his hands on his chest looking heavenward while he waited for the alcohol to leave his system.

In the dimness, Beth reached for him. Her pale hand slipped across his belly and slowly cupped his privates. A jarring terror jolted him. HT bolted for the front door but was overcome by nausea. He veered toward the bathroom. As he fell to his knees, he knocked Beth's little beeswax candle and tray into the toilet. The bathroom went black. He offered up the contents of his gut—heaving, hacking, retching.

Light streamed in from the bedroom when Beth turned on her lamp. "Hand Talker, are you alright in there?"

He was in no mood to respond. He stared for a moment at the broken bobbing bits of cracker—flotsam adrift in the whiskey-wine-water mix—and the brass tray submerged in the murk below like some once-treasured golden paten on the seafloor. *What the hell just happened?* he thought. He managed to shut the bathroom door with his foot. For now, darkness was better.

HT LIFTED HIS HEAVY LIDS. His eyes gradually focused. The red shawl Beth wore was wrapped snake-like around her neck and torso. She offered him a small plate with fruit and a glass of apple juice.

"Good morning Lovie. Are you feeling better?"

'A little,' he signed.

"Here is your ring."

He snugged the yoostsah back on his paralyzed finger.

"When I found you last night, you told me that you've done terrible things. That I deserve someone better than you. I am ready to listen now. You can tell me. I promise I won't be judgmental."

Somber, HT looked sideways at her, remembering her dead lover. He motioned for his mud-stained notepad.

He scribbled: ***I just said that because I was drunk***

49

CHRISTMAS COMMUNIQUÉ

LA RONGE, SASKATCHEWAN
DECEMBER 25TH, 2015

AUNTIE MILLIE OPENED THE OVEN DOOR. Rich aroma wafted forth when she bent back the foil and tested the golden-brown bird.

"It's ready Nate. Would you take it out please—and carve it?"

"Sure thing Auntie."

"Hand Talker," she said, "bring the potatoes and stuffing and rolls to the table please. Bring the butter too. I'll get the gravy and cranberry sauce. Beth— you stay right there. We'll get it. You're our guest of honor today, eh. You should be taking it easy. Would you like more mint tea Dear?"

Beth nodded.

"How far along are you?"

"Five months."

"And how long till you go on maternity leave?"

"I don't plan to—I hope to be working up to the last minute. My kids really need me."

"Well you'll need to take time off at some point, right? Maybe you could fly back home to see family for a week or two."

"Maybe. But traveling abroad pregnant is not something I would relish."

"Then take your lovey dovey with you—to help out."

Beth smiled at the thought of it. "I have not seen my father in over a year. I suppose he would like to meet Hand Talker—although he really does have this thing about trappers."

"It seems maybe he passed that trait along to his daughter, eh?" said Nate.

'Yes,' signed HT. 'He did.'

"Hand Talker," said Auntie Millie, "would you please go check on Macha?"

HT entered the main room. Macha knelt by the Christmas tree, her head low. She peered up at him, tears streaming down, making her thick eyeliner run so she looked like some sort of sad circus clown. She reeked of body odor and perfume and cigarettes and alcohol.

"I miss my Sonny, Honey."

He held her for a while. When she'd composed herself a bit, they entered the kitchen together.

Beth noticed the dark vertical lines below Macha's eyes and gave her a reassuring smile.

"What a feast," said Auntie Millie. "Okay, let's eat. Would you say the blessing for us Beth?"

IN THE MAIN ROOM by the tree they took turns handing out and opening presents. When it was HT's turn, he withdrew several newspaper-wrapped bundles from his packbasket and passed them around.

Macha went first. She carefully removed the paper from her square, flat package, exposing a remembrance album HT created for her with copies of all the photos of Sonny he'd been able to compile. She squeezed it to her chest and mouthed the words 'thank you.'

Then Nate opened his. Inside were a half-dozen hand-carved and painted wooden fishing lures. "Thanks there Cousin. Ya know I'll put 'em to good use."

Auntie Millie went next. Nested inside her misshapen package was a set of beautiful birch bark baskets etched with Dené and Woodland Cree designs. "Hand Talker, these are amazing. You've become quite a craftsman."

'Go ahead,' he signed to Beth. 'Your turn.'

She ripped the paper away, revealing a pair of handmade beaver fur mittens. Her eyes went wide and began watering. Her face flushed.

"You bloody—"

'You don't like them?' he signed, nudging her.

"You bloody wild man. Of course I like them. I absolutely love them. They're gorgeous. You made these for me?"

He nodded.

"They're so soft. They smell so nice."

He scribbled: ***That's woodsmoke from the tanning process***

"It's the best gift ever. Thank you so much Lovie."

'From the heart,' he signed.

Beth's cell phone buzzed from the table across the room. She went and answered it.

"Yes. Yes. Alright." She sat on the couch beside HT. "Okay, I am sitting now. So tell me. What is it that is so important? We are celebrating Christmas here mind you."

Thirty seconds passed while Beth listened to the communiqué from the British Consulate official. Then she fainted.

Auntie Millie dabbed Beth's face with a cold wet cloth. "Wake up Dear. Wake up."

Beth's eyes opened. Her head gyrated as she moaned and sobbed and cried out 'no' over and over.

'What is it?' signed HT.

"No—no—no!"

'What?'

"My father."

'Tell us.'

"They say they found him—hanging."

LATE THAT NIGHT BY CANDLELIGHT, HT faced Beth while she laid there in bed on her back racked in grief. The silver yoostsah on his hand rested atop her bulging belly over her umbilical scar.

"I'll be leaving tomorrow for the funeral."

He nodded.

"My mother is gone. Yuri is gone. And now my father. I have no one."

'You'll always have the baby and me,' he signed.

50

SOLOMON

EGG LAKE REGION, SASKATCHEWAN
MARCH 21ST, 2016

ONE MORNING HE HEARD A PLANE CIRCLING the lodge. HT stepped outside, glanced over at Dog and squinted skyward. The floatplane made a final pass, then touched down and motored to the beach.

Cousin Nate climbed out, then helped Auntie Millie traverse the pontoon onto shore.

HT gave each of them a puzzled look. Nate sported a pink camouflage jacket. Instead of his usual work boots, he wore designer mukluks. Auntie Millie's long dress and flowing hair were gone. She now sported a butch haircut and blue jeans and had on Nate's old work boots.

"You seem surprised Cousin," said Nate. "Bein' all alone out here in the bush, I guess the world is just passin' ya by. Ya told me to be true to myself, eh."

"Where's my hug?" said Auntie Millie. "We decided to drop in on you now that Beth's on spring break. She's only got a week off. Besides, I've never seen your place out here on the lake."

The bush pilot helped Beth exit the plane. With his help, she waddled along the float and scooted herself down onto the gravel below. The last time HT saw her was during Christmas. He was amazed at her immense belly. She seemed ready to burst.

They kissed hard and bear-hugged, her roundness getting in the way a bit.

'Should you be out here?' he signed.

"I'm fine Lovie. Don't worry about me. I'm not due for three more weeks."

The floatplane motored away from shore and throttled up. It took off, then circled east.

"Hold that baby in, eh Beth," said Nate. "He won't be back till suppertime."

The group made its way toward the lodge. HT scaled the ladder to the cache. He opened the tin-covered door and held up his fur hangers for them to see.

'35 squirrels, 6 lynx, 18 marten, 5 red fox, 1 cross fox, 11 weasels, 10 beaver, 22 muskrats, 2 otters and 5 mink,' he signed.

"How come no wolves?" laughed Nate.

'We prefer to avoid each other.'

"Ya did good this season," yelled Nate.

'No,' signed HT. 'Not good. The animal numbers are way down. Trees are dying. Something is wrong out here on the land. Something terrible is happening.'

Inside the lodge, Auntie Millie and Nate made themselves comfortable on HT's chairs. Beth and HT sat on the edge of his bed. He stroked her belly as she scratched Dog behind the ears.

"Did you feel him Lovie? He kicked."

HT nodded. 'He?' he signed,

"Yes, it's a boy," she smiled. "You're the last one to find out, aren't you? That's what happens when you choose to live out here like a wild man."

"Do you think the baby will grow up to be like him?" said Auntie Millie.

"He better not," said Beth. "I don't know if I could take another one like him."

"No, there aren't too many folks like Hand Talker," said Nate. "Most folks would die or go crazy livin' alone out here. From what I hear, ya didn't get along so well with 'em at first. So tell us Beth. Have ya changed your mind about Native trappers like that guy sittin' there next to ya—or do ya still hate 'em all?"

"Ouch," she said.

"Now Beth, ya know I was just kiddin' ya, eh?"

"Ouch—ouch. I must be having a contraction."

Auntie Millie looked toward the empty beach and grimaced,. "I told you this might happen," she sighed. "But you just *had* to see your lovey dovey, didn't you? Aoo'!"

She got up and hobbled over to the young woman.

"Let's have you lay down, okay Dear? Hand Talker, we'll need some clean sheets and towels—whatever you have. It's probably just false labor, but you never know. And you Nate. Make yourself useful, eh. Crank up the woodstove and make sure the kettle's full. I'll need a pan of boiling water to sterilize a few things just in case. And get that Dog out of here."

BETH GRUNTED AND GROANED with each new contraction. HT circled the lodge time and again. He stopped now and then to wipe sweat from his forehead and neck. Meanwhile, Nate sat in the shade covering his ears. Hours passed. Well into the afternoon the spasms grew closer together until Beth moaned and cried out nearly non-stop.

Her cries halted. Seconds later, the sound of a wailing infant could be heard. Then the wailing abruptly stopped. HT and Nate exchanged worried looks. Once more HT began pacing around the lodge.

Perhaps fifteen minutes later, Auntie Millie shuffled outside cradling a small blood-spotted bundle. She set it atop Dog's house and quickly hobbled back inside.

HT and Dog approached the bloody bundle. Chin on his chest, he melted to the ground. Dog nuzzled him while he silently wept. Nate placed his hand on HT's shoulder.

Auntie Millie stood in the doorway. "Aren't you boys coming in?" Then she noticed HT's expression. "Oh sheez. I'm so sorry Hand Talker—I should have explained. That's just the afterbirth. Beth and the baby are fine. Come and see for yourself."

Beth waved feebly and lifted the tiny infant from her breast. "Solomon, would you like to meet your father?"

HT caressed Solomon's soft scalp and touched his lips to the newborn's forehead. HT and Auntie Millie and Nate sat on the edge of the bed.

When Auntie Millie nodded, Dog hesitantly stepped inside and went to greet Beth and her new baby.

Lumbering, shuffling sounds came from outside. Beth shot HT a concerned look.

'That's your other baby,' he signed.

"What other baby?"

A yearling moose ducked its homely head through the open doorway and let loose a guttural groan.

"Why hello Gertie," said Beth. "What a big girl you have become."

HT got out his flute. He played the *Beginning Song* while Beth quietly sang to Solomon and Dog and Gertie.

Undated Poem by Hand Talker

MY FAMILY

Asdzaa Nádleehé [Mother Earth] *clothes my lover in morning dew,*
decorates her with sacred stones, chiming shells
and pollen and blows four breaths of life
as I craft a birch bark cradleboard
lined with the finest of furs
for our little son of Sun.

51

THE GOOD, THE BAD AND THE UGLY

EGG LAKE REGION, SASKATCHEWAN
JUNE 20TH, 2016

ETH HANDED BABY SOLOMON to HT. The pilot held her hand while she stepped down onto the gravel beach.

HT hugged her hard and gently squeezed Solomon. 'He has a lot more hair,' he signed.

"Yes. And he has your eyes and your appetite Lovie."

'You brought a lot of stuff,' signed HT as he and the pilot unloaded the plane.

"Well, it *is* for the entire summer after all. I have my schoolbooks and papers. And I have lots of food and clothes and nappies. Luckily for you I am breastfeeding Solomon. Otherwise, you would be up at all hours of the night mixing formula and warming bottles over the woodstove," she laughed.

Making multiple trips, HT lugged Beth's boxes, suitcases and bags into the lodge while she and Solomon lounged atop the bed.

After he'd finished, Beth noticed how crowded the lodge had become. "There is no room for your papa," she told Solomon. "I guess he will just have to sleep outside with all of his plant and animal friends."

'Maybe sleep with Dog,' signed HT.

"Maybe you should," she joked.

'Did you see that?' he signed.

"See what?"

'Solomon signed to me. He copied me.'

"No. That is not possible. He is only three months old."

'He did Beth—look. He did it again.'

"Crikey! He signed 'maybe' and 'Dog.' Did you see that?"

HT nodded.

"But Lovie, babies don't begin to speak till they are eight or twelve months old. His mouth cannot pronounce any words yet. But maybe he can learn to sign like you Hand Talker. Come on. Sign for him again. I want to see if he is actually copying what you say, or if he just knows how to make the sign for 'Dog.'"

'No. More than 'Dog.' Watch.'

HT repeated the hand signs he'd already made. Then he rapid-fired signs to Solomon about his plans for the summer months. After he finished, the baby stared intently at his father. Solomon began making vigorous hand motions. And although his movements were slower and more rudimentary, he was clearly trying to copy many of his father's motions.

HT got out his notepad and pencil stub.

Our baby is a little Einstein

"No Lovie. He is sort of the opposite. Einstein did not speak until he was four or five years old—a delay in communication. Something quite different is happening with Solomon—and it is absolutely amazing. I took a class on early childhood development at university and there was never a mention of anything like this. Every parent likes to think their child is brilliant of course, but I think it is going to be different with our little Solomon. He is a very special boy indeed."

He takes after his mom

Beth smiled and whispered: "Well, then I better watch it with my cursing from now on, right Solomon? Maybe you understand *everything* I am saying to your father."

'Maybe,' signed Solomon.

BETH WOKE TO THE SMELL of frying bacon. She stretched and crawled out of bed. HT poured her a mug of tea. He held Solomon in the crook of one arm while he fiddled with the spatula. She took a seat and he handed her the baby.

"Why good morning Solomon. What did that wild man father of yours do to you? What is this Lovie?"

He took out his notepad.

It's a Dené diaper—He won't need the ones you brought

With skepticism she examined the trainers HT fashioned from a pair of Solomon's bottoms by cutting off the legs and stuffing the remaining part with sphagnum moss.

"Won't it be rough on his skin?"

He handed her a loose piece of moss.

"It is quite soft."

It's naturally antibiotic too

"You mean to tell me I brought hundreds of nappies out here for no reason?"

HT smiled and shrugged.

'Look,' he signed, handing her a loop of fabric.

She turned it over in her hands.

"What is it?"

He helped her sling it diagonally across her back and chest. Then he spread the fabric strip in front and inserted Solomon.

'He can ride in front or back,' explained HT. 'Or be hung from a tree.'

"Where did you learn these baby tricks?"

'Good teachers. And my books.'

"Speaking of babies, where is my Gertie? Is she still around?"

'Yes. After breakfast we'll look for her.'

HT LED THE WAY to where he'd seen Gertie browsing on willow shoots the previous day. He whistled, but she was out of earshot. They followed her tracks through the network of muddy trails through and around myriad willow and alder patches. As he tracked her, he observed where several wolves entered the trail and followed the yearling moose. He saw that Gertie's stride had lengthened as she trotted and then ran ahead of the small pack of advancing wolves.

He stopped and faced Beth and Solomon. 'We stop here,' he signed. 'You shouldn't see this.'

"Why? What's wrong Lovie?"

He stepped forward and pointed to a water-filled wolf track in the mud.

"Is that what I think it is?"

He nodded. 'Let's go back,' he signed.

"No. I have to know what happened."

'Please—Beth—please. Let's go back.'

She refused.

"Gertie is my baby."

'She's not your baby. She's a wild moose.'

"I raised her."

'You know what we'll find.'

"Yes Lovie. I know. But I have to see it for myself."

He paused for a time. Then he directed Dog and Beth to hang back while he continued tracking Gertie and the wolves. He found clumps of loose hair on the ground where they'd nipped her hind quarters. Then he found where they first drew blood. The tracks became more erratic after Gertie left the trail and zig-zagged in her attempt to evade the pursuing pack. The wind was in HT's favor when he crept around the final patch of alders.

Gertie was on the ground. Her neck was stretched tight by a large gray wolf with her bulbous snout in its grip. Two more wolves were feeding on her through a gaping hole they'd gnawed through her rectum and genitalia.

The wolf holding Gertie spotted HT and Beth. It bolted for cover. A second wolf followed suit. But the third wolf was head-deep inside Gertie's pelvis, ripping and gulping chunks of offal from her abdominal cavity. There was a dark stripe across the wolf's side and HT noticed one of its hind legs was bent upward near the hock at an acute angle.

Beth screamed in anguish.

The wolf exited its gnaw-hole, glanced at the humans and loped away on three legs. Dog gave chase, but returned when HT whistled. HT and Beth and the baby approached the fallen moose. Deep in shock, Gertie's eyes remained fixed in place while she continued her useless throes and front leg kicks. Her sides heaved. Her nostrils sprayed blood. She feebly lifted her head. HT took the axe from his pack and swiftly severed Gertie's spine just below the base of her skull.

Beth's cheeks were flushed and shiny. "They are so bloody evil—eating my baby while she was still alive!"

'For people things are good and bad and ugly,' he signed. 'But it is not that way for them. Life brings death. Death brings life.'

HT wrapped his arms around Beth and Solomon.

52

THE PEGLEG

EGG LAKE REGION, SASKATCHEWAN
JANUARY 12TH, 2017

THE BITTER NORTH WIND chilled HT's exposed cheeks as he and Dog trekked toward the next trap set. This winter the snow was late again, but now a few flakes were finally drifting down. He rubbed his itchy nose. Soon there'd be a fresh layer on the ground—snow to help him track down and kill the trapline thief.

HT experienced a similar problem that first season when Henry Yellow Bird was stealing his catches. Now a different thief was giving him grief. Each day HT and Dog would check the line during the day. He regularly rebaited. But the thief would visit the sets at night and eat the new bait and any catches, including those he needed to feed Dog and to add to his own store-bought food supply. The thievery had gone on for two months. Due to the unwanted visitor with an immense appetite, their meals became more and more meager. HT could find no tracks or other evidence of the thief's identity on the snowless frozen ground and Dog wasn't interested in following its scent trail. Despite his years of wilderness trapline experience, he was at a loss as to who or what was stealing from them.

Upon reaching his last set, he found only an empty trap and a discarded marten tail. The set was rigged to lift his catch high in the air, out of reach of anyone or anything. Yet the thief simply knocked down the lift pole and stole the marten, once more thwarting HT's efforts.

During the long trek back to the lodge he formulated a new plan.

HT ROSE EARLY and added a log to the woodstove. He poked his head outside. It was ink black. Snow was still falling. The wind had picked up. He made a batch of hotcakes and topped them with syrup and his last handful of dried blueberries. After downing them with a mug of tea, he took something down from the wall pegs above his bed normally only used by Cousin Nate during the annual moose hunt: the high-power rifle that he obtained when the poacher tossed it aside and plunged to his death in the hot spring. HT pocketed a handful of cartridges. Today he would travel alone and light—no Dog to frighten the thief away—no packbasket to slow him down or interfere with his movements if he happened to get the opportunity for a shot. This morning he would take only the rifle and his knife.

HT jogged quickly along the trail, this time running the trapline in reverse. He'd taken the reverse route before in an attempt to catch the thief, but without the benefit of fresh snow for tracking. He stopped at a pile of boulders, scooped out a seat at the base of one, and tried to get comfortable and blend in with his surroundings. In the early morning gloom, with the rifle over his knees, he patiently watched the trail. Nearby, raven wings flapped and flashed through the black spruce spires.

In the distance something large and gray moved along the trail. He watched while it slowly approached through the swirling snow. But the wind went squirrelly and hit him from behind. The figure stopped for a time, seeming to stare his way. It disappeared from the trail. Whatever it was evidently winded him, then left.

HT waited till the wind shifted again. He went to the place where the thief stood and examined its tracks in the drifting snow. '*Mą'iitsoh* [wolf],' he concluded. Yet this timber wolf was different from other wolves. In the tracks he saw where it approached him along the trail, traveling on three legs instead of four. But when the animal scented him and stopped, the stump of its fourth leg showed in the impressions—a pegleg. The wind was gradually erasing its tracks and those from his mukluks.

He leapt forward in pursuit. The tracks of the limping lobo led him through thick alders, then onto a ridge. At the crest, he saw where it milled about and watched its backtrail. Then the tracks dropped down the other side of the ridge into a valley and crossed a frozen slough.

HT kept to the trail. He found where the wolf gnawed the scattered remains of a moose—an old kill site. *It's been kicked out of the group because it's injured,* he thought. *It's taking a big chance coming here where the pack made a kill. If they catch it, they will kill it.*

As he continued the chase, he saw where the pegleg humped ahead through the snow on its three good legs back up and over the ridge and re-entered HT's trapline area. *The damn thing is completely dependent on me for its food supply,* he thought.

When he pressed forward, he found where the wolf entered a dense patch of alders. But now, instead of threading his way through the tangle of low trees, the trapper circled ahead. On the far side of the alders he saw there were no tracks. Downwind, he found a tamarack trunk and hunkered against it. With the rifle snugged into his shoulder, safety off, he guarded the thicket. The wind howled and bit at him, blowing with fury, creating horizontal snow-blow. It was an all-out blizzard.

After a time, the pegleg emerged from the tangle. It stood there, quartering toward him. HT recognized the dark stripe across its side and the broken, perversely angled hind leg, most likely broken from a well-aimed moose kick. His vision clouded while he tried to focus the crosshairs on the wolf's vitals. Blowing snow obscured his vision for a time. Then, when it cleared, he held steady on the thief's chest and gently squeezed.

Kpoomf!

The wolf bolted across the clearing and vanished into the treeline. HT waited. Finally, he crossed to the edge of the thicket where he found a few drops of blood. A clump of loose hair clung to the nearest alder trunk. He searched for tracks, but they'd already been erased by the wind. Over the next several hours he thoroughly scoured the area where the pegleg disappeared. He found nothing—no tracks or blood trail or body—in the cold, empty land.

After a time, the boreal wind subsided a bit. HT stopped searching for the wounded wolf and returned to the boulder pile where he'd waited early that morning. Once more he sat and leaned against the big rock, frustrated. He berated himself for only further injuring the animal.

Scanning downtrail, he watched the location where the pegleg had first appeared. And then he saw it. A skinwalker stood there upright at that same place in the trail, facing him—tall and gray—brooding. Its hackles were raised. Its fur robe flapped loosely in the crosswind. The witch-wolf watched him. Its ominous yellow eyes were unblinking. On the pad of its paw, the apparition brandished a wildly flickering flame in front of its ivory-studded jaws. The flame flashed bright gold. HT's vision blurred.

Instinctively, he raised the rifle, released the safety and fired. He sprinted along the trail to the spot and searched for tracks and signs of a hit. But there was nothing. Only virgin drifting snow.

UNDATED LETTER FROM BETH

My dearest Hand Talker,

Happy birthday Lovie! I do hope you enjoy this special day. I hope too that you like your present. Nate told me he thought that it was something you may find useful. It is from the Trading Post (Bob's family said to tell you "hello").

I just want to say thank you again for being such a big part of our lives. You are a fantastic partner and lover for me and an amazing father and role model for Little Doc [Solomon]. Although you are away from us much of the time, we always feel safe knowing that you are there whenever we need you.

You have often told me that you wish you could do something to better protect the land and the living things of the Earth. The best way to do that Lovie is to spend more time with people and to connect with those who have similar thoughts. I realize it may be difficult for you to do that, but I will support you if you decide to do so. Your Aunt Millie is quite involved in the community, as was your own father. You can do it too if you set your mind to it Lovie.

Please know that I am always with you, especially during your dark periods. I think of you each day we are apart. If you ever want to talk to me about things that happened in your past that are bothering you I am here to listen (or you can write it down for me if that makes it any easier). You stood by me when Yuri disappeared, and now I am here standing by you. I want to help, so please don't shut me out Lovie. Remember that you are the best thing that has ever happened to me and our "Little Doc."

Always yours,

Beth

OOOO XXXX OOOO

53

INFERNO

AT FIRST THE WESTERN BREEZE bore just a faint hint of woodsmoke—a slight gray haze—while it gently wafted through the clearing beside the lodge. Gradually, the smoke increased till, after a week, it was clear that a large wildfire was growing even larger as it approached Egg Lake. All the while, fire patrol planes, super scoopers and air tankers from Barber Field flew over the lake, worked the flanks of the fire, then returned to La Ronge to refuel or load up on more retardant.

Each morning and evening HT and Dog would scale the low hill behind the lodge to check on the fire's progress. After each trip, HT would report his observations to Beth and three-year-old Little Doc.

'The fire is about 20 kilometers away,' he signed one day.

"Should we leave?" said Beth.

'No. But we should pack just in case.'

"What's going on?" said Little Doc.

'We're getting ready,' signed his father. 'We may need to leave. The fire is getting closer.'

HT placed his most treasured possessions—his crucifix, flute and jish—in the bottom of his packbasket. He stacked his favorite books close to the door. In the end, a large pile of belongings lay ready to go. But his and Beth's packs could hold only so much. And the canoe couldn't possibly hold the three of them and Dog, plus all the things HT had heaped together.

A few mornings later HT climbed the hill. It was windier than before. The glow from the flames was now only a few kilometers away. He returned to the lodge and indicated it was time to load up. Beth and HT each made multiple trips to the beach. But in the end, the canoe held only a fraction of the items they intended to bring. They put the remainder under a canvas tarp weighed down with beach cobbles, away from any trees or other combustibles.

At midday, a massive smoke column became visible from behind the hill. The wind steadily pushed the megafire toward the lake, herded on each flank by the government's fire planes.

"Where's Dog?" said Beth. "I haven't seen her lately."

'I don't know,' he signed. 'But we can't wait. We have to go now.'

HT and Beth and Little Doc boarded the heavily loaded craft and shoved off. Despite the extra weight, they made good progress. Then HT felt the windshift on the back of his neck. Over his shoulder, he watched the fire's giant smoke column collapse on itself. Within minutes, the wind across the lake increased and the forest behind them began to glow. He paddled hard. The waves grew higher till their splashes crested the gunnel, slowly filling the canoe. HT changed course and let the wind push him along, now aiming for a long grassy spit projecting out into the lake. Beth bailed. From his seat amidships, Little Doc watched in wide-eyed amazement as the drama unfolded around him.

Trees along the western shore began to blaze bright orange. The roaring fire behind them raged high in the sky. Soon, ember-filled gray and black smoke plumes blocked the sun.

Several times the canoe threatened to swamp, but HT righted it and paddled onward while Beth shifted cargo around and furiously bailed. When they ground to a halt against the spit, Beth disembarked with Little Doc.

HT sprang forward, dragging the heavy craft into the protection of a mud hollow. He dumped its contents and flipped it and packed the outer edge with moist black silt. He grabbed what belongings he could and signaled for Beth and Little Doc to join him in the makeshift shelter below. The three of them crawled in, clutched each other and waited.

The west wind was strong. Steady. Without warning a wall of hot gas rocked the canoe. Fiery embers swirled while the family hunkered tight against the cool mud. The fire front approached. It curled and blackened the grass as it raced across the spit toward them. The furnace around them grew hotter and hotter, till breathing became difficult. HT put all his weight against the lip of the gunnel to keep the canoe from flipping. He curled his body over Beth and Little Doc. A firebrand found its way inside and landed on Beth's arm. She tried to bolt, but HT snuffed it out and held her down. They clawed deeper, creating breathing spaces for each other. The hot gas was suffocating—nearly searing their lungs. Little Doc screamed when HT and Beth pinned his head into a hole in the muck. They choked on the harsh smoke. The inferno blowtorched the land around them. They moaned in anguish.

Half an hour passed as the heat and smoke gradually dissipated. When it was safe, the three of them emerged from their shelter into a coal-black moonscape surrounded on three sides by water. Their clothing and hands and faces were streaked black with mud. HT and Beth and Little Doc coughed and kissed and hugged one another.

'I can't believe we made it,' signed HT.

"You saved us," she said.

'But we should have left sooner,' he signed.

"Yeah," said Little Doc, "what in the bloody hell were you two thinking?"

"The important thing is no one got hurt," said Beth. "We are alive. I think if we would have left earlier we surely would have capsized and drowned out on the lake. Those waves were monstrous—crikey!"

Their cargo was scattered across the end of the spit. Most items were fire-damaged. HT examined the canoe. There was a long line of blackened wood and several holes where blowing embers collected and burned through the hull during the firestorm. They spent the afternoon regathering and sorting their belongings.

That evening, a floatplane flew in and circled the lodge site. It turned and followed the meandering shoreline. HT and Beth waved. The plane set down near them and motored to shore. Nate and the bush pilot stepped out.

"Thank God," said Nate. "We didn't know where ya were at. How the heck did ya survive it?"

Beth pointed to the hollow area where the canoe lay. She told how they'd hid beneath it and dug deep in the mud.

"That's why Little Doc is so grubby, eh?"

Nate hugged the boy.

'It's good you found us,' signed HT. 'The canoe has holes.'

"In other words," laughed Beth, "can we catch a ride?"

"There's room," said Nate. "Cousin, we flew over your lodge. I'm sorry, but it's gone—burned and collapsed. And it looks like your trapline is mostly burnt up too. Everything is completely cooked—vaporized. The trees and animals— nothin' could've survived that inferno. Guess you'll need to find another line of work. Any idea what that'll be?"

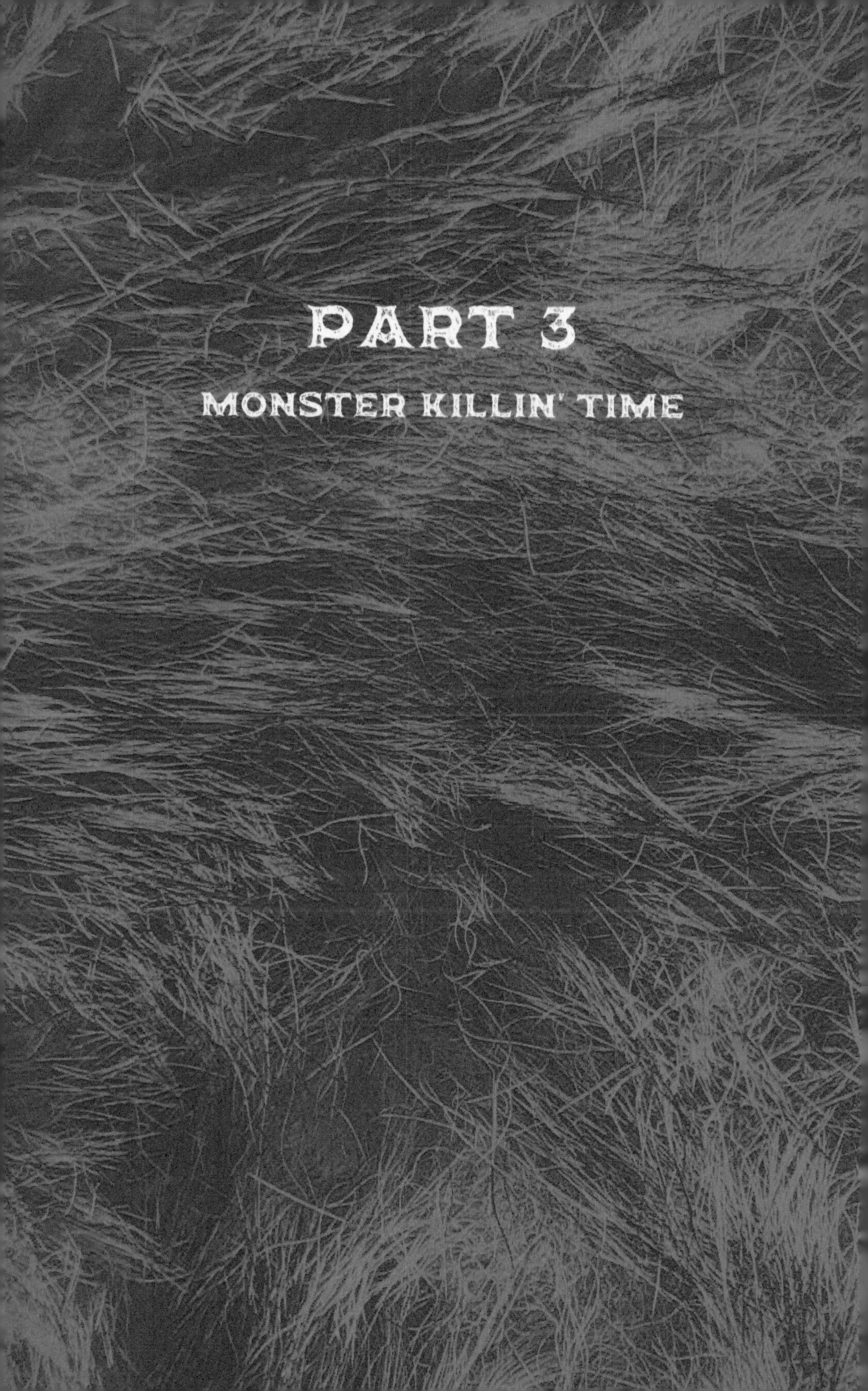

PART 3
MONSTER KILLIN' TIME

54

FAMILY PHYSICS

LA RONGE, SASKATCHEWAN
OCTOBER 3RD, 2023

"GOOD MORNING CLASS. We have some special guests with us today. Mister Hand Talker Judd and our son Little Doc are here to help me teach physics—the topic of our science class this month. Also, with us is their cousin Mister Nate Cookman. Mister Cookman and I often interpret for Mister Judd because he is mute. He is unable to speak orally. Today you will see how he uses sign language and notes to communicate. That is how he got the name 'Hand Talker.' Many of you are members of the Lac La Ronge Indian Band, so you are probably already aware that Hand Talker is the current National Chief of Canada's Assembly of First Nations."

Nate stepped forward. "I'll be interpretin' for Mister Judd today since we go way back. I've known 'em more than twenty years, eh."

HT waved 'hi' to the kids, then began signing to Nate.

"He says he'd like to open class for ya with a song. But first, he wants to know if ya have any questions for 'em. I see a hand there in the back row. What's your question, eh?"

"Is it true your cabin got burnt up in a big fire?"

HT signed to Nate, while Nate told the class about the family's narrow escape from the firestorm and how HT's lodge, Dog, his trapline territory and most of his belongings were burned. He explained how humans' burning of fossil fuels was driving climate change which, in turn, caused bigger wildfires and other problems around the world. He told of the Assembly of First Nations' initiatives to help slow climate change by switching from fossil fuels to renewable energy sources like geothermal and solar and wind and hydro.

Then HT played a healing song on his flute while Nate thumped a moose hide drum. Beth sang along using Native words she'd learned. Little Doc ignored them all as he busied himself on his computer. His nimble fingers flew furiously across the keyboard as he mentally analyzed trillions of data bits and bytes uploaded to the cloud by hundreds of thousands of engineers, mathematicians and scientists around the globe.

When the song ended, a girl in the front row raised her hand.

HT nodded.

"How come you hunt and trap Mister Judd? Why do you hurt those poor animals?"

"That is an excellent question," said Beth. "Mister Judd, please do explain yourself."

HT thought for a moment, then signed again while Nate translated.

"Mister Judd says the Dené and Cree have always fished, hunted, trapped and gathered. It's how we fed and clothed ourselves. It's how we survived, eh. It's why we're here today. Many of your relatives here in the North still do these things for the same reason. For an animal or fish to die from a bullet or hook or to freeze to death overnight in a trap is more peaceful than a slow death from starvation or gettin' eaten alive by a predator, eh? It's true some kinds of traps do cause pain. To reduce it, the government adopted best management practices put together by a group of experts.

"Mister Judd says gatherin' animals and fish also helps prevent over-crowdin'. When there's too many of 'em in one place it can damage the land or cause sickness among 'em."

"Like with snowshoe hares?" asked a student.

HT nodded, then continued signing.

"Mister Judd says, 'Yes, and like with people too,' eh. Not long ago there weren't very many people on Earth at all. Now there's eight billion. That's why we're seein' die-offs from diseases. There's too many of us. It's somethin' no-body wants to talk about. And now with all the burnin' of fossil fuels, we're ac-tually destroyin' our life support system. But HT is signin' to me that this is a physics class not an ecology class. So let's talk about physics, okay?"

HT drew a sketch on the board. 'What's that?' he signed.

"Some kind of trap maybe?" said a boy.

HT signed to Nate.

"Yes, it's called a taiga deadfall trap. And it kills the animal instantly in case ya were worried about that. Traps like this were one of the ways First Nations people used to get their food. And maybe some fur or leather too. Now they mostly use more modern ones."

HT clicked his tongue and signed for Little Doc to continue the physics lesson. The skinny kid went to the front of the room.

"Keep it simple for us, okay Little Doc," said Nate.

Little Doc gave him a thumbs up.

"Hi guys," said the boy. "I just solved an important physics problem. Let me show you—it'll be really quick, I promise." Little Doc stood tiptoe and scribbled on the board.

$$U \approx \left\{ [energy \leftrightarrow matter] \xrightarrow{\delta} spacetime \right\}^{\infty}$$

where π and Λ oscillate inversely at rate c relative
to dynamic equilibrium Ø at any measurable
frame of reference or world point

"It's pretty basic really," said Little Doc, "Einstein already used the 'Special' and 'General' theory names. So how 'bout we call it the '*Universal* Theory of Relativity?' Or maybe just the 'Theory of Everything.' What do you guys think?"

The room was silent.

"You see, right now the standard models are incomplete. That's why physicists are incorrectly interpreting the age of the Universe to be 13.77 billion years and their understanding of dark energy and dark matter doesn't fit. But when you tack this on to the models, you get a much different result, right? That funky arrow in the middle means variable one-way flow by the way. If you happen to be a creationist or believe in time travel, just try to pretend it's not there, okay?

"It all comes down to the superposition of paleo phenomena within the Hubble volume. The leading physicists can't see the forest—reality—for the trees—all the small-scale mathematical models they make. They keep trying to chop the 'in' off the word 'infinite.' But they'll get it right once they extrapolate the energy-matter patterns inward and outward to build better maps. Historically, our maps have *always* gotten larger and smaller. Now that the James Webb Telescope and detector upgrades for the HL-LHC at CERN will be giving them a clearer view, that should help, right?"

"How old are you?" asked one of the students.

"I'm six."

"You're six years old—in Grade One—and you're teaching high school?"

"Well, I skipped Grade One. And high school."

"You're in college?"

"No. College didn't work out too well for me. So now I'm a freelancer."

"What's that?"

"I teach myself. Mostly with online resources. My mama and papa let me do it."

The kids laughed.

Beth cleared her throat. "And no, you cannot all become freelancers if that is what you are thinking. Alright Little Doc. Back to your father's drawing. Please explain the science behind it."

"Okay. I'll start with a qualitative explanation."

Little Doc pointed up at the sketch.

"The taiga deadfall trap can be thought of as a simple machine, right? The heavy object—the rock or log—is basically a tilted plane held up by a lever—part of the trigger mechanism. Here's the lever stick. And here's the fulcrum where the lever stick rotates on the support stick. When the trap is set, everything's held in place by the weight of the heavy object transferring energy among the parts. Then, when an animal wiggles the bait, the energy is released and the object falls and squishes the animal. But as you probably already guessed, the trap can also be explained *quantitatively* using a variety of mathematical approaches. Who wants to hear about some of those?"

No hands appeared.

Yeah, I guess math can be a bit boring if you're not into it. Or even scary if you can't understand it. But try to remember that it's just a bunch of ways people invented to help them map reality and figure stuff out. It gives them a guesstimate of reality. For example, your math teacher probably expects you to know that 1 apple + 1 apple is exactly equal to 2 apples. And in math that's true. But in the real world, those 2 apples are similar, but not equal—not if you consider that equation on the board, right?"

"Solomon," said Beth, "I happen to be their math teacher. Don't confuse them."

"Sorry about that Mama. In that case, you guys might need to ignore what I wrote there about π being variable instead of constant. Astrophysics and astronomy are my real passions. Who wants to talk about the northern lights—aurora borealis? Or maybe the James Webb Space Telescope?"

The kids' hands flew up.

55

DREAMIN' BIG

LA RONGE, SASKATCHEWAN
OCTOBER 3RD, 2023

THEY HUDDLED IN AUNTIE MILLIE'S snug living room around the coffee table while the fire quietly crackled in the woodstove. HT, Auntie Millie, Beth and Nate were strategizing on how to unite the scattered Dené bands and tribal nations. Back in the corner of the room, Little Doc hovered over his laptop computers. His small fingers flashed and flew across the four keyboards.

"Hand Talker," said Auntie Millie, "as National Chief of Canada's Assembly of First Nations, you already have a big advantage here in the north. Given your good name recognition, all the Alaskan and Canadian Dené bands will likely support you. So I think your focus should be on the Navajo, Apache and Hupa communities down south. Those are the Dené groups with the most potential voters. At Dinétah [Navajoland] you'll get strong backing because you're still a member there and your dad was a chapter president. Everybody remembers Jess. They trusted him."

'I agree,' signed HT. 'Nate, do you still want to manage and translate for me?'

"Sure thing Cousin. I'm behind ya on this one. Like Auntie says, we need central leadership so all the nations can work together on common goals. I'll be there with ya durin' the campaign and afterwards if ya happen to get elected President. Ya know I'll work real hard, eh."

'And you Beth?' signed HT. 'You hate cameras and publicity. You even changed your last name to help stay hidden. Should we do this?'

"It is your life and your career Lovie. If you are elected, Little Doc and I will just have to adjust to it. I will support whatever decision you make."

"Me too Papa," chimed in Little Doc from his corner.

'Okay Nate,' signed HT. 'We'll visit every Dené nation. We'll stop at each one in Canada as we go north. Then circle through Alaska, Then head south along the coast. But like Auntie said, Navajoland is key. They have the most voters. If we lose there, we lose the race.'

Auntie Millie cleared her throat and gestured at the stack of papers and note-books on the table in front of her. "Very well. Maybe we can use some of the ideas I've been collecting here over the years. Tonight we'll hash out the mission statement and interim goals and guidelines for the United Dené Nations. After that, maybe we can work on voting procedures. We should set a date for the election. Years ago, when I helped Petey co-found the Assembly of First Nations with some other chiefs, we learned that to make something big like this happen—with so many players involved—we had to just jump in with both feet and take the bull by its horns. I suggest we aim for March. The sooner the better, really."

Nate nodded. "Sounds good. I'll work up a ballot template to share. Each nation can customize it and add names to it as election day approaches. Let's set the election for a Saturday so folks don't have to miss work to go vote. That should make for a higher turnout, eh?"

'Auntie Millie,' signed HT, 'I wish you could come with me and Nate.'

"Me too. But you know my arthritis won't allow that kind of travel. Besides, your social media manager over there, Little Doc, says he'll help me support you from here by computer. He's got information on all my contacts and can help me connect with all the Dené chiefs and tribal chairpersons and administrators. We can help support the campaign from here."

Auntie Millie rose and pushed her aluminum walker aside. "Sheez. I can't believe this is really happening. Aoo'. You're finally rising up, eh Hand Talker? Now rise that skinny butt of yours up off the Chesterfield and help me move it." They slid the big couch away from the wall.

She reached into a slit in the backside upholstery and withdrew a pouch. "Here. Take it Nephew. I've been saving up for this moment for a long time. I want you to have it. You and Nate are going to need it for food and gas. Of course if you lose the election, you'll have to repay every single loonie!"

56

BIG STORM A COMIN'

MANCHESTER, ENGLAND
OCTOBER 31ST, 2023

FOR A MOMENT, the tall and pudgy prophet remained silhouetted in the pub doorway. His yellow-orange aura faded as he entered and carefully shut the door. His eyes slowly adjusted to the dimness. The place was nearly empty. There was a short, hawk-nosed man with cropped, pure white hair sitting in the shadows. The prophet went and slid into the empty space beside him. Together, they faced the door.

"Person—woman—man—white rabbit—TV—007," whispered the prophet.

"What?"

"That's the password, right?"

"That's some words and a number. What do you want?"

"Will you talk to me?"

"We're talking aren't we? Who the hell are you?"

"A big storm cometh," whispered the prophet. He stroked his long red silken necktie. "But the armor of God will protect us on Judgment Day."

"I said, who the hell are you?"

"I'm the Anonymous Prophet of the Patriots. That's what everybody calls me."

"Really? Quite a name you got there Mate."

"You've probably seen the stuff I posted online."

"No. Haven't seen it. You better not have been followed here you bloody fool. Open your shirt."

"Why?"

"To make sure you're not wired."

The Manchester man discreetly patted-down the prophet's pant legs and checked his wide torso for wires and tape.

"Okay, you're clean. So what gives—Prophet? What do you want from an old bloke like me? The name's Stonehocker by the way. Roger Stonehocker."

The prophet frowned. He glanced sideways to make sure no bobbies were listening in. "I know who you are," he said. "I need some credentials—to get inside the Family's estate. I need some other things too. Here's a list. And instructions. A colleague of mine said you'd be willing and able to do it."

Roger unfolded the paper and read it. "You know this will cost a pretty penny. Can you afford it Prophet?"

"Not a problem. My donors will gladly cover it."

"When do you need all this?"

"End of March like it says there in the note. Deliver everything to me at that time and place and you'll be greatly rewarded."

"That's not how it works Prophet. I'll need half up front. That's half a million quid. Up front. Hard cash. None of that cryptoshit."

The prophet left the pub. He returned a few minutes later rolling a big dark plastic suitcase. "It's all there. You can count it. Half a million pounds. And at no extra charge I threw in some of my Sea-to-Lake® herbal infusion supplements, Holy Land Brand® olive oil and MyPeterPowerPills® pecker-perker-uppers. I sell them online. When you run out, just go to MyPeterPowerPills.com to get more—only $19.95 a bottle plus shipping and handling."

Roger grinned. "Thanks Prophet. Care to join me for a pepperoni pizza and a pint of ale?"

"Pedophiles eat pepperoni pizza," said the prophet.

Roger slammed his fist on the table. "Fuckin' Yank—calling me a peedo?"

"No Roger. I'm just saying that where I come from—New York City—and all over the world really—there are these Satan worshiping cannibals that run the pizza joints. They serve up pizzas with pepperoni sausage made out of little Christian babies and fetuses born from the child sex slaves they keep chained up in back of their pizza joints. They break the kids' legs so they can't run away. There's an international ring of them—pedophiles—that have sex with the kids and sell pizzas with sliced baby sausage. It's super tender. And tasty, right? So if you don't mind, I'd prefer we order something else on the menu. I really don't want to support that sort of business enterprise. Besides, I can't handle spicy food like that too much anymore." He rubbed his chubby tummy.

"You've gone bonkers Prophet," laughed Roger. "Hey, maybe I *have* heard of you and your followers after all. I bet you're one of those Yanks who thought there was a spaceship behind that comet quite a while back. And then all you blokes swallowed a bunch of pills and flew away to join the alien Lizard People. But you decided to return to Earth. Am I right?"

An awkward silence ensued as the prophet stared at Roger, unblinking.

"I'm just joking with you Mate. How about a shepherd's pie to chase down your ale? It's on me." He patted the big dark money-filled suitcase.

57

A Claim Jumper

Navajo Reservation
Autumn 2023 – Mid-March 2024

ALL FALL AND WINTER, Cousin Nate and HT campaigned hard on a shoe-string budget. They drove from place to place in Auntie Millie's old sedan. Depending on where they ended up each night, they slept on people's couches, or shared fleabag motel rooms or an old tent. They even camped out behind a barn or a billboard a time or two.

From Alaska to Mexico, from the Pacific Ocean to the Great Plains, at each Dené nation they visited, HT and Nate found the members receptive to the idea of creating a grassroots inter-tribal coalition to be called the 'United Dené Nations.' During the day, Nate—in his pink camo neckerchief—discussed logistics and provided the formative and electoral documents to the leaders and their staff, while HT—in his black headband—met with prospective voters and handed out flyers promoting himself as a presidential candidate for the organization. Each evening, with Nate interpreting, HT described his grassroots vision for the UDN to local groups of men, women, youths, elders, ranchers, forest workers, firefighters, police officers, educators, and traditional handcrafters and artists.

Election Day was drawing near when one evening Nate returned to the motel room in a foul mood. "Hey Cousin, we have a serious challenger, eh."

'Who?' signed HT. 'Not Jon. He said he's too focused on local issues. He doesn't have time to run against me.'

"No, it's not Jon. Have ya heard of this fella called 'Wolf Man Keetsal?'"

'Of course,' signed HT. 'When I was little, Wolf Man ran against my dad. Everybody at Dinétah [Navajoland] knows him. He's that chapter president I told you about—the golfer. To impress people, he used to travel around with a huge wolf-dog. He preyed on everyone's fears. He retired so he could play more golf.'

"Right. Anyway Cousin, Wolf Man decided to come outta retirement. He's runnin' against ya for the UDN presidency. And from what I hear, he's well on his way to gettin' his name put on the ballot at *every* Dené nation. Worse than that, he's supposedly workin' behind the scenes now to keep your name off the ballot at Navajo. There's a Navajo Nation law on the books that requires ya to be a resident for your name to be on a Navajo ballot."

'But the UDN is for *all* Dené nations,' signed HT, 'not just Navajo. And I *am* a Tribal member. I'm living at my mom's hogan. My umbilical cord is buried there.'

"I already checked into it Cousin. For residency ya gotta live at the rez for at least a year. You've only been livin' there for five months off and on. Wolf Man knows it, eh. He's been writin' letters to the Elections Committee about it. I'll do some brainstormin' and see what I can do, but, unless that law gets changed or revoked within the next week or so, we're outta luck. The number of voters at Navajo is more than all the other nations combined. Plus Wolf Man's been contactin' the other nations and competin' with us for those votes too."

'To prove residency, I can stay at the hogan until election day,' signed HT. 'Beth and Little Doc are coming for spring break. So, next week I'll be out there anyway.'

"There's somethin' else ya need to know Cousin."

'What?'

"Wolf Man's tryin' to get ya kicked out of the Tribe, eh. Get ya disenrolled. He's claimin' that since ya been livin' up in Canada for so many years, you're not Navajo no more. He's askin' for an audit from the Vital Records Office—to verify ya've got the blood quantum needed to be on the Tribal rolls. And he's callin' for ya to take a blood test too, eh. Apparently he's been goin' around sayin' you're not even a real Indian."

There was a blur of motion as HT spun and punched a fist-size hole in the drywall.

NATE DROPPED OFF HT in front of the hogan, then quickly drove away.

HT checked the water level in the trough, then strolled out to the lambing ground. There were four more newborns since the last time he'd checked. Back at the hogan, he cooked a quick supper, then hiked to the neighboring ranch.

'Thanks for watching over things,' he signed.

"You're welcome," said his cousin Jimmy. "It's been a good trade for us.

We needed the extra pasture. How's the lambing coming along over at your place?"

HT held up four fingers.

"Good," said Jimmy. "Keep an eye out though. Ben's been having problems. There's a mạ'ii [coyote] that's been killing his lambs. He's lost five so far. He's had to set out traps and snares."

'Will do,' signed HT. 'Can I borrow grandmother's truck?'

Jimmy went inside the hogan and returned with the keys. "The tank's close to full. Use it as long as you need it Hand Talker. I'm telling everybody I know to vote for you. But you oughta hear what some folks are saying about you. Politics is full of lies—at least with Wolf Man around. I'm just fed up with all of it."

HT started the old truck and drove back to the hogan.

For a long time he sat in his father's old chair. His eyes settled on his mother's broken crucifix hanging once more in its place of honor above the hogan door. Then he scrutinized the ceremonial war lance hung high on the opposite wall. The President of the Navajo Nation had presented the honorary spear to his father when he was first elected Chapter President. HT got out his black headband and secured it using the traditional knot. He rose and lifted Jess's war lance from the wooden pegs.

58

CLASH AT THE OLD CORRAL

NAVAJO RESERVATION
MARCH 19TH, 2024

ON THE OUTSKIRTS OF GALLUP, the old rez truck approached the towering hilltop house. Yellow light spilled from the tall windows, flooding the sprawling dormant lawn below. A fancy black pickup with tinted windows was parked in the driveway under a metal halide light. Its custom license plate matched the nickname of the owner: *'WOLF-MAN'*

HT passed the house and circled across to the far corner of the golf course parking lot and pulled into a space.

He trotted across the moonlit fairway, hopped a fence and approached one of the living room windows.

A man inside shouted: "Hey Riz. We're running late Woman. Pick a sexy dress and paint your damn face. Just do what you have to do, okay Sweetie? I'll be out in the truck listening to Frank Sinatra."

The big man slammed the front door. The truck engine revved.

Riz's high heels clicked raucously as the raven-thin woman hurried across the living room. She pulled the front door shut behind her.

HT listened to the roar of the vehicle fade into the distance. When it was clear, he crept around the outside of the house, checking each door and window as he went. A bathroom window was ajar. He removed the screen, raised the window and entered.

The long hallway was lined with photographs of the big sturdy man posing with his various friends and political cronies and several judges. In the dimness, HT examined images taken of Wolf Man with a man he recognized from his boyhood—the healer known as Sam—now an old man.

In the living room was a massive stone fireplace decorated with bows and arrows and a lance arranged around a gold-framed photograph of Wolf Man with his dead wolf-dog. From the room's walls hung other photographs and paintings of wolves. Attached to one wall was a huge home theater screen facing a long black leather couch. HT scanned the spines along the bookshelves. The topics ranged from 'group psychology' and 'political science,' to 'hypnotism' and 'witchcraft' and 'how to become a billionaire.'

In the dining room he picked up a glossy election mailer from the white tablecloth. In the middle of it was a photograph of HT and Nate, each cousin draping an arm across the other's shoulder. But the photo had been doctored. The printed image showed what looked like a piece of black tape over HT's mouth. Nate's lips were now scarlet, making it appear he had on lipstick. And HT's traditional black headband was now pink, matching the scattered patches of pink on Nate's camouflage neckerchief. Below the photo it read:

'Save Dinétah! Don't let this canadian commie and his faggot sidekick take over our homeland. Fight the foreigners. Vote for a real Navajo. Somebody who's able to speak for you. Somebody who belongs here and knows how to spell Diné the write way. Your generous contributions are the only way we can deal with these grave robbing coyotes. Give while you still can. Elect Chapter President "Wolf Man" Keetsal as the very first United Diné Nations President!'

HT's cheek and neck muscles twitched. *What the hell is Wolf Man thinking? Words like this could get someone killed.*

Then his thoughts turned to the note he'd written for Beth's boyfriend. With just a few deceitful words, he'd sent that poor naïve man Yuri off to his hopeless battle against the muskeg muck. A torrent of guilt washed through him yet again. *It should have been up to Beth to decide her future—not me—not by killing him.*

Then HT noticed the boxes stacked along the wall behind him. One was open. Inside he saw more flyers like the one in his hand. *There must be tens of thousands of them*, he thought. His face reddened. His vision clouded. His heart raced.

He resumed his search. In the lavish bathroom and master bedroom he rifled through drawers and shuffled through shelves, but found only packets of old love letters and gaudy clothes and jewelry and trinkets of the man and his wife. Then he spied it. There, hung in a dark corner, was the tanned skin of the man's enormous gray wolf-dog.

HT bolted out the front door. A short time later, he backed the old pickup into Keetsal's driveway and loaded all the boxes of flyers into the bed. He took down Wolf Man's feathered lance from its place over the fireplace.

As he drove toward the Gallup sewage ponds, the tall man's gleaming truck came into view.

Wolf Man and the craven woman pulled into their driveway and parked up against a short section of retaining wall he'd hired a couple migrant workers to build during the heat of the previous summer. A four-day project for them. *Never did pay those morons*, he laughed to himself. *Funny how people believe whatever the hell you tell them.*

The couple listened while Old Blue Eyes crooned *My Way* through the truck's audio system. Wolf Man wrapped his thick stubby fingers around Riz's spindly claws and leaned toward her till their heads nearly touched. When the song ended, he flipped on the interior light and checked his ducky-doo in the visor mirror. He swept a few loose hairs back in place, grinned a fake grin, then ran a twisted tongue across his ultra-white plastic dental laminates.

They got out and started up the walkway. Once more he grabbed her hand. Riz squinted and looked away, hoping that for once he would *not* launch into his regular nightly tirade. But he did. She'd never tell him of course, but she wished then that for once he'd just shut that dog-mouth of his. And for once he actually did. Wolf Man's stream of heated hyperbole halted when he noticed Jess's war lance protruding from his front door.

THE HORN OF THE DUSTY 4X4 SUV sounded. HT poked his head out the hogan door. Two Navajo Nation policemen stood next to the old horse corral looking at the dilapidated remains of a sweat house. The older one dabbed water from the trough onto the back of his thick neck.

"Hand Talker! Hey there Buddy, I haven't seen you since junior high," said Officer Begay. He dried his hands on his uniform. "How you doing?"

They shook hands.

"Hand Talker, meet my partner in crime. This is Tucker Benedict. Hey, can I borrow your outhouse Buddy? I really gotta go after all the coffee and the bumpy ride out."

HT pointed behind the hogan. He offered his hand to Tucker, but the officer declined to shake.

When Begay was gone, Tucker scowled. "You stole those flyers didn't you?

You goddamn Canadian half-breed. Don't you get it? We don't want your kind around here. You wanna take over and tell us all what to do. I hear you wanna put a bunch of those cancer-causing wind turbines up on the high mesas and shut down all the coal-fired plants. My dad used to work at one of those plants. You're not shutting down nobody. What you and your boyfriend are gonna do is pack up and leave. Today."

Tucker shoved him hard. "And if you two don't leave on your own, me and the boys will proudly put you on a bus back to where you came from. You got that?"

HT gritted his teeth. The knuckles on his clenched fists whitened, but he held himself back.

"They say you're not even Diné. You've got no right to wear that." Tucker reached up and tore off HT's headband and threw it in the dirt. Then the young officer forced HT to his knees and put his hand on his Glock model 45 in 9mm German Luger with Ameriglo Bold sights. HT looked back and forth between the stack of cobbles by the trough and the gray fox tattoo on Tucker's gun arm.

"You goddamn grave robbing coyote," said Tucker.

HT reached for a big white cobble on top of the pile.

"Hey!" said Begay. "What the heck's going on? You two look like you're ready to fight or something."

"Nah," said Tucker. "Hand Talker was explaining to me how these rocks are used for sweat baths. Then he went and tripped over his own feet. Did you get dizzy or what Hand Talker?"

"Right," said Begay. "Tucker, take your hand off your weapon."

Tucker didn't move. HT snatched his loose headband from the ground and stood. He and Begay glared at the young officer. Tucker glowered back. Begay turned on his body cam and touched his hand to his own weapon.

"There's no threat here Tucker. Stand down. Now."

Tucker blinked and let go of his gun. He flung a sneer at HT, then got back in the SUV, slammed the door and began blasting commercial pop tunes on the radio.

Begay switched off his camera. "Sorry about that Hand Talker. Tucker's been put on probation. He'll likely get fired this week. Until then, I really gotta watch him. I used to think he was a decent cop. But it seems that him *pledging* an oath and *keeping* an oath are two very different things. He's been slowly going rogue. Not using common sense anymore. He was trained at the academy to be objective. To be a peacekeeper, not a warmonger. But now Tucker believes anything and everything he hears and reads. Then he turns around and acts on it. He's a cop who goes around making bad situations worse. It's completely nuts."

HT nodded.

"So, I have to ask if you know anything about a robbery over at Wolf Man Keetsal's place? Wolf Man claims his spear and a bunch of boxes were taken. He thinks you're involved somehow since you guys are running against each other. His security camera footage shows a truck in his driveway."

HT shrugged and pulled out his notepad.

I don't own a truck

"When I brought your dad's spear into the station for evidence, they said they'd be dusting it for prints. Listen Hand Talker, I've seen those flyers and I would've done the same thing myself. Things are pretty heated in town among all the voters right now. Wolf Man's got everybody riled up. They're all yelling and cussing at each other. He's got Navajos fighting Navajos. It might be safer for you to stay out here till things cool down a bit, okay?"

HT nodded.

"None of this election stuff even matters now Buddy. You must not meet the legal requirements for residency. Last night the Elections Committee kicked you off the ballot."

59

BARE TO THE BONE

NAVAJO RESERVATION
MARCH 24TH, 2024

GRINNING, OLD MAN SAM removed his hands from his naked patient's oily lower abdomen. "Remember that time I healed the sickness in your belly when you were a little kid?"

HT nodded.

"You can get up now. You're healed again. Sorry about all the blood this time."

HT rose and squatted there, eyes straight ahead, somber.

"What'll you do now?"

HT motioned northward.

"Back to Canada already, huh? But Hand Talker, I thought you were running for United Diné Nations President. Everybody's gonna vote on Saturday. I was hoping maybe you'd stick around here awhile. We really need somebody like you. We need new leaders—leaders who respect healers like me."

HT sat there, unmoving.

"You're healed," repeated Old Man Sam. He set a bloody little bone on the wool blanket between them. "There's the ugly thing that was stuck inside you. It's from a dog or a wolf I'm pretty sure. A ch'įįdii [evil spirit] put it in there somehow. Maybe when you were asleep. Good thing I took it out, huh?"

HT glanced down and recognized it as a lamb's cannon bone. He stared at the dying flames through the tempered glass in the door of the woodstove.

Old Man Sam shifted his weight and carefully slipped the empty plastic blood-bag into his back pocket.

'I need a *real* medicine man, not some quack,' signed HT.

"What's that? I don't understand hand talk too well. Anyway, you can pay me now—whatever you think is fair. How 'bout a young ewe?"

60

QWACKANON AND THE A-HOLE PROPHECY

CAMBRIDGE, ENGLAND
MARCH 27TH, 2024

THE PROPHET made his way along the walkway. From time to time, he stopped and peered at his reflection in the upscale Cambridge shop windows. He'd check his hair and tie, then carefully look behind to make sure no one was tailing him. Motorists rumbled past on the narrow cobblestone street.

He entered the resort hotel restaurant.

"Give me your biggest New York steak—medium rare. With freedom fries. And a bottle of your most expensive wine."

"A special occasion Sir?" said the waiter.

"Just take my order, okay."

"Sir, we don't serve freedom fries. Would you like to order French fries instead?"

"Bring me some fried chips. UK style. Nothing French. Understand?"

The waiter returned a short time later.

"This is our best wine Sir. Would you care for a sample?"

"You're not listening. I said I want your most expensive wine. Not your best."

While he waited, the prophet polished his manicured nails. His steak arrived a bit underdone. He sliced off the edges and set them aside. He drenched the undercooked center part of the steak in ketchup, threw it against the wall, then proceeded to eat the edges.

The waiter returned and noticed the red mess on the wall.

"Sir, is something wrong?"

"Oops. I had a little accident. You can clean that up. By the way, these French fries are the greatest ever."

After dinner, the prophet returned to his room and retrieved a large dark suitcase. Outside, he made his way down the walkway, then entered an ornate garden. He took a seat on a gilded bench. Fifteen minutes or so later, Roger

Stonehocker's white-capped head bobbed behind a nearby hedge. The man glanced furtively from side-to-side and behind, then joined the prophet on the bench.

Roger started to say something, but the prophet cut him off. "Stop. First I have to make sure you're not a lizard or a robot. Tell me the secret password."

"What? Uhhh, okay: 007—person—woman—man—bunny—TV—awhhh shit Mate! You know who the bloody hell I am."

"Close enough. Now I know you really *are* Roger and not just some fake guy. By the way, you would've gotten extra points if you'd have listed the words in the right order."

"Whatever. Anyway Prophet, I read some of that stuff you posted online. I have to admit I never thought I'd be making fakes for somebody so—uhhh—unstable shall we say?"

"You're not my first choice for a business partner either. But a deal's a deal, right? Besides, it's too late to fire your ass."

"Fuckin' Yank."

"Bloody Brit."

They laughed and slapped each other on the back. The prophet slid the heavy suitcase over to him. Roger handed the prophet a black briefcase. Inside was a folded orange uniform with shoulder patches, an Emergency Services ID on a lanyard, a badge, a set of keys and a small bubble wrapped bundle.

The prophet pulled out the bundle.

"Careful with that thing," said Roger. "I already put the battery in. That's one hot potato you've got there—locked and loaded—ready to go. He gestured toward the hotel parking lot. It'll take out an entire block."

The prophet carefully unwrapped what looked sort of like a garage door opener. He gently turned the little gadget over in his hands, then set it on the bench between his legs. "Stand back and stand by," he said.

"Who're you talking to?"

"You'll find out soon enough. Like I told you before, a big storm cometh."

"Okay. Uhhh. Anyway. Listen Prophet, about that stuff I read online. It seems you're not so anonymous. Wikipedia says the 'Anonymous Prophet of the Patriots' is Dr. Alex Joe Bananas."

"No. It's Bannonis—not Bananas. Doctor of Crypto-political Philosophy—

Hillsdale Collegial Institute of Liberated Theocracy—Nostalgia, Michigan. Plus I got a mail order certificate in Financial Schematics from one of those universities over in the Caymans.”

“Then you *are* Alex Joe, right?”

“That’s right Roger. You’re really really right. Except you’re wrong. I’m no longer Alex Joe Bannonis. I’ve been transformed. Now I’m T2.”

“What’s that supposed to mean?”

“I got metamorphositized—by God—to get ready for Judgment Day. Here—give me your hand. Now put it right here in the middle.”

Roger touched the man’s broad belly.

“Push hard. Harder. Tell me what that feels like?”

“Sort of like Jello I guess—or maybe a giant boob.”

“Exactly. God did that to me during my metamorphositizationing. So now I’m actually made out of a liquid metal-plastic alloy—Titanium-Teflon amalgamate—also known as ‘T2.’ My QwackAnon colleagues say they discovered it online. Supposedly they were following a trail of bread crumbles—hints—that were dropped by this White Rabbit guy on the way to one of his truth holes. He baits people in so they can find the *real truth* instead of all that fake truth.”

“What in the bloody hell are you talking about Mate?”

“It’s true. Really. That’s why I’m all squishy inside now—just like in that second Terminator movie, right? Only for me it’s *real*. I’ve always been a super-duper dude. But now I’m pretty much indestructible. For example: suppose the two of us are standing back there in my hometown out on Fifth Avenue and you accidentally shoot off my leg with a howitzer or something. It won’t matter at all. Believe me. The New York City coppers won’t even bat an eye because all my blood and meat and skin and bone chunks will just flow like mercury right back into a brand-new leg. All healed-up, right? That’s why the elites call me ‘T2.’”

“But you said the elites are a bunch of pedophiles and cannibals.”

“Yes. Some truly are Satan worshippers—baby-biting vampires—serial killers—folks like that. And we’re at war with all those kinds of guys and gals. But some elite folks on the other side of the issue are actually my QwackAnon colleagues—my supporters and donors. You’ll understand better once you read all the web posts and find the clues and learn the code—monkey around a little in all the rabbit holes. It’s all right there online. Early on we never bothered to encode our messages. But then the elite cannibal network started to decipher our comm patterns on the World Wide Web using some of those sneaky Al Gore rhythms. They homed-in on our vibes the same way spiders do on *their* webs to capture bugs, right? So us good guys had to switch to randomized messaging. Now everything's communicated in an unbreakable code up in this massive cloud thing. And the beauty of it is that everything is completely random. Get it? You just need to keep an open mind with all the stuff you read."

"Yeah, I get it now," said Roger as he averted his eyes. "Garbage in, garbage out. Anyway, uhhh, T2 is it? I've been wondering what made you decide to do something as dangerous as this?"

"I'm doing it for the kids of course. My QwackAnon colleagues and I are kind of like modern-day messiahs—kid saviors, right? The British Royal Family heads up the Fake Snake—this satanic pedophile network that's responsible for trafficking and sexually abusing and cannibalizing kids all over the world. Not the *real* Royal Family of course. No. They're being secretly held—imprisoned— in the Tower of London by the vampire guards and alien lizard dudes. The head of the Fake Snake is this group of imposters—look-alike Royal Family robots made in China with surgical plastic and controlled by the MSM. That stands for 'mainstream media.' So you see Roger, I actually have no choice really. I was chosen by my Qwack buddies to remove the head of the Fake Snake—to decapitate it. My mission is to save the *real* Royal Family and all those millions—could be billions—of child sex slaves."

"You mean the ones with broken legs—the pizza kids, right?" said Roger. "But what happens after you decapitate that Snake thing?"

"Then the Christian patriot military takes over of course. Obviously, a lot of people will be going straight to jail."

"Obviously," said Roger, rolling his eyes till they nearly fell out.

"And once more the world will be guided by biblical truth."

"Guided by a global military don't you mean Mate?"

"But that won't matter because they'd be led by the Prophet—by me—T2. And I know a thing or two about biblical truth. Believe me. Like that bunch of commandments carved on a rock the Pope keeps under lock and key. And I know my bible verses. Two Corinthians for example. Personal stuff like that."

"That's not a bible verse."

"Exactly. Most people wouldn't have even known that, but I definitely knew that."

"So Prophet—T2—you're basically saying you want to rule the world someday. That's pretty ambitious Mate. But you don't really believe all that other bullshit do you? Sounds like some of your colleagues might just want to be the Prophet once you're out of the picture. And what I don't understand is how you expect to rule the world someday if everything ends for you tomorrow?"

"Like I said Roger, I'm not going to die. My hair and blood and fat and meat and guts and shit like that will just flow right back together. I'll come out a perfect winner. Didn't you watch the movie?"

"But what if all your chunks and droplets and stuff happen to get way too spread out? What then?"

"I've planned for that. There's this babysitter of mine—"Flynn" Arnold—an ex-soldier. His code name is 'General Jesus.' He may have gotten fired from his regular job, but he has real high level intelligence. He's almost as genius as me. And stable too. Anyway, Flynn says he's got my back and is there to pick up the pieces and watch over my kids and everything if anything goes wrong at all. A win-win situation."

"Maybe a *Flynn*-win situation," mumbled Roger.

T2 shrugged, then looked away.

"Listen Mate, you're taking a pretty big risk. If you follow through with this plan of yours, you could easily end up like that Humpty Dumpty fellow."

"To be a winner like me, you need to be committed to losing most of the time."

"I agree you need to be committed."

They were both quiet for a time.

Then T2 spoke. "What about you Roger? Why did you decide to help out? What's *your* beef with the Royal Family?"

"Well for one thing they let too many bloody fugees onto the Island." Roger lifted his shirt over his head, turned, and showed T2 the face of the British National Action group leader he'd had tattooed on his upper back.

T2 pushed aside his tie and unbuttoned his shirt to show Roger the tattoo on his chest flab. The image appeared to have recently been created in the mirror using a black Sharpie.

"What's that supposed to be?"

"It's from the Prophecy. It's the Alpha-Omega symbol—the beginning and the end. It means I'm the Chosen One. Chosen by God to lead the billions of patriots around the world through the coming storm."

"Really? All I see is a big 'A' on top of what looks like a big hole. A-hole. Anyway, you've got your A-hole Prophecy Qwacks and I've got my White Brotherhood." Roger gestured at his tattoo again. "Some of us old timey Brits just want to be able to run our own country without all the blackies and brownies and slant eyes and women and kids and cripples and homos being involved, right? Make it like it was back in the good old days when the *real* men were in charge and all those women and rest of them knew their place—make the United Kingdom great again."

"I think you hit the nail on the head," said T2. "You sound just like my dear old dad. He was a *real* tough guy—not a damn phony like..."

T2 was silent for a moment.

Roger pulled out an antique pocket watch and flipped open its worn cover. "Time for me to head out Mate. That ID and badge will get you through the front gate. The rest is up to you. Be careful with that button between your legs."

T2 smirked and mischievously waggled his manicured fingers above the little gadget.

Roger backed away. "Good thing we're on the same team Prophet—Alex—uhhh—T2. Whoever the fuck you are. Because you're one dangerous deranged dude. I'll see you on the other side Mate."

T2 swallowed hard and grinned a grim grin to himself while the white supremacist disappeared into the cool evening gloom with his suitcase.

T2'S PALE VIOLET EYELIDS slowly opened. *Damn,* he thought. *It's still there.* Instead of it being just some dark dream, he woke to see his stretched-out red necktie actually hanging there from the hotel room chandelier. In the late hours of the night, the imported silk didn't support his weight, having ripped just above the slipknot. Not to worry. No need for the tie this morning. Instead, he'd be wearing his new open-collar one-piece Emergency Services uniform.

After showering, shaving, dressing, and primping his combed-back hair, he went out to the parking lot and located the freshly painted ambulance provided by Roger.

T2 turned the key. A BBC news report blared. He slammed the tuner button till he found something a little more relatable—a shock-jock talk show. He adjusted the seat and mirrors, then pulled out of the lot into the heavy traffic and headed north toward the village of King's Lynn.

Thirty minutes later, he turned off the thoroughfare and entered the grounds of the Family Estate. A guard at the gate checked his ID and waved him through. He looped the vehicle around and found a suitable parking space with a clear field of view.

T2 looked in the rearview, rolled down the windows and breathed deep of the cool country air. The smell of fresh-mown grass reminded him of his time as a boy at the sprawling academy campus. He popped a few pills, closed his eyes and reflected on those lonely years.

A woman with a baby stroller interrupted his thoughts. He gave her the time and she hurried on her way to the nearby church. He checked his Rolex over and over as he waited. Seconds ticked by. Then minutes. Then an hour had passed.

He got out a roll of medical tape from the first aid kit and pocketed it.

A uniformed bobby approached the open window and said something to him. Once more he produced his ID. The bobby scrutinized T2's photo on the laminated card and stared at his shiny new badge.

"I've been recently assigned to them," explained T2. "Just here on stand-by in case of a health crisis or other emergency. Some of them are quite old you know."

"Just checking," said the officer. "You never know."

"I know, believe me. Anyone could be a bad guy these days—pretending to be someone they're not, right?"

The officer walked away.

T2 mentally reviewed the timetable. His plan was on schedule. Now for the final task. He unwrapped the little gadget Roger had provided and carefully taped it to the steering wheel. T2 stared at its red button and reflected on the immense sense of power it gave him. Aware of his rising erection, he pulled out his white silken hanky and unzipped his fly. But the sudden erection went away just as quickly as it had arrived. *Worthless pills!* he thought. *They never did work worth a damn.* He tossed the empty plastic vial out the passenger window.

Angry and grimacing, he refocused his attention on the big doors at the top of the steps where the woman and infant had disappeared. T2 momentarily thought of his ex-friends and ex-colleagues and ex-business partners and ex-employees and ex-wives and ex-lovers and ex-children and his seventeen ex-grandchildren back in the States. *What a bunch of losers.*

A bell tolled. People began streaming from the church.

He started the engine. *Patience*, he told himself. *Not yet.*

T2's phone rang. He glanced at the number and ignored it. The phone kept ringing. Exasperated, he finally answered, "Oh, hey Ginni. I'm really busy right now. What's up? You know you're not supposed to call me direct. What's that? No. Remind the Judge that I'm the boss and I'm doing it *my way*. And tell Vlad he better turn over every single copy. He claims there *are* no copies and it never even happened. But I know better. I was there. Vlad's not the only tricky dicky dipping his wicky around town. Remind him I still have *his* file. Tell that baby-face commie if he doesn't comply, that I'll have my people take him outside and knock the crap out of him—then break his legs—then grind him into sausage. Then I'll cook him in a pizza pie and eat him and shit him off the Brooklyn Bridge myself. Tell him that's the deal. On second thought Ginni, forget all that stuff. Just ask Vlad again to *please* hand over every single copy." T2 pressed 'End Call.'

The enthusiastic crowd members chatted among themselves in little groups in front of the church. T2 carefully studied them. He recognized the tall thin elderly king standing a bit off to one side among a cluster of Royal Family members. The king was flanked by uniformed bobbies and a BBC news crew. *There!* he thought. *The head of the Fake Snake.*

Pedal-to-the-metal, T2's ambulance shot forward with incredible speed. Bodies and umbrellas and baby carriages tumbled and flew. Dozens of people were crushed as the heavy vehicle plowed through the crowd of churchgoers. T2 veered toward the king. He flipped on the wipers to clear the red spray. The human obstacles became an increasing impediment, eventually bringing the ambulance to a halt just short of the astonished group.

"Welcome to Judgment Day you bunch of phony fakes!" He locked eyes with the king. His thumb twitched involuntarily above the detonator.

A bobby stepped forward, drew her weapon, aimed and squeezed. Sear disengaged. Hammer struck firing pin. Pin dented primer. Sparks flared. Powder ignited. Expanding gas pushed the bullet downrange through the barrel where it parted the fresh English countryside air, pierced the blood-streaked windshield, grazed the inner corner of T2's right eye, perforated his orbital bone, mushroomed between his fluid-suspended cerebral hemispheres, exited his thick cranium, punched through skin and hair, then penetrated the vinyl upholstery and polyurethane seat cushion of the fake emergency vehicle. Newly lobotomized, T2's head whipped back into the soft cushion, then bounced forward like a boxer's speed bag and slammed into the detonator while he polluted the atmosphere with his methane one final time through the seat of his orange jumpsuit.

61

BENEATH THE GRAY-HAIRED PARCHMENT

NAVAJO RESERVATION
LATE MARCH 2024

IT WAS WINDY AND CLOUDY when Beth and Little Doc landed in Albuquerque. From there, she rented a car and made the long drive to Nitzee's hogan near Gallup. They arrived at dusk. HT had a hot meal of mutton stew and cornbread waiting.

After supper, the three of them crawled beneath their woolen blankets. That night there was a commotion outside. For more than an hour, the small flock of sheep called out.

In the morning, HT went to the lambing ground to investigate. After a quick search, he found the bloody remains of a slain newborn. Beside its remains were the fresh tracks of a coyote. While backtracking it from the kill site, HT observed where the coyote had exited a dry wash, entered the lambing pasture, and then returned the same way.

Back at the hogan, he opened the long wooden chest against the back wall of the hogan. He withdrew a kit fox skin quiver of steel-tipped arrows and his father's sturdiest serviceberry bow. He replaced the bowstring, whetted the arrowheads on a stone, and dipped each one in a paste of spring water and white ash from the woodstove.

In the evening and all through the following day, HT fasted as he readied himself to eliminate the predator. All the while, Beth and Little Doc busied themselves in and around the hogan.

Late that afternoon, HT returned to the edge of the killing field with the bow and quiver and a bleating, kicking lamb. He tethered it in the open and built a brush blind at a place where the wind was favorable. After taking a few practice shots at a nearby mound of duff, he ducked into the blind and constructed an earthen hassock. Then, bow-in-hand, he knelt upon it.

He waited in ambush while the lamb incessantly called out for its mother. Darkness arrived. HT remained kneeling there for hours, half-asleep and dizzy from thirst and fasting. To him, the killing field seemed to be in constant motion—a kaleidoscope of blurry gray and black and white shapes and shades. Finally, in the fading starlight of false dawn, the killer revealed itself.

One twisted gray-blur seemed different to him from all the other grayness. It emerged from the deep shadows and crept into the clearing and halted for a time. When the gray-blur moved again, HT recognized it for what it was. Yee naaldlooshii. A skinwalker. A witch-wolf prowling in the night. And now it was slinking toward his blind, snuffling the ground here and there, scenting the dew-covered grass, sniffling and whiffling the desert wind. But instead of wild prey, the creature coveted something else as alluded to in the Diné legends: a kid to catch unaware in the darkness, away from the safety of the hogan; a child to devour; a young girl to vomit out; a helpless boy to leave lying out there somewhere in a broken heap.

The gangly witch-wolf roved across the killing field, loping toward him along a sinuous path. As it drew near, HT saw it wore a gray fur robe wrapped around itself, the edges hanging loosely from its belly. Over its mane was a macabre necklace of what looked to be jerked penises—trophies of its exploits over the eons. And tied perversely atop its long pointed snout it wore an asshole from one of its ruined prey which it circumcised and cut-out years before—an asshole tied there no doubt to remind it of the hunt and allow it to re-live the kill-thrill over and over and over ad infinitum—so it could relish the trail of tears and bloody tails it left behind.

The skinwalker made a beeline for the bleating lamb and, with a sudden lunge, seized it by the neck. HT watched in horror while the beast ripped the lamb's throat, tore open its soft belly and wolfed down its warm liver in huge bloody gulps.

Instinctively, he drew the bow and released. All hell broke loose. The skinwalker screamed an ungodly screech as the arrow pierced its rib cage. The injured demon dog raced helter-skelter across the pasture and tumbled abruptly at the far edge, then dragged itself into the tree cover.

Bow-in-hand, HT leapt forward and sprinted after it, pursuing the hellhound into the dark shadows. He heard the wounded thing thrash and yelp in a frenzied fit up ahead. Finally, he spied it. The hideous creature was crawling along the ground like a furry sidewinder. Its dried, warped pelt flapped as the witch within the skin writhered about in panic, attempting to escape. He slung another arrow at the slithering gray mass, but missed. It squirmed away and sheltered behind the twisted roots of a gnarled, half-dead cedar.

Unable to flee, the skinwalker flailed on the ground. Bloody bubbles burbled from the arrow wound each time its side heaved. HT delved deep into the jaundiced eyes of the veiled witch. In the dimness, a gold-capped canine tooth flashed. There, watching him from behind the papery mask, was the school principal—Father Phil—that damned trickster! Once a giant of a man standing six-foot-six, he seemed now so incredibly small and pallid and naked. He laid there injured and afraid—cowering behind his dog skin vestment—hiding beneath the gray-haired parchment that he clenched so tightly.

HT was enraged. A third arrow would not suffice for what he knew he must do to this cursed man-beast. The wounded abomination deserved to be defrocked—crushed to hell—stoned to death. He searched for a serviceable rock, but found only crumbly sandstones as he staggered here and there in the pre-dawn starlight. He needed something with which to kill that thing—the tormentor—that had dogged and bedeviled him all of those years. He remembered the pile of cobbles at the old corral.

NEWS MEDIA TRANSCRIPT
MARCH 28TH, 2024

Chris: - This is CNN. Chris Wallace here filling in for Anderson Cooper. We have breaking news tonight. If you're just tuning in, there are reports of an explosion this morning in Norfolk County, England. A large plume of smoke can be seen in this early footage we received from our news crew. There are reports of many dead and injured at the scene. We go live now to our London correspondent, Isa Soares. Hello Isa. Could you provide us with an update?

Isa: - Yes Chris. I'm here outside Sandringham Estate in Norfolk, England. The crew and I were here on assignment covering the Easter Weekend events when at 9:37 this morning there was a massive explosion in the direction of the Estate. At this time, its cause is not yet known. At least 20 persons were reportedly killed in the blast and dozens more injured, some of them critically. Over 100 persons are unaccounted for. The number of dead and injured will likely climb as we receive updates from first responders.

- Okay, I do have an update for you Chris: we now have confirmation of 28 dead and at least 50 injured.

- The explosion could not have happened at a worse time Chris. Services at Saint Mary Magdalene Church at the Estate were just letting out and we know the steps and plaza were full of departing worshipers. The scene was reportedly in utter chaos as emergency responders rushed to assist the injured. The ones I've spoken to say there is a large crater where the explosion occurred and the surrounding area is covered in debris and bodies.

- Thank you. This just in Chris. It has been confirmed that members of the Royal Family are among the missing.

Chris: - Isa, I'm interrupting with an update we just received here in New York: the BBC reports some members of the Royal Family were killed in the blast and other Family members are being taken to an undisclosed location for their safety. The report states that populations downwind are being evacuated as a precautionary measure—Isa, did you hear that?

Isa: - Yes Chris. Indeed I did.

Chris: - Isa, you and the crew need to evacuate now. You need to go upwind.

62

ASHES TO ASHES, SHIT TO SHIT

NAVAJO RESERVATION
MARCH 30TH, 2024

AWN WAS BREAKING when he reached the twisted, lightning-struck cedar. The sheep killer lay tangled in its exposed roots. HT raised the white stone high overhead, preparing to hurl it. But it was too late. Exhausted, dehydrated, he lowered his weapon and set it beside the dead animal—a mother coyote. The reflection in her yellow eyes was beginning to fade a bit as her corneas slowly glazed over. His broken arrow protruded from the still steaming wound in her side.

Then, as he stared at the dead animal, HT remembered what he'd blocked from his mind all this time. He allowed himself to finally relive the events of that bloody long-ago night—to face the godawful truth: Father Philip Garghant, the tall priest with long yellow hair, had tried to do those terrible things to him yet again. But HT avoided the man's trickery at the dinner table. He went to bed hungry, thirsty. He laid there in his bunk with the broken crucifix over his heart. He waited. He prayed.

Late that night, under cover of darkness, Garghant crept through the dormitory rooms. His long arms reached for the boy. They struggled. Unable to scream for help, HT lashed out with the crucifix. The fluted end sliced deep across the man's cheek, creating a gaping wound and hideous flap of flesh. The boy bolted down the hallway, closely followed by the enraged priest. Outside in the snow, HT spun and faced his powerful assailant. He hefted the loose chunk of marble and slung it with everything he had, hitting his mark. Skull-cracked, the priest collapsed in a heap. The boy took up the stone, mounted the stunned man and bashed in his front teeth. The man gurgled and choked and spat, spewing several ivories and a gold. Then HT struck Garghant's forehead again with his makeshift weapon. He vividly recalled how those haunting eyes twitched and flashed in the lamplight. Warm blood spurted and sprayed while the priest's gangly body bucked beneath him in a dreadful dance of death. When HT dropped the stone, the massive man's face was a mangled mess steaming in the winter night's chill.

Unbeknownst to HT, Archbishop Moreno's cover-up man had concealed his killing of the priest. Officer Valdez arrived first on-scene. He quickly loaded the pedophile's oversized body into the trunk of his cruiser. Later, he stripped it of clothes and stuffed it in a rusty culvert far out on the frozen prairie east of Denver. Back in Denver, the archbishop told anyone who bothered to ask, that Garghant abandoned his vows, packed his things and left without explanation. That spring, a family of coyotes found the hidden corpse, gnawed the putrid flesh and bones down to nothing, then unceremoniously shat it out.

HT's body sagged. *It is finished,* he thought. *Yé'iitsoh* [Big Giant] *is dead.*

Cotton-mouthed, he gagged and coughed as he stared at the beautiful, lifeless canine on the ground in front of him. Her charcoal-black lips were stark against the linen-white fur of her chin and chest. Her bib was streaked crimson from the ripping of her prey. To HT, the grinning, golden-eyed bitch resembled an enraptured sister in her habit, lying twisted in a state of ecstasy, freshly washed in the blood of the lamb.

He thought about the coyote character—the trickster—described in the stories of his boyhood. He dipped his fingers red and savored the salt-tang taste of the sheep killer's lifeblood while he reflected on their early morning encounter. The neighbor's snare—now twisted, knotted and broken—still hung from her neck. There was a pink gash atop her muzzle from a recent fight with another coyote—one which perhaps got a little too close to her den full of pups. And then HT noticed miniscule movements inside the gash. He peered close. A tiny fly larva—a maggot—wriggled about there in the open wound. He'd seen it before with his father's horses when they'd gotten caught-up in barbed wire—the maggots cleaning dead stuff from the punctures—helping the animals' painful oozing wounds to heal.

The coyote was unusually gaunt, her muscles atrophied. The teats along both of her hairless sagging udder strips were swollen and leaking milk.

Those pups must be close by, he thought. HT followed the coyote's dew trail, backtracking her movements through the trees and grass. He saw where she'd dragged her bloody body on the ground. In her tracks he observed her panicked flight across the meadow. He saw the curving path she'd taken to the kill site near his blind. Further along he noticed where she'd killed and eaten a mouse at the place he first spied her movements in the starlight. He continued on the coyote's backtrail till he found it.

The den was halfway up an open hillside at the head of a dry wash. In front of the entrance was a reddish earthen mound plastered with mother and pup tracks and tiny droppings. But there were no tracks of other adult coyotes—no helpers— just those of the mother and her litter. Now he understood why she'd resorted to killing lambs instead of the usual gophers, mice and rabbits.

He hiked back to the hogan and returned with an old shovel. After stripping off a swatch of the coyote's hide, he buried her remains at the base of the lightning-struck tree, her grave capped with the big white stone.

63

Cleansin' Time

Navajo Reservation
March 30th, 2024

L ATE THAT MORNING, HT, Beth and Little Doc left the hogan and hiked together to the coyote den with the shovel and a cardboard box containing the swatch of hide from the dead mother. They widened the entrance, gathered up the pups and returned to the hogan. HT shredded some roasted mutton and gave it to them. He watched Beth and Little Doc play with the growling, wrestling, nipping pups.

"Here Papa," said the boy.

HT stroked the wriggling pup. It licked him and bit at the yoostsah on his rigid finger with its needle-sharp teeth. Half-smiling, he held it close for a time and contemplated his experiences with coyotes and wolves and dogs and skin-walkers. *All this time I was just being superstitious*, he thought. *There was never anything to fear*. He handed the pup back to Little Doc and stepped outside.

He opened the sheep pen gate and leaned against a weathered post. Old odors permeated him—the scent of cedar woodsmoke and sheep dung. The small herd of ewes and newborn lambs calmly filed out in search of good grazing. HT thought about what occurred earlier that morning when he defended the flock— how he'd shot and killed the mother coyote. *Some must die so that others may live. That's how life works.*

And yet, after killing the coyote, a sense of emptiness—a brokenness—remained in him. He wandered over to the old horse corral. His eyes settled on the stack of cobbles by the water trough and the pile of decomposing branches nearby—the scattered remains of his father's sweat house. HT recalled what took place there long ago. It was a place of cleansing. A place of renewal. A place of healing and balance. He would do a sweat bath like his father did with the other men and HT and his brother Shash Yáázh when the two of them were little kids.

And this time the sweat bath would be done differently yet again. Just like the stories HT had heard so often as a child were a little different each time. For, during the years he lived at Egg Lake, he'd learned that things never remained the same—that everything changes with the circling of the moon and sun and stars and seasons. He understood that, as with Changing Woman [Mother Earth], change was the very heartbeat of the Universe.

He headed toward Jimmy's place to borrow the old pickup again.

BETH AND LITTLE DOC brought fresh-cut branches from the back of the truck over to HT. He bent them and tied them in place. When he'd finished, a new dome-shaped framework sat atop the site of the collapsed one. They wrapped a couple old canvas tarps around it and hung a blanket for a door.

"What is it?" said Beth.

He scribbled: ***Táchééch—Sweat house***

They dug a small pit inside.

Outside, they cleaned out the old fire pit. HT dug deep in the scorched red earth. He lined the empty pit with twelve river cobbles of varying colors from the pile.

With his firemaking kit, he showed Little Doc and Beth how to kindle a new fire in the old way—something he'd learned from a young Diné man while on the campaign trail. HT twirled the long thin elderberry spindle between his hands above the split cottonwood stick, placed the smoldering ember on a pad of shredded bark, then gently blew. Soon, the smoking tinder bundle burst into flame. He set it in the pit and built a fire on top. One by one, Little Doc added dry branches.

HT went to the hogan. He took the broken crucifix from its place above the doorway, then slid his father's wooden chest to the center of the floor. Inside he found the Naayéé' Neizghání [Monster Slayer] mask used by his father for the Blackening Rite after his return from the war in Viet Nam. HT got the jish [medicine bundle] from his duffel.

Back at the fire, he stripped off his shirt and handed it to Beth. He knelt, opened the jish and removed a small pouch of iron ocher powder. With the sharp end of the crucifix, he slowly sliced two tilted lines in the brown skin over his heart. He rubbed the healing powder into the fresh, bloody cuts, permanently reddening them.

HT thumped the fallen cross tattoo with his palm. 'Now I understand how all the ugliness got inside me,' he signed. 'This is so I will never again forget what happened.'

Looking skyward, he held the broken crucifix tightly to his chest for a time—remembering. Then he signed to Little Doc and Beth: 'This thing belonged to my mom. She walked on [passed away] many years ago. And I no longer need it. So I am giving it back to her.' He gently set the crucifix in the flames. Beth and Little Doc looked at each other. They watched the plume of pungent smoke rise from the burning molten plastic. As the black cloud dissipated, the polished pot metal Christ figure slowly turned to slag and dripped through the ashes and bled into the red earth below, becoming part of it once more.

HT donned the mask. He spread his arms, then snorted loudly. 'I am Naayéé' Neizghání,' he signed. 'I killed Yé'iitsoh [Big Giant]. That fucking monster is dead.'

Together, the family heaped heavy branches high on the new fire. It crawled and flared and hissed and lurched and roared into a fire whirl. HT removed his mask.

That evening, when the bonfire was reduced to coals and ash and the cobbles glowed white-hot, HT scooped them into a metal bucket. The trio stripped and entered the sweat house. They closed the blanket door behind them. HT poured the hot stones into the pit.

Little Doc lit cornstalk slivers one by one while his father signed, scribbled notes on his pad and scratched a little feathered stick in the sand, with an occasional click of his tongue or soft whistle. In the flickering light HT told them of the four sacred mountains of Dinétah. Then he smudged sage and made an offering of pollen and corn meal in each of the four directions. He pointed to the yoostsah on his hand and explained the various meanings of the stone's color and how its rounded six-sided outline matched the outline of his mother's hogan. He told how, when he was an infant, his umbilical cord dried, fell off and was then buried nearby in the traditional manner.

The family sweated into the night while HT relayed the Diné legends he remembered from his boyhood. Then he recounted the story of his own life to them. Toward the end of it, he circled back and told them how the religious beliefs adopted by his mother while living at the residential school had influenced his own beliefs—how after her death he spoke with a Franciscan friar in Gallup about maybe becoming a priest himself. He described being sponsored by the arch-bishop and going away to attend the Church-run school for boys in Denver.

HT stopped and hung his head. His shoulders slumped and his body shud-dered and went nearly limp. He remained that way for a long time.

Shimmering heat waves rose from the twelve hot stones like Niłch'i Dine'é [Wind People]—waiting for him to say it—to say what needed to be said. Finally, he lifted his head and shoulders. He allowed his eyes to rise and look beyond Beth and Little Doc at the sinuous crimson shadows shapeshifting about on the motor oil-stained canvas covering the sweat house.

He told of Father Phil's friendliness. He told of their hugs and their playful wrestling and how the other students who'd also wrestled with the tall priest jok-ingly called him 'Father Feely' behind his back. HT told of the man's long talks with him while the two of them secretly drank whiskey together. He described how Father Phil later preyed on him because HT was mute—unable to voice his protests. His chest began to heave. Salty rivulets welled and flowed from his bloodshot eyes when he described the dinnertime druggings he'd experienced and his dim recollections of the late-night rapes that followed.

Little Doc dropped his makeshift candle and threw out his thin arms. "But Papa, you were just a kid."

HT coughed and wheezed and nodded while his son struggled to relight the cornstalk sliver. When there was light again, HT lowered his head and confessed how he lashed out at Father Phil that final night at school, cutting him, and how the priest pursued him barefoot out into the snow. He admitted turning and fighting back and ending the man's life. 'I killed it—the whorer—the whorer.'

"It's okay Lovie," said Beth, her eyes brimming and spilling over. "He drugged you and did those terrible things to you. He was chasing you. Who knows what he would have done had he caught you. You had to defend yourself. I'm so sorry that it happened to you. Thank you for finally telling us. Is that why you were hiding out there in the bush all those years?"

'Not hiding,' he signed. 'Looking.'

"Looking for what?"

'Hózhǫ́ [peace]. And the part of me he stole.'

"Did you find them, Lovie?"

He paused. 'I found hózhǫ́ out there with the plants and animals—the water, earth and sky. But the kid part of me is gone forever. Dead. Inside I am still messed up.'

Once more HT slapped the swollen tattoo. 'It was not just one man who hurt me. I have read of it. There were many of them—too many. They failed me and the other kids. They failed all of us. But I can never give up. For many years I was dead inside. They killed the kid in me. But now I understand what happened. My spirit rises.'

The telling of his story freed him—like the rolling away of a heavy stone that had pressed and crushed and entombed him all those years—allowing some light to finally fill the dark void.

He slipped the heirloom yoostsah from his finger and handed it to Little Doc. 'Be careful when you choose who to trust,' he signed to his son in the flickering light. 'Some people think only of themselves. At first they are nice, but later they betray the ones they are supposed to care for.'

"Will you forgive them Lovie?" said Beth. "Can you?"

'I don't know. But I will try.'

HT gestured toward the entrance.

Naked—shiny with sweat—the family emerged from the sweat house into the dawn of the new day. Laughing in the early morning light, they jumped in the trough and poured handfuls of cool water atop each other's heads.

"What's that?" said Little Doc. He pointed at a black fly-like speck in the eastern sky just above the blinding sun.

'A crow or raven maybe,' signed HT.

The black speck drew closer. Then a low hum could be heard. The humming intensified as the object ominously approached. The three of them stared at it. Now an engine could be clearly heard. The machine began to thump loudly.

"It's a helicopter," said Little Doc. "Sikorsky UH-60M Blackhawk—9,000-pound lift—151-knot cruise speed—runs on two GE T700 engines—1,630 horse-power."

They remained in the water trough as they watched the roaring black copter circle overhead. It eventually set down between the hogan and the corral, blasting them with billowing red dust and sand.

A trio of men climbed out and approached them while the pilot wound down the mechanical bird. Little Doc recognized Nate's pink camo neckerchief and gave him a thumbs up.

"Good mornin' Little Doc. Kinda early for bath time isn't it Kiddo?"

The boy smiled and flipped him off.

Beth shot Little Doc a warning look.

"But Papa does it all the time."

"He has a paralyzed finger," she said. "You don't."

"Hey there Prez," said Nate.

'Prez?' signed HT.

"Long story," he said, grinning.

Then he nodded at Beth and curtsied.

"How are ya this fine mornin' your Majesty?"

She cocked her head. "What's going on Nate?"

"Your secret's out Beth. There's no more hidin' for ya, eh?"

She gave Nate a puzzled look, then pulled her arms tighter across her chest and looked warily at the two men standing beside him.

"Ya haven't heard?"

"Heard what?"

"Then I betcha haven't heard the news about Hand Talker yet either."

"We can't get anything out here Nate," said Beth. "My phone lost service. There's no telly. Little Doc uses solar for his computers of course, but we can't get an internet connection."

"Well it's all over the radio too."

'What is?' signed HT.

"The votes from all the nations were tallied up. Ya won it hands down Cousin. Wolf Man Keetsal is contestin' the count. And there's this other fella too—a recently fired cop. They call 'em 'Tucker the fu—' oops! Sorry Little Doc, but you'll need to cover your ears."

'Oh that guy,' signed HT. 'Yes, I've met him.'

"Anyway, the whole Navajo Nation is in an uproar because yesterday mornin' this fella Tucker and a gang of like-minded folks took over the Admin Center and Council Chamber over at Window Rock. Wolf Man organized 'em, riled 'em up and told 'em to all go there and fight like hell. So that's just what they did, eh. There was a riot. A bloody battle. They ended up hurtin' a bunch of Tribal officers and admin staff who were tryin' to hold the line. Some of 'em are in terrible shape. They may not survive.

"Anyway, the Navajo Home Guard had to deploy. Tucker's gang and the Navajo Nation administration are in a standoff. President Jon is tryin' to convince 'em that overthrowin' the government is not the way to go. It's an act of treason. But Tucker's claimin' that they're doin' nothin' wrong at all. He's callin' for a new election. And Wolf Man's hidin' out in his fancy house out at the golf course whinin' and yappin' about how he's the one who really won and how all the old ladies countin' the votes committed fraud. Tribal elders are sayin' Wolf Man needs to be dealt with in the old way—banished. His cronies don't know what to do. He's got 'em all buffaloed. It's a real mess Cousin."

'But how did I win? People were not even allowed to vote for me.'

"Wolf Man's supporters kept your name from bein' printed on the ballot, but the Elections Committee added a line for write-in candidates. The people were behind ya. A landslide victory. Not even close. They must've got tired of all his fear mongerin' and lyin' and hatin'—pittin' the Tribe against itself.

"In a couple days you'll be sworn in as President of the United Dené Nations. And since you're already National Chief of Canada's Assembly, you'll be presidin' over an area of Native territories coverin' roughly half of North America. Betcha weren't expectin' that, eh?"

Not sure how to respond, HT just sat there for a moment in amazement.

'And the helicopter?' he signed. 'For me?'

"Don't ya wish, eh? No, Cousin, that beautiful bird belongs to Kirtland Air Force Base. Which brings up the real reason we flew out here." Nate looked down for a moment. He kicked a nearby cobble. It rolled, then clunked eerily against the trough, causing ripples to splash against the three occupants.

"A terrible thing happened, eh Beth. There's no easy way to say it. There was another car bombin' ya see—a big one I'm afraid. Saint Mary's Church at the Family Estate was targeted and lots of people were killed and injured. I'm so sorry for ya Beth."

He gestured toward the two men in suits. "This is Secretary of State Halsey and UK Ambassador Armstrong. They're sayin' that apparently…"

"Tell me Nate."

"Apparently you're the heir apparent—to the throne—of the Commonwealth of Nations. So anyway Beth, Hand Talker's gonna be President of the United

Dené Nations. And you're gonna be Queen Elizabeth III. What do ya say to that, eh?"

Their mouths went agape. HT and Little Doc embraced Beth as she began to cry.

Nate stayed quiet, not knowing how to help. When Beth finally looked up, he spoke. "Well then, why don't ya just relax for now and let it soak in a bit. And then at some point we can start gettin' ya prepped for the ceremonies. Ya know— the inauguration—the coronation? Ya might need to be wearin' some clothes for that, eh—so you'll be dressed proper for all the pictures they'll be takin'."

Beth broke down again, crying even harder this time.

64

NEW CLOTHES: LEGACY .45

NAVAJO RESERVATION
APRIL 1ST, 2024

FOUR YOUNG KIDS CRIED OUT in unison as they burst through Wolf Man's recently patched front door and fled down the walkway. "He's naked!" They raced across the driveway and nearly collided with the reporters, videographers and Navajo Home Guard members positioned along the sidewalk.

"Who's naked?" said a reporter.

"My granddad. He's totally naked. And he's got a gun."

Inside, Riz turned to her adult children.

"Go with the kids. Now. Stay with them. I'll handle this."

Riz gently guided Wolf Man from his place in the center of the living room, down the long hallway, back into the steamy master bathroom. She turned off the shower faucet and threw his pile of sopping wet clothes in the hamper. Together, they stood facing the fogged-up gold-framed mirror. He laid the heavy handgun on the polished white marble.

"What's wrong?" she said.

"Don't you smell that? I'm so damn dirty! The stank won't wash off."

"Talk to me."

"The toilet's plugged-up again. Why the hell can't they make toilets that *work*?"

"Talk to me,'"

"Okay. Well, you know those people who died over at Window Rock?"

She nodded.

Beads of sweat decorated the big man's jowls. He leaned in and whispered: "T'áá aníí ásht'į [I did it]."

"What's that? Speak up. And say it in English for me please."

"Aw, never mind Riz. It's no big deal. Really."

"C'mon. You need to tell me—to get it off your chest."

Wolf Man started to say something, but his jaw suddenly clamped shut and his expression became a defiant glare. Then he spoke: "I know people are blaming it on me. But it wasn't my fault. It was those damn morons that stormed the Admin Center. They did it. Not me."

"No. You can't lie your way out of it this time Sweetie. You sent me all those emails and twats too, remember?"

"Not 'twats' Riz. They used to be 'tweets.' Now they're called 'posts.'"

"Oh? Anyway, I saw how you told Tucker and the rest of them to go do whatever it takes to shut it down. Those people you call 'morons' only did what you told them to go do. Your words got people killed. And now all those poor boys will be going to jail because of you. Did you hear your friend Ashléé died?"

"Yep. War is hell. Things like that happen in war."

"It was an election not a war. You're the one who turned it into a war."

"But I didn't lose," he whined. "Those old ladies counted wrong. And there was tons of fraud. I'm telling the truth this time."

"C'mon, your own dear Auntie Ruby and Cousin Shayéé stayed up all night counting those votes. And you never ever ever tell the truth, right? We both know you're a professional phony boloney. A lot of your supporters know it too. The same way they know you lost. It's simple: those people just wanted you to be their leader. They like all the things you stand for—and stand against. Some people just love to hate. And you gave them what they love by telling them who to hate."

"But Riz, you don't understand. The Wolf Man *never* loses. And I sure as hell didn't lose to some dumb, gray-eyed half-breed who can't even talk right. I'm not a loser like him."

"Listen Sweetie, *everybody* loses now and then. But don't worry. This is the last time it'll happen to you."

"Riz, go tell the grandkids to keep their traps shut about seeing me with no clothes, okay? Loose lips sink ships," he growled. "Go tell them right now. And when you're done, bring me some new clothes."

Riz went around to the dark corner of the bedroom, then returned. "Here's your new clothes." She draped the skin of the giant wolf-dog over his head and down his bare backside, then picked up the Springfield Armory pistol, chambered a round and forced it into his meaty paw.

Riz looked him square in the eye. She squinted. "Listen. Everybody knows you were standing naked out there in front of the grandkids holding a gun to your head. The kids ran outside yelling about it. Remember all those reporters and soldiers out front? You know how the hogan hotline works. The news is all over Navajoland by now. They say when this is over you'll be charged as an accessory for those people getting hurt and killed at the Admin Center. Because you started the whole thing. I can't let you drag the family through a mess like that."

"But—"

"Just do what you have to do, okay Sweetie? I'll be out in the truck listening to Frank Sinatra."

He reached for her hand, but she jerked away.

Riz squinted at him one last time, wiped the fog from the vanity mirror, then turned and left him alone.

Wolf Man clutched his Legacy .45 auto. He glared at the hideous skinwalker staring back at him. "I wasn't naked," he howled.

65

CHANT OF CHANTS

BUCKINGHAM PALACE, LONDON, ENGLAND
APRIL 22ND, 2024

THE YOUNG QUEEN HESITATED. She adjusted her heavy crown, took a deep breath, then stepped forward to the podium at the edge of the balcony.

"Thank you. Hello everyone. I am so sorry that the recent tragic events have led us to this moment. We all feel the loss of my dear Uncle Charlie, my cousins, and all of the others we lost on that dreadful day. There were so many. Too many. I know everyone is still in shock. But we will make it through this challenging time—together. Now that our loved ones have been laid to rest, I want you each to know that things are going to be different around here from now on. It won't be like it was before. Obviously.

"First, I would like to address the elephant in the room as it were. My Granny-mum never told me this directly, but before she passed away a few years ago, I did find out that she disapproved of my relationship with Hand Talker Judd, a Native American man. She told those around her that she was concerned about maintaining the *purity* of the Family. Some of you may have similar concerns. All of us here loved Granny-mum dearly and we will always remember her kind acts in support of those less fortunate. I would never say anything to diminish her reign or tarnish her legacy. But I need to remind everyone that it was this same kind of thinking we actively fought against during World War II when white supremacists took the idea of genetic purity to the extreme. The Commonwealth of Nations is incredibly diverse. And no nation, religion, race or person within it is superior to another. As your new Queen and as Supreme Governor of the Church of England, I am keenly aware of that fact. Therefore, the Oath of Supremacy to the Governor will no longer be administered or accepted. I encourage each one of you to look within yourself—to examine any prejudices you may hold—and to try to move beyond them. We need to come together to celebrate our shared humanity.

"And this brings me to my first proclamation as Queen: it is time for the Monarchy to end." Beth removed her diamond-embellished crown and set it on the podium.

The people below gasped in unison. There were shouts of disapproval.

"The Monarchy will be phased out." She pulled out her hair pins and freed her golden tresses. "The surviving Family members and I have agreed to liquidate the Monarchy's assets. Most of the proceeds, as well as the sovereign grant, will be used to fund a lifesaving initiative which I will be announcing momentarily. It is the right thing to do. Please understand that these funds are desperately needed elsewhere. The world is changing ever so quickly. We must respond appropriately. During the coming transition, my support staff and I will remain available to the Prime Minister and to members of Parliament in an advisory capacity."

The crowd grew more and more restless.

"Excuse me. Please allow me to explain. My Granny-mum, my Uncle Charlie, and now me—none of us ever asked for this office. Instead, it was forced upon each of us. But I have come to believe that power should reside with officials who are duly elected by the people. Certainly not with a person or a family that *holds control* over people through threats or coercion. And certainly not with someone like me who simply *inherited* power because of my genetics. I am sorry to break with tradition, but the time for change is overdue. Thank you all for your steadfast loyalty to the Crown and for the tremendous love you have shown my family for so many years—for centuries actually. And please don't worry. I assure you we will all be just fine as we move forward.

"Now Hand Talker wishes to address you all. As you probably are already aware, he is the leader of the newly formed United Dené Nations of North America. Please hear him out. Unlike so many people and organizations today, he stands for truth telling. Hand Talker is mute, so his cousin Mister Nate Cookman will translate."

Nate stepped forward. HT stood beside him and began signing.

"Hand Talker says hello and 'Happy Earth Day' to all of ya. He says that his heart is broken. That he waited too long to come forward. That we all waited too long to do somethin' about the fossil fuel burnin' issue, eh. And now we're passin' over the tippin' point. Our oceans keep warmin' and risin'. Our coral reefs and kelp beds and fish are dyin' off. The storms are a lot stronger than before. The forests around the world are burnin' up. Hand Talker's own forest burned up, eh. All the ice and frozen soil and mud up north and down south is quickly meltin'. Hand Talker says that his son Little Doc tells 'em the gas comin' from all of this meltin' is goin' to be way worse than anyone expects. He says Little Doc might be a kid, but he knows more about science than any adult. Little Doc understands reality—the way the world works. He's the one that unified all those models they use in physics, eh? Anyway, the other day, Little Doc explained it to his dad this way: that humanity is leanin' on the tip of a knife—ready to plunge into it. He says that by treatin' the Earth like one big gold mine instead of the garden it is, that we're settin' fire to our one and only home when we're trapped inside, eh. Hand Talker says that for years the youngsters have been cryin' out to the powerful ones, sayin', 'Hey you guys, listen up. We're bein' fucked!' Older people heard 'em, but they did little to stop it. He says it's time to put a stop to it. He says we need to ignore the folks denyin' it on TV and the internet because they're just gettin' rich doin' that, eh.

"Now Hand Talker says he's done talkin' and he wants to offer up a song to all of ya. It's called the *End Song*. It's the one Dené folks sing when someone dies. 'Cause the livin' things of the Earth are passin' away faster than we can count 'em. He says he just wishes peace to all of ya durin' the tough times ahead, eh."

Nate proceeded to rhythmically beat his moose hide drum. Cedar flute in hand, HT began playing the *End Song*. Beth went and stood beside him. She closed her eyes and started humming. And then, like when she was on the stone slab by the creekside pool near his lodge, she opened her turquoise and jet eyes and smiled. Her pink-flint lips parted, exposing exquisite rows of polished white shell. Beth sang her *Song of Songs* to the people. The two songs intertwined and merged into one. Auntie Millie and Little Doc and the other guests began singing. And as people around the world listened to the music on their phones, computers, TVs and radios, they too joined in, chanting the ancient *Chant of Chants* everyone seemed to know—the chant of love and life and death.

When the chant ended, the crowd went silent.

Beth cleared her throat. "As mentioned earlier, my son Little Doc has a plan—a worldwide initiative—to possibly save some of the living things and some of our young people—before it is too late. Earlier today, the Prime Minister, the Chancellor, Hand Talker and Little Doc and I met with the Secretary-General of the United Nations. He agreed to present the plan to the General Assembly in an emergency council this afternoon. Little Doc, would you please explain to everyone why your plan is needed?"

The kid walked to the podium with a large poster board. Beth held it up for the crowd and the multitude of TV cameras. In the center of the poster was an image of the planet Earth with a few words printed in large letters above and below.

HT lifted his son till he was level with the cluster of microphones.

Little Doc met the crowd with bold bright eyes. His father's oversized yoostsah hung from a string around his neck. Little Doc threw out his thin terra-cotta-colored arms. "Hi guys. I know I'm just a kid. But when no one is listening, kids need to speak up so adults can know when something terrible is happening. Like Papa said, we're crossing the tipping point. Our future is being taken away from us kids by paid liars and paid deniers. The Earth's ecosystems are collapsing because everyone is being told it's all fake and they don't need to radically change their ways.

"In less than 200 years, people have increased CO_2 in the air by 50%. The scientists all agree this is true. It's the energy interests and their political slaves who keep telling you it doesn't really matter. And now they're calling kids like me ecoterrorists. All of this lying has to stop!"

Little Doc pointed to the words on the poster and shouted into the microphones, *'STOP STEALING — FROM THE KIDS'*

The crowd roared its approval. Some began to chant, 'Stop the steal. Stop the steal.' The boy raised his arms to quiet them.

Overhead, several black plastic rotary wing kamikaze dwarf drones drifted into view and zeroed-in on the brave boy on the balcony below. HT glanced up at the trio of crow-like unmanned aircraft. The drones hovered there for a moment, then suddenly dipped.

"Okay guys, here's the plan," said Little Doc.

There was a whir of blades and rush of air. Chaos ensued as HT clutched Little Doc to his chest and leapt backwards through the doorway.

we walk on in beauty
    it is finished
    it is finished
    it is finished
    it is finished in beauty

ACKNOWLEDGMENTS

First, I hope this story can shine light on the remaining diverse families, bands, tribes and nations of Dené [meaning 'The People'—also known to many as Athapaskans or Athapaskan speakers] and help them celebrate the heritage they share. Special thanks to my Apache, Dene/Dené, Diné [Navajo], Natinixwe [Hupa], Tolowa Dee-ní and Wailacki friends and colleagues. I respect and admire you and your ways. May your own healing journeys take you where you want to be. To the few Native Americans who might take offense that a white man shared a story about a multicultural Native character, I encourage you to look within yourself—to examine your prejudices—and to try to move beyond them.

Thanks to my family for their patience and love. Special recognition goes to my now-deceased animal-loving veterinarian / rancher grandfather. He taught me how to remove porcupine quills from dogs and cancerous eyeballs from cattle, how to catch brook trout and beaver and, hopefully, how to tell a story.

I extend my gratitude to numerous persons who assisted in properly grounding this novel in its many locales including Colorado, Wyoming, Montana, New Mexico, Saskatchewan, Victoria (Australia) and England.

I appreciate the generous support of the following people who helped make the completion of *Hand Talker* possible:

<u>Critique readers</u>: Alexandra, Brian C., Darryl, Dean, Hillary, Jacilyn, Jan, Jerry, Jimmy H., Michael, Michele, Paula, Robert and Sharon

<u>Editing</u>: Brian C. and Slim

<u>Moral support</u>: Chuck, Dan, Dewey, Greta, Harry, Jim N., Julie and Soledad

Finally, I need to acknowledge the creators of the various fictional characters, fairy tales and hoaxes alluded to in the closing chapters:

¤ Jim and Ron Watkins and Paul Furber, the pranksters who allegedly initiated and promoted the QAnon conspiracy theory phenomenon

¤ Lewis Carroll, creator of the white rabbit character in *Alice in Wonderland*

¤ Wilhelm and Jacob Grimm, authors of *Hansel and Gretel*

¤ Samuel Arnold, author of *Humpty Dumpty*

¤ James Cameron and William Wisher, creators of the T-1000 character in the film *Terminator 2: Judgment Day*

¤ Hans Christian Andersen, author of *The Emperor's New Clothes*

ABOUT THE AUTHOR

Born a proverbial "mutt" of mixed Northern European ancestry, Johnny "JD" Doeskin grew up in north-central Colorado. After high school, he studied the natural sciences and anthropology while building a multicultural family. JD has lived and worked in several other western states and two states in Mexico, spending much of his professional and personal time serving and learning from Indigenous North Americans. He is a life-long outdoorsman, proficient in a variety of primitive living skills. Besides the natural world, his passions include regenerative agriculture, working outdoors, oil painting, and visiting antique and thrift stores and traveling with his wife. They live in the heart of the rural Midwest. *Hand Talker* is his first novel.

Author's note: Net proceeds from this book, if any, will be directed toward causes that support victims of abuse, particularly among the Dené. Because most indie books never generate a profit, readers can be a part of this support effort by discussing this book and these causes with others.

INDIGENOUS TERRITORIES UNDER HAND TALKER'S LEADERSHIP
NORTHERN DENÉ
Auntie Millie's house in La Ronge, Saskatchewan
SOUTHERN DENÉ
Nitzee's hogan in Dinetah
N
TRADITIONAL LANDS DEPICTED
United Dené Nations of North America
Canada's Assembly of First Nations
Jointly-administered territories